I0553274

She wants the truth, but it may cost her more than she thinks...

An ex-patriot-American living in England, magazine reporter/editor Casey Rowan wakes to find one best friend murdered and another seriously injured. Casey is determined to find the killer, despite running afoul of the detective in charge of the case—a blue-eyed Scot named Rod Carlisle, who considers her a prime suspect. As Casey gets closer to the truth, losing her heart to the sexy cop isn't the only thing she risks. Now *her* life is danger, too.

He wants her, but he may have to choose between love and duty...

Rod has no patience with civilians who interfere in police matters, even hot little numbers like Casey. Though he tries to keep things professional, Casey's beauty and spunk are hard to resist. He warns her that what she's doing is dangerous, but he only succeeds in alienating her. She refuses to listen and goes off on her own with disastrous results. Now Rod's in a race to find the killer before the woman he loves becomes the next victim.

Was he really going to leave her? If she could just make him understand that she had to know the truth...

As Rod swiveled on his heel, his face expressionless, and gestured around the room, the house suddenly seemed a fragile barrier against the world.

"Look how easy it would be to break in here," he demanded. "They just didn't want to—next time, who knows? It could be a letter bomb exploding in your hall. You were seen documenting the events in Bradford. Now they've warned you. You keep digging, ignore what happened here, and me, then I can't keep you safe."

"I'm already in the firing line, as you say. I wanted to help Tessa, and now I need to keep digging for my own safety."

"No, you don't. You could take a holiday. Go back to America for a while. Just back off, Casey."

Stung that he now wanted to get rid of her, she said bitterly, "Hardly my fault I ended up in the middle of a riot."

"No, that wasn't your fault. Can I trust you to leave things alone from now on?"

"You want me to sit around and wait for someone to..." Her voice trailed off at the horror of it.

"No. Will you go away for a while?"

She frowned and shook her head. "This is my home. What good would running do? I'll have to come back sometime."

He grabbed his jacket and walked to the door. "Well, don't ring asking me for information." He wrenched the door open. "Your obsession with this case just adds to my worries, and it seems to be doing you no good either. Again, I repeat, for Christ's sake have done with it."

She watched him through the window as he left.

KUDOS for *Murder in Devon*

Murder in Devon by Maggi Andersen is more than a standard murder mystery. Sure, there is all the suspense you'd expect when Casey Rowan, an American ex-patriot and reporter wakes in the country home of old college friends to find one murdered and the other barely alive. What's more, Casey finds herself "a person of interest"—in more ways than one—of Detective Inspector Rod Carlisle, a man from whom any red-blooded woman would be more than happy to raise their arms and receive a personal pat down... Andersen has crafted a sharp, twisting plot. *Murder in Devon* does not hand over its secrets easily, but drags you along and keeps you riveted until the last page. Her characters are real, filled with humor and pathos and you want so much for Casey to find the killer but also for her to achieve a sense of peace at the tragic loss of her friend. Maggie Anderson has a new fan and I can't wait to read another of her novels. – *Taylor, Reviewer*

Murder in Devon by Maggi Andersen is a murder mystery as chilling as the wintry English countryside it is set in. When American ex-patriot, Casey Rowan wakes to find her best friend murdered and his wife barely clinging to life, she knows her life will never be the same. But she doesn't know that soon her own life will be in danger. The sexy hunk of a detective, Rod Carlisle tries to warn her—once he stops thinking of her as his prime suspect—but Casey isn't big on listening...a fast-paced, riveting tale of greed, politics, murder, and two people trying to find room for love while standing on opposite sides of a police investigation. He has to operate within the law, and she is willing to break the law to get to the truth. This suspense-filled page-turner deprived me of sleep, supper, and my usual email-and-chat fix in the evenings. I simply couldn't put it down. You'll want to visit this one over and over again. – *Regan Reviewer*

MURDER IN DEVON

By

Maggi Andersen

A BLACK OPAL BOOKS PUBLICATION

GENRE: ROMANTIC SUSPENSE/MYSTERY

This is a work of fiction. Names, places, characters and incidents are either the product of the author's imagination or are used fictitiously, and any resemblance to any actual persons, living or dead, businesses, organizations, events or locales is entirely coincidental. All trademarks, service marks, registered trademarks, and registered service marks are the property of their respective owners and are used herein for identification purposes only. The publisher does not have any control over or assume any responsibility for author or third-party websites or their contents.

MURDER IN DEVON
Copyright © 2009 by Maggi Andersen
All Rights Reserved
Cover Design by Maggi Andersen
All cover art copyright © 2012 All Rights Reserved

PRINT ISBN: 978-1-937329-34-1

First Publication: 2009 — CASEY'S LUCK

All rights reserved under the International and Pan-American Copyright Conventions. No part of this book may be reproduced or transmitted in any form or by any means, electronic or mechanical, including photocopying, recording, or by any information storage and retrieval system, without permission in writing from the publisher.

WARNING: The unauthorized reproduction or distribution of this copyrighted work is illegal. Criminal copyright infringement, including infringement without monetary gain, is investigated by the FBI and is punishable by up to 5 years in federal prison and a fine of $250,000.

ABOUT THE PRINT VERSION: If you purchased a print version of this book without a cover, you should be aware that the book is stolen property. It was reported as "unsold and destroyed" to the publisher, and neither the author nor the publisher has received any payment for this "stripped book."

IF YOU FIND AN EBOOK OR PRINT VERSION OF THIS BOOK BEING SOLD OR SHARED ILLEGALLY, PLEASE REPORT IT TO: lpn@blackopalbooks.com.

Published by Black Opal Books http://www.blackopalbooks.com.

DEDICATION

For my children

There are treasures beyond compare in the ocean. If you seek safety, stay ashore. — *Sufi saying*

PROLOGUE

The wind ruffled the curtains at the open French doors, and moonlight slipped into the darkened room. The knife dazzled as it slashed through the air. A startled cry failed to wake the slumbering woods, followed by a stumble and a spray of blood. Moments later, the wind blew at the curtains again, the shadowed room silent but for a labored breath, dying with the night.

CHAPTER 1

January 2001, Devon, England:

Why did the house feel so cold? Casey leaned her elbows back onto the narrow bed as the memory of the past few weeks ran through her mind, tightening her stomach. She'd hoped to escape the trauma of a broken relationship by returning to England, but the break-up seemed to have taken a piece of her she wasn't sure she'd get back.

The roughly plastered walls had been painted crisp white since her last visit, and the acrid smell of turpentine hung in the air. Glad of a distraction, she tucked her hands under her head and studied the changes in the room. The Tudor ceiling-beams had been newly stained, and curtains patterned with birds and flowers covered the lead-light windows. She smiled at the thought of Don perched on a ladder with a paintbrush and pulled the duvet up around her shoulders. It was almost nine. The others would be downstairs preparing breakfast. Don loved to cook her and

Tessa the great English breakfast. Bacon, sausage and eggs, his cure-all for a heavy night.

Knowing she had to get up, she lifted her head. It began to throb from the toxic mix of jet-lag and red wine. She rose and quickly donned her gown and some oversize sheepskin slippers—an impulse buy at Miami airport. Shuffling over the slippery timber floors, she pulled back the curtains.

The six acres of private woodland Don and Tessa prized so highly stretched out before her eyes. The wind had died down in the night, leaving the lawn bristled with white frost and the pond frozen over. Behind the stone wall, the silent, dripping woods began like the edges of a ragged blanket covering the hills. She shivered at the sight. English countryside in the winter failed to charm her. It seemed lonely and dark. Some miles beyond the woods lay the Devon coastline and the cold, oily waters of the English Channel.

She opened the door and walked out onto the landing, realizing someone must have closed her door during the night. The house was deathly quiet. She descended the sixteenth-century staircase, each step creaking louder than the last. She halted on the bottom step, which cracked like a pistol shot into the silence. Disconcerted by the echo it left and the lack of response, she felt her skin prickle at a thumping noise from the kitchen.

"What's the matter, Soc?"

The despondent tabby cat stood on the kitchen table, rocking it against the uneven stone-flagged floor. He arched his back, and she stroked him. He replied with a deep, throaty meow.

"Where do they keep your food?"

She searched the cupboards and found a tin. Blanching at the fishy smell, she filled his bowl and replenished the water in his other dish.

With a purr, Soc leapt to the floor and ate. She plugged in the electric kettle, wondering if she should take some coffee up to Don and Tessa. It was late for them.

Reaching for the kettle, she hesitated, aware of the range of strange noises thatched cottages could make.

Caffeine would help, she decided and poured a cup, carrying it into the hall. She paused at the hall table to study a photograph in a gold frame—herself and Tessa in their caps and gowns. Like bookends standing on each side of Don, drinking champagne in the crowded Quad at Oxford. In the misty air, her rebellious brown curls tipped her mortarboard to a drunken angle, creating an untidy counterbalance to petite Tessa, her red hair a neat plait over her shoulder.

As she replaced the photograph, a deathly sweet, unpleasant smell assaulted her senses. She moved towards the sitting room doorway and faltered.

The doors to the terrace stood open, and the leaves had blown in and nestled at the foot of Don's chair. He sat just where she'd left him the night before.

The cup and saucer slipped from her fingers and crashed to the floor, spilling coffee over the rug. She stumbled over them.

"Don?" His eyes remained open. A stream of blood ran from the corner of his mouth and mixed with the hairs of his neatly clipped beard. The front of his shirt, saturated in blood, pooled into his lap.

She placed her hands on his shoulders to shake him awake. "Don?" The moment she touched him, her legs buckled, and she fell into a crouch at his feet. His glasses lay beside her on the floor. Her bloodied hand hovered over them. *Don't touch them.*

A labored but bubbled breath floated through the room. *Tessa.*

Casey jumped to her feet and scrambled to the other side of the room. Brownish blood spots splashed across the green linen sofa. Tessa lay behind it on her stomach, the back of her ivory nightgown stained bright red, fanning out to a reddish-pink.

"Tessa, Tessa?" Casey touched her gently, but she didn't stir. She looked just like a waxy porcelain doll some child had thrown down in a corner, limbs akimbo.

She grabbed the phone from the table near the door and dialed.

"What service do you require?"

"*Ambulance.* Someone's been hurt. I think she's dying."

"What's the address?"

Her mind went blank. What was the damned street number? She took a huge breath to steady herself, and the number emerged. She leaned back against the wall. Through the open door, she heard rustling in the trees across the lawn. Her heart hammered, and she ran to slam the terrace doors shut. As her clumsy, trembling fingers shoved the bolt home, she saw it. The deer stood stock still, watching her. Suddenly spooked, it bounded away into the woods. She scoured the bare, wintry branches for further signs of life, afraid of what she might find. Could those ghostly trunks shield a murderer? Or was he still somewhere in the house?

∽∾∽

"Are you with me, Ms. Rowan?" The words pulled Casey's attention back into the room. She took a sip of cold, sweet tea from the mug. Someone's hand reached for her cup, and she moved her gaze up to a pair of concerned blue eyes.

"Ms. Casey Rowan? I'm Detective Chief Inspector Carlisle, of the Devon and Cornwall Police." He squatted beside her. "I realize you're in shock. Is there someone I can call?"

She bit her lip hard, needing to feel something. She wanted to scream and cry, but a cold vacuum seeped through her insides, and a sharp pain at the back of her throat sealed the scream inside. She'd stayed by Tessa's side until they'd taken her away. Don was gone too, packed into an airless body bag, zipped up tight. "I have to go with Tessa," she begged him. "Will you take me to the hospital, Inspector..."

"Carlisle, Ms. Rowan. There's no point in going to the hospital right now. And you can't stay here. Is there somewhere we can take you?"

"I have to know if Tessa is going to be alright."

"The hospital will ring you." He looked down at her left hand, where she clutched her mobile so tightly her knuckles were bloodless.

"Is there somewhere you'd like to go, Ms. Rowan?"

Casey shook her head. The tears flowed and eased the pain in her throat a little. She sniffed and wiped them away with the sleeve of her dressing gown. "Someone has to take care of Soc." She struggled to gain a hold on herself, not recognizing the strange, high-pitched voice.

"Who's Soc?" A policewoman came to stand beside the man.

"Socrates is Don's cat."

"I see." The policeman stood and spoke into the policewoman's ear. Casey didn't try to listen, her attention drawn to another policeman securing tape to the sitting room door. A fourth packed away his video camera. Be careful of their things, she wanted to say, pick up the cup I dropped.

The blue-eyed man left the room.

"Come on, love." The policewoman took Casey's arm. "Now, don't you go worrying about the puss. We'll find someone to take care of him. First, we'll go up and get dressed. Detective Chief Inspector Carlisle has found somewhere for you to stay."

Casey opened her mouth to protest. "Right near the hospital."

She shivered and wondered if she'd ever feel warm again.

CHAPTER 2

Casey stood at the window and stared down into the street. She wrestled with a strong desire to pack up and leave, knowing she couldn't. It was three o'clock in the afternoon, and hours had passed since they'd brought her to the boarding house. The phone rang, and warmth surged through her chilled body at the news Tessa had made it through surgery, her condition serious but stable. Casey snatched up her bag and ran the short distance to the hospital.

The sight of a police constable guarding the door of Tessa's room shook her. Tessa remained unconscious. She lay still, tucked neatly into the bed. Her arms and hands, with their long manicured nails, stretched out beside her. A tube in the back of her left hand connected to a drip. While she had a redhead's translucent skin, now it looked solid, like veined marble under Casey's tanned fingers. She found herself unprepared for the sudden, fierce jab of anger that hit her stomach, knocking the air out of her.

"Who did this, Tessa?" The hoarseness of her voice invaded the quiet room. Tessa's eyelids, with their fine tracery of blue veins, didn't stir. The machine went on with its pulsing beat.

"Rest now, darling." Casey lowered her voice. "When I come back, I know you'll be better."

She left the Royal Devon hospital and crossed Barrack Road, darting in a reckless fashion between a bus and lorry, wondering how people could go calmly about their business when Don was dead.

As she reached the pavement, the lorry's indignant klaxon sounded close behind her, but she didn't look back. Donald's death was front-page news, and someone also wanted Tessa dead. The police obviously thought so, too. But how long could they protect her?

Casey was eager to start looking for answers, but just as quickly, the newfound energy faded, and she dragged herself back to the guesthouse. Stretched out on the candlewick bedspread, she watched the breeze suck the awful chartreuse net curtains in and out of the open window. The room had grown icy cold, but she didn't get up to close it.

☙❧☙

Tessa remained unconscious the next day. Returning to her lodgings, Casey found Detective Chief Inspector Carlisle waiting at the gate.

"Ms. Rowan, I need to ask you a few questions. Are you feeling stronger?"

"Yes, thank you," she fibbed. It struck her how good manners persisted even in the worst of times.

He led the way to two overstuffed armchairs placed in "conversation mode" in the front room. They sat and looked at one another. For the first time, Casey took in the details. On that fateful morning, she'd remembered only Carlisle's blue eyes. She now saw he was a Scot, midway through his thirties. Tall and slim with straight, dark brown hair. Good looking, some would say, appearing reasonable and kind. But appearances weren't to be trusted.

"How is Mrs. Broughton?"

"The same," she replied, watching his long tapered fingers open the notebook.

He wore a plain silver ring on his right pinkie finger, but his left hand was bare. This man would be leading the investigation into Don's death? Somewhere between the hospital and here, she realized grief hadn't rendered her weak—it made her angry and tough. Her mind clear as a bell, she already had her plan mapped out. She wouldn't sit and wait for developments—she intended to take an active role in this investigation. Even though she knew the police wouldn't welcome her involvement. For this reason, her interest in Carlisle equaled his interest in her.

"When did you arrive in Devon?"

"Thursday night, the five o'clock train. Don picked me up from the station."

"Was it your habit to stay with them often?"

"Yes, but I've been away for the past three months in America. I only arrived back last week."

"Plain you haven't spent the winter in London. You have quite a tan." He smiled, making her aware of his well-shaped mouth and nice teeth.

She caught herself smiling back and shook her head. "Key Largo."

"I know of it. Bogart and Bacall?"

"Filmed at Warner Brothers."

He grinned briefly then turned business-like again. "You were friends, then. More with one than the other?"

"The three of us were good friends."

He wrote something in the notebook, and she tried to read it. Failing, she raised her eyes to find him watching.

"You didn't hear anything after you went to bed?"

"No. We had a few drinks, and I was tired."

Carlisle raised his eyebrows. "You slept pretty deeply then?"

She nodded, ignoring his unspoken suggestion she might have drank too much. "I didn't hear when someone shut my door during the night."

"You don't know who it was?"

"I thought it was Tessa."

"Can you give me any reason why someone would want to harm either of them?"

She fought to keep grief from her voice. "None whatsoever."

Tears pricked her eyes, and she rubbed them away savagely. "Do you think it was a burglary?" A random attack would mean Tessa would now be safe. Although she asked, she'd begun to doubt it.

"Too early to say, but it's looking increasingly unlikely," he said, confirming her thoughts. "Mrs. Broughton's jewelry and other valuables appear untouched. We'll need your help to make an inventory. Can you think of anything they might have taken?"

She forced herself to wander, in her mind's eye, through every room of their home. She stopped at the sitting room door, her mind refusing to go in. "Tessa had some nice silverware, a tray and tea service her mother gave them. What about the music system, the DVD player and television?"

"All still there." He rose and walked out of earshot, his phone to his ear, then returned. "Anything else?"

"Don's laptop? It's a silver Mac."

"I'll check on it."

"Perhaps they were interrupted?"

"Maybe." Carlisle changed tack. "Could Mr. or Mrs. Broughton have been involved romantically with someone else?"

"No," she scoffed. "They were a *very* loving couple." She remembered the twinge of envy she'd quickly buried at the sight of them holding hands and walking together.

Carlisle looked at her and waited for her to go on. "Do you mean could a lover have committed a crime of passion?" She shook her head. "You're on the wrong track there."

"What time did you go to bed?"

"It must have been around midnight. I heard Tessa follow me up. Don never went to bed before the early hours. He was listening to music. Could it have been Tessa they wanted?"

"At this stage, you know as much as we do, Ms. Rowan."

She looked at her hands. "Not much, then."

"It's possible Mrs. Broughton disturbed the intruder or intruders and they panicked and didn't finish the job."

Thank God they'd failed. Her mind went back to the hospital room and Tessa. Should she ring?

Carlisle shifted in his chair. "You say you've known the Broughtons for about ten years. Can you tell me more about them?"

She thought back to the first time she met Don. He was the quintessential Englishman with the ironic sense of humor, but his superior intelligence and sheer guts made him distinctive. His life and hers had a kind of symmetry. They both understood what it meant to be alone in the world.

"I was reading English and fine arts. Tessa, philosophy and physiology." She looked away. "And Don was an investigative reporter. He also had a radio show on BBC Radio 2—music and current affairs on Sunday afternoons."

"I read *The Times*. I enjoyed his column."

She glanced at him gratefully. "Tessa and I had just begun our degrees when we met him. He was in his early thirties and left Oxford years before."

Her mind traveled back over the past. As his celebrity status grew, Don attracted an enormous readership. He believed in social justice and political reform and scathingly condemned elitism. A furious opponent of the political status quo throughout the world, he could still see the funny side of life. He often tempered his strong beliefs with wit, and the Brits, not short of a sense of humor to get them through the bad times, loved him for it.

"And you, Ms. Rowan?" he said, interrupting her thoughts. "I believe you're a journalist also?"

"I'm deputy editor of *Hers* magazine." She reflected on how Don had ribbed her. *A woman's magazine? Can you really publish such drivel? Where's your social conscience?*

Hers wasn't like that, she'd argued, believing it at the time. She'd taken part in its inception, and they'd all started out wanting to make a difference. To chronicle the changes for women in society. They'd aimed to inform and advise women, but Casey never could convince Don she hadn't sold out, and his respect was important to her. There were pieces she'd fought for and took pride in, like the one on female circumcision, and the interview with Benazir Bhutto. Don admitted those articles had clarity and import, but that didn't change his mind.

And he'd been proven right. The team at *Hers* was naïve and idealistic. The standard didn't last, and the magazine slipped into the mold of many others, pandering to the reader's thirst for celebrity news.

"Miss Rowan?"

She found herself locked in the past again and shook her head to clear it. "Sorry."

Carlisle lit a cigarette. "Could something he'd been involved with have dangerous repercussions for him?"

She glanced at the "No Smoking" sign he disregarded. A law for the police and another for the rest of the public? The sign hung incongruously above the fireplace, and she knew Don would have laughed.

"Don was working on his autobiography." Carlisle raised his eyebrows. "He'd mentioned it in his column, and possibly his radio program, but I doubt it would have stirred up trouble. To my knowledge, it wasn't about exposing anything new."

Don hadn't talked about his work on Thursday night. They'd all had a lot to catch up on, but for him to fail to mention it had been unusual. Now that she thought about it, he'd looked tired, sitting back and allowing her and Tessa to do most of the talking.

"A grudge then, from the past?"

"I'm sure Don made a few enemies along the way. He could be single-minded when it came to a story." She remembered him years ago, when she'd just begun her career, his expression intense, telling her a good journalist never steps away from the truth.

Carlisle stubbed out his cigarette before he'd finished it. "Trying to give them up." He shrugged and gave a half-grin.

Casey nodded in commiseration.

"Perhaps someone had a reason for not wanting those memoirs published?"

"I don't have any idea, I'm sorry. You could talk to Don's publishers, and Tessa would have worked with him on it. You'll have to wait and ask her."

It was hard to pinpoint anything specific through the densely packed years of Don's career. But there was something.

"It may not be important, but there was an incident about four years ago. Don received a death threat."

"Go on."

"Lord Rupert Morris-Smythe threatened Don. Do you recall his father, Lord Harold, the Tory politician? He was mixed up in a prostitution racket and found guilty of fraud. Don was involved in the exposé."

"I remember. A Profumo type affair."

"The press pounced on the comparison. It was a tawdry business. One newspaper labelled him *Lord Pimp*. He couldn't take it and committed suicide."

Carlisle wrote something in his notebook. "What was Broughton's involvement?"

"Don wasn't after Lord Harold. He wasn't in the habit of attacking individuals." She ran a hand through her hair, the need to defend Don and respect his memory overwhelming her. He was gone. *Gone*. "He was *never* a moralist—he was more concerned with causes. Lord Harold's son, Rupert, wrote Don a hate letter. Threatened to kill him."

"What did he do about it?"

"Nothing." She shrugged. "The letter seemed the end of it, and as I said, it was years ago."

"Anything else?"

She shook her head.

"What about Mrs. Broughton? She has her own practice, doesn't she?"

"Yes. She works with victims of domestic violence. She counsels some of the perpetrators as well." Shortly after becoming registered, Tessa turned her back on an elegant practice in London to become involved in real nitty-gritty work with the less fortunate.

"Has she had any success?"

"With the perpetrators, you mean? Rather limited, I'm afraid."

"Aye, its learned behaviour, isn't it? We have to reach them when they're young, to stop the cycle of violence. Can you remember any particular cases which might be relevant?"

"Tessa didn't go into details. Client confidentiality." Casey didn't have to think far back. "She was involved in a court case only a few months ago. Her psychometric assessment ensured a murderer would remain behind bars for life. An Irishman named Gavin Holmes."

Carlisle began to write.

"He and two other men raped and murdered a young girl in the Kilburn area."

"Anything more you can add?"

"Well, Tessa's involvement attracted some publicity. I have the newspaper cuttings back at my flat in Richmond. Holmes appealed against his life sentence on the grounds he wasn't capable of the standard of verbalisation contained within his 'confession.' He couldn't express himself as well as his statement indicated. Tessa tested the limits of his comprehension of the statement by paraphrasing its content sentence by sentence. Holmes was, in fact, cognizant. In Tessa's opinion, he was extremely taciturn and uncommunicative. She felt when interviewed he would have sat dumbly, you know, staring into space and saying very little."

"So he forced the police to formulate statements for him?"

"Precisely. Then he'd agree to what was documented, even though the words and phrases weren't his."

Carlisle paused and clicked his pen. "Mrs. Broughton sounds like an interesting woman."

Casey wondered if he was a man who loved women. Women would most probably pursue him. Men like him were quite often spoiled. Annoyed, she gathered her thoughts. "Yes, she is. Tessa's evidence had a lot to do with the appeal being rejected. Holmes and the other two. Cleavy...Daniel's his first name, and Brian Black—they all got life imprisonment."

She waited for him to finish writing. "He eyeballed Tessa in the courtroom, made her skin crawl. Will you find out if they're still in jail?"

"I will. Anyone else?"

"There could be, but nothing I'm aware of. Why would anyone come all the way down to Devon? Tessa lives and works in London."

"There's no telling what some people will do. At this stage, it appears Mr. Broughton is most likely the target. Where's Mrs. Broughton's practice?"

"Camberwell."

"I believe her parents have been staying with their elder daughter in Manhattan. They're on their way home. What about Donald? Does he have family we should contact?"

"No, Don was an orphan. He became fiercely determined to rise above it. Driven, I suppose you could say. Plus sheer brilliance got him into Oxford."

Feeling the police would concentrate on Don and leave Tessa unprotected, she decided to lay her cards on the table. "After Tessa's parents arrive, I'll make a few enquiries of my own. Look into some of Tessa's contacts."

Carlisle frowned. "No, Ms. Rowan, I'd rather you didn't interfere with the processes of the law. No amateur sleuthing, please. It could hamper our investigation and might put your own life in danger."

"Detective Chief Inspector, one of my friends is dead. The other is seriously injured and may still be at risk."

As cold-blooded fury pounded through her veins, a plan took shape. Because she'd returned earlier than planned from America—ran away, if she was honest—she still had two weeks of extended leave left. She would check with the hospital first thing in the morning. Hopefully, Tessa would have regained consciousness. If not, her parents were due to arrive later in the day. She would take Don's car and head up to Camberwell to Tessa's practice to check through her files.

"Don't you get any foolish ideas, Ms.Rowan. Stay put until Mrs. Broughton recovers."

"I have no intention of it, Inspector," she said brusquely. Don had taught her to go after a story, and this was one story she couldn't afford to pass up.

Carlisle took his displeasure out on his tie, reefing it to the side. The design had little hits of aqua, which matched his eyes, a color much like the waters off the Florida Keys. He met her gaze, and the tone in his voice held a warning.

"Are you used to getting your own way, Ms. Rowan?"

"If you think I've enjoyed a charmed life because I went to Oxford, Inspector, you're wrong. Like Don, I've worked hard for what I've achieved."

He paused and watched her. She felt her face redden and bit her lip, afraid she was losing it.

She opened her mouth to fight on, and he said mildly, "My instincts tell me you're an educated, intelligent woman. Too smart, surely, to find yourself on the wrong side of the police."

Neatly, he diffused her anger and left her to wonder at her own behavior. She watched him walk out the door, smoothing back his hair. Long for a policeman, it hinted at insubordination, which she found rather interesting. Fleetingly, she wondered about his personal life.

He turned, interrupting her reverie.

"Ms. Rowan? You were, of course, the last person to see Donald Broughton alive. At this stage you remain a suspect."

CHAPTER 3

Detective Chief Inspector Rod Carlisle walked into Superintendent Thomas Kennerton's room at Middlemoor HQ. Tom leaned back heavily in his chair, causing it to give a screech of protest.

"Sit down, Rod."

Rod obeyed. Taking out his pack of cigarettes, he offered one to Tom. His office remained a haven in a smoker's shrinking world.

"I have to give 'em up." Tom waved the packet away. "Doctor's orders." He grimaced.

"That's rough, Tom, but we all should." Rod put the packet back in his pocket.

Tom tapped the papers on his desk. "Damn it! This is the fourth murder we've had in as many months."

Rod watched red blotches break out on Tom's face. They'd pension him off if he didn't watch out. Or he'd die on the job.

Six months ago, Rod had hovered on the brink of death himself. He now struggled with tiredness, not only from his injury, but also from feelings of grief and guilt he was endeavoring to work through with the police psychologist. He shook his head in bemusement. Instead of taking extended leave, he'd requested a transfer away from Scotland Yard's SO13. Somewhere quieter, and here he found himself in the midst of a celebrity murder, which would throw a lot of media attention his way.

"It's a first for this area," Tom continued. "We'll have to watch our budget, and it doesn't help we're under review from the Home Office Working Group. We'll get a lot of pressure to solve this one—it's high-profile stuff. We have the press clamoring for details, and I've set up a conference. We don't want them messing this up. What can we safely give them?"

Rod shrugged. "The truth. We have absolutely nothing yet. All we can say is at this moment, there's no apparent motive. Officers are trying to piece together."

"Yeah, okay." Tom smiled, and the angry flush faded. "What did you get from Ms. Rowan?"

"She says she went to bed a bit worse for wear, slept heavily, and heard nothing."

He picked up the photo of the three of them at Oxford Rod had dropped on the desk. "What's your gut feeling about this girl?"

"I doubt she's involved."

Tom took a gulp of coffee and grimaced. "Can't get used to it black." He sighed and held up the photo again. "Rowan's a looker, if you like the type."

"Not bad," Rod said casually—too casually, apparently, for the sharp, older man raised an eyebrow.

"That doesn't affect your gut feeling?"

"Certainly not," he answered swiftly. At first glance, Casey had appeared grief-stricken and brittle, but the defiance in her big, hazel eyes challenged him. Made him suspect she was tougher than she looked.

A spasm gripped Rod's side, evoking a painful memory. He had a desperate need to prove to himself he was a good cop and a good mate. He wished, for the hundredth time, things would've turned out differently. If only he could pick up the phone and talk to Pete. The voice, they say, is the hardest to remember. He cautioned himself to be careful—now was not the time to get distracted. He knew Tom would evaluate his performance.

"What about lovers, ex-wives, ex-husbands?"

"Donald and Tessa were married for seven years. Happy by all accounts."

"Well, someone wanted them dead," Tom said bluntly.

"Rowan might prove to be a problem, though."

"Oh?"

"She's a journo, on a mission to find the truth."

"Christ. That's all we need." Tom took a loud slurp of coffee and put down the cup with a gesture of disgust. "Warn her to keep out of our way." He tapped the photo. "She could well be involved. Looks a bit like a *ménage à trois* to me. Some of these people are too well educated for their own good."

Rod wondered if a twinge of jealousy lay behind the remark, but Tom was on the move. He'd fished out the silver pocket watch he always carried. Rod knew its history. At one time it belonged to Tom's grandfather, but it gave Tom a rather anachronistic air he could ill afford.

"Time." Tom stood and searched his pockets for the nicotine chewing gum. "Let's get to it, Rod."

With the files tucked under his arm, Rod followed Tom into the meeting room where photos of the murder scene were thumb-tacked to the whiteboard. He felt a familiar kick of nausea hit his stomach. Would he ever grow inured to the endless, gruesome deaths of decent people? The murder team perched around the room, waiting for the meeting to start. None of them looked particularly pleased to have him there.

Kennerton held up his hands, and all conversation in the room halted. "Okay. I'm sorry it's Saturday and some of you have given up your weekend. I've called this emergency conference because of the particularly nasty aspects of this crime. This is a homicide, a double homicide if Mrs. Broughton dies. I know you're all keen to get on to it, so I'll put you in the hands of Detective Inspector Rod Carlisle. As I'm sure you're all aware, he has joined us from the exalted atmosphere of New Scotland Yard."

"Good afternoon, ladies and gentlemen." Rod walked straight to the board and wrote down the names of Lord Rupert Morris-Smythe, Holmes, Cleavy, and Black. And he included the other information Casey had given him.

He returned to pick up a file on the desk.

"We have the post mortem report on Donald Broughton. It was rushed through this morning. Death was caused by blood loss resulting from one right-handed knife thrust through the thorax straight into the heart. Blood spatters and the angle of the wound show us his attacker stood above him. There are no wounds on Broughton's hands to suggest he might have tried to repel his attacker and no other evidence of a struggle. The depth of the stab wounds to both Broughton and his wife would indicate the same attacker. Someone pretty bloody strong. They were discovered around nine o'clock, Friday morning, Twentieth February."

Rod looked up from the report. "Impossible to establish an accurate time of death. On Donald Broughton, rigor mortis was developing. His core temperature would have been affected by the cold. The door was left open, and the temperature during the night dropped below minus five. Somewhere between two a.m. and four a.m. was the time of death. Then we have Tessa Broughton, alive, but seriously injured. A single stab wound of great force to the back, damaging a lung. She remains unconscious."

"Is she expected to live?" PC Anita Jennings leaned forward in her chair, eyes shining—with compassion or interest in celebrity, Rod couldn't tell.

He put down the report. "Too early to say."

"No obvious signs of forced entry?" asked DS Danny Singh, a thin, young cop with sharp brown eyes and a bad case of acne.

"We're not sure how the killer got in at this point, but we know he exited via the sitting room doors, leaving them open. We have a partial footprint, plus blood spots of type AB. The same blood type as Tessa Broughton."

"What about the weapon?" Singh continued.

"Not found at the scene, but we believe it to be a large knife. Non-serrated, about the size of a carving knife, and we believe it was used to attack both." He scanned the room. "We have a PC posted outside Tessa's hospital room. The person who found them and raised the alarm is

Ms. Casey Rowan. She was staying with them for the weekend. Ms. Rowan is a thirty-year-old American who works as an editor with *Hers* magazine."

"Oh, my mum loves that mag," Jennings said.

"Aye, thanks for that," Rod responded dryly. "Rowan lives in Richmond, Surrey. For the present she's residing in a guest house here in Exeter, near The Royal Devon & Exeter Hospital, where Tessa Broughton is recovering."

"Surely Rowan would have heard *something*, sir?" ventured Singh.

"She says someone closed her bedroom door during the night." Rod folded his arms and leaned back against the desk. "I think we should keep an open mind on the motive and circumstances at this stage. As you're aware, the crime-scene people have been through. Donald Broughton's laptop is the only item confirmed missing. Nothing's obviously damaged or disturbed, but we'll wait for evidence. It's an isolated cottage, and the closest neighbors are at least five miles away by road. The cottage is stone and thatch set on eight acres of private parkland twenty-five minutes' drive from Exeter. Nearest town is Honiton. This was their holiday home and not their principal place of residence. That's in Fulham. Let's hope Mrs. Broughton regains consciousness and can tell us something soon. If not, we'll have a lot more ground to cover."

Rod looked around the room. "We need to get to know our victims. I want to know about Donald's business associates and what he wrote in his column for the past six months. Need to know what was going in his autobiography. We'll talk to his publishers, find out who his friends were and where he's been lately. Then we'll probably have to do the same for Mrs. Broughton." He pointed to the board. "There are two leads to chase up, first a death threat made four years ago to Donald by a Lord Rupert Morris-Smythe, just after his father Lord Harold committed suicide."

"That's a waste of time. Stone cold," Tom said, throwing down his pen.

"There's also been a knife attack reported in Exeter some hours before the murder." Rod glanced at Tom and frowned. "Chances are it's unrelated, but we'll have to check it out. PC Jennings? Will you get onto it, please?"

"Right, gov."

"Tessa Broughton is a psychologist," Rod continued. "Part of her practice is to work with the victims of abuse and domestic violence. Her psychological opinion in court helped put an Irishman, Gavin Holmes, away on a murder charge. DS Singh, you can do the check on him and his cronies. Contact the local borough and see what the word on the street is—if he has any loyal friends on the outside. I'll take a trip to Pentonville Prison and pay him a visit. Tessa has an office at Camberwell. We'll bring in the local boys if nothing turns up in the next few days."

Rod leaned forward and rested his hands on the table. "Donald Broughton also had a Sunday radio show on BBC 2. I want to know if that produced any hate mail. We have quite a job to do. So, let's get on it."

There came a murmured chorus of agreement.

"DI Barry will be in charge of delegating duties. Colin?"

Rod sat down as Colin Barry stepped forward and began to supervise the scenes of crime officers. His face and body appeared far too heavy for action, more suited to playing Santa Claus in a Christmas pageant. Rod wouldn't count on him to watch his back in a siege, but could he say the same about himself? In the last tragic operation, he'd performed to the best of his ability. Or had he? It was a question he constantly asked himself, even though the Board had acquitted him of any wrongdoing.

Barry began to detail all the mundane necessities of investigation. The legwork just might turn up a lead, a trigger, however small, which could set up a line of inquiry.

CHAPTER 4

On Sunday morning, Tessa still hadn't regained consciousness, and Casey took a cab back to the cottage. In the distance, a line of men searched through the fields, disappearing into the misty woods. A few reporters still hung about, and her presence now caused a rumble of interest. An older man in a wrinkled suit and unattractive stubble wrapped up his kabob breakfast and strolled towards her with a young woman photographer in tow.

"Ms. Rowan, could you give me a little of your time? I believe they found you at the murder scene, covered in blood. What's your relationship to the deceased?"

"I've nothing to add to the police report." A flash from the photographer's camera startled her. "What paper are you from?"

"The Sun."

Damn. She opened the gate and walked quickly away into the garden, pulling out her mobile and dialing.

"Hers."

"Hello, Jenny, it's Casey. Could you get me Hugh Bailley or Geraldine?"

The senior editor at *Hers,* Geraldine Broadhurst, came on the line, her voice flooded with sympathy. "Oh Casey! What a god-awful thing to happen. How's Tessa?"

"She's still unconscious, Geraldine."

After Casey rang off assured of any help she might need, she approached the old stone house wrapped with crime scene tape.

She had permission to get the things she'd left behind, and a young police constable met her at the door. "You can go through," he said, "but I'm afraid I'll have to accompany you."

"That's fine." Casey silently cursed, making a mental note she needed to get Tessa's keys. Inside, the quiet felt eerie. It seemed all the warm vibes of a house well-loved and filled with laughter had been sucked out, leaving an empty space. Even Soc was gone, off with the nearest neighbor, a couple of miles down the road. Casey didn't want to be here and vowed never to come again.

They walked down the hall, and she caught sight of the chair, now stained dark with blood, where she'd found Don and her bile rose. She followed the policeman up the stairs to her room, and he waited while she stuffed her remaining things into her overnight case.

As she worked on a way to get rid of him, the doorbell chimed. He disappeared down the stairs, and she took the opportunity to dart into the main bedroom.

Tessa's side of the bed was rumpled, but Don's pajamas remained folded on his pillow. On his bedside table lay his extra pair of reading glasses and a manuscript he'd been asked to endorse. She grabbed Tessa's handbag from the dresser and rifled through it. Aware the muffled hum of conversation downstairs had ceased, she headed back to her room and zipped up her case.

The young constable returned.

"I'm right now, thanks," she said.

Casey glanced at him and noticed he'd cut himself shaving. He looked much too young with his fresh pink complexion, and she hoped she wouldn't get him into trouble.

"Permission's been given for me to take the car."

He nodded, slid the car key off Donald's key ring and handed it to her.

The task lay ahead of her.

CHAPTER 5

The traffic was surprisingly light. Casey watched the speedometer climb as she sped up the M5 motor way to London. Over the last few years, she'd curbed a tendency to drive too fast, but grief seemed to have changed that, too. Don's pallid face appeared in her mind, and she took the corners at a dangerous speed.

Close to three hours later, she headed down the Old Kent Road in Camberwell and miraculously found a parking spot near Tessa's office, pulling into the curb just as the two o'clock news came over the radio. She sat for a few minutes and listened for any new reports on Donald's murder but heard nothing.

It was one of those familiar, grim London days with smoky gray clouds rolling over the rooftops. When opened the door, the cold air touched her skin like a clammy hand. She wrapped a scarf around her neck and slipped on her coat.

She crossed to a sandwich shop and bought a bread roll filled with salad and cheese and a take-away coffee. She returned to her car and ate quickly, hoping the food would provide enough energy to get her through a demanding, stressful, and emotionally taxing day.

Tessa's neat office suite smelled musty, as if shut up for a long time. It felt odd to be here without her. Unlawful, too, but Casey felt sure Tessa would support her on this. She slipped into the bathroom and used the facilities, attempting to wash the fatigue from her face before adding lipstick and combing her hair.

She went to the office window and threw it open. With a decisive snap, she pulled on a pair of rubber surgical gloves from the chemist and opened a drawer in the steel filing cabinet, removing a bundle of files.

Sitting behind the desk, she began to look for clients who fit the criteria or profile she'd worked out for herself. Cases Tessa handled during the past year. Someone's partner who might have felt Tessa's help was interference, or who blamed her for the break-up of their relationship. Anyone possibly dangerous.

An hour and a half later, she'd narrowed the possibilities down to five. Three men and a woman, plus a brain damage case she thought bore some investigation. She turned on the photocopier, copied the case notes, and replaced the files before locking up.

She reached the street to find a group of black youths clustered around Don's beloved old red MG sports car. They wore their strange, baggy uniforms, pants several sizes too big that hung off their young, thin bodies. Casey sensed their silent envy.

It began to rain, and for a moment she sat and listened to the thud of heavy raindrops on the canvas roof. It reminded her of snuggling down in bed and listening to the rain on the roof as a kid, but in London the rain wasn't revitalizing, it was just plain dreary, and she couldn't conjure up the comfort that sound once had for her. The patter of drops increased into a deluge.

Windshield wipers on high, the stop and start business of negotiating London traffic beginning, she headed east on the Camberwell New Road. Her next stop was Don and Tessa's new riverside townhouse in Fulham. They'd moved in while she was in America, and she would see it for the first time. Tessa had asked her to housesit next month while they went to Manhattan to visit her sister. She had written the alarm details along with the address and new phone number in Casey's diary.

Almost an hour passed before she turned left into Fulham Road.

Driving down the narrow lane, she checked to see if anyone was there. The phone rang, and Don's message came on the line. She braked in shock.

She sat and stared blindly through the windshield for a moment, then drove on through the blur of tears and rain. She approached the cream-painted brick wall, pressed the button on Tessa's key ring, and parked in the garage beside Tessa's powder-blue Mercedes Coupe. Holding a newspaper over her head, she ran for the front steps. Freezing rain soaked into her scalp and crawled its icy fingers down the back of her neck all the while.

The house was an impressive post-modernist blend of old and new. In the center of the wide frontage stood a glossy black door with a heavy brass knocker. Box hedges acted as sentries. Careful not to touch the door with her fingers, she slid the key into the lock and used it as leverage to push it open.

She called out, her words echoing through the dark hallway, and crept forward, her heart pounding. A sound like a trapped animal began to peel through the house. Abandoning any pretense of stealth, she flew down the hall, wildly searching for the alarm keyboard Tessa had told her about. She reefed open the door and punched in the numbers. Silence descended, and she sighed with relief. She shakily wiped the door handle of the cupboard with a tissue and turned to study the house.

The living areas were of an open-plan design. Through a wall of glass, a stone terrace at the rear of the building bordered a parterre hedge and gardens. A path led down to a marina bobbing on the mist-shrouded Thames. Night fell early in winter, so she would have to hurry. She couldn't risk putting on lights.

She turned back to the sitting room. It had Le Courbusier style seats and chrome and glass everywhere, Bauhaus in the twenty-first century. On a wall at the far end of the room hung a painting with brilliant red-orange oil on canvas. She moved closer and examined the signature. The name, Wassily Kandinsky, made her gasp and put out a tentative finger to touch the painted surface. It was real.

Retracing her steps, she headed for the other wing of the house.

The drum of her heels on the parquet floor echoed through the hall. Something seemed very wrong. Don had been very successful in his chosen profession, but it wouldn't have made him the millions of pounds required to buy this kind of luxury. Their previous house had been humble by comparison. At what point did they start wanting so much more?

She pushed open the door to the main bedroom with her fist and stopped. The room had been ransacked, cupboard doors hung open and drawers overturned, their contents spread across the floor. She backed up against the wall, her eyes darting across the room. When did this happen?

The scene sent her heart pounding so hard her ribs began to hurt. She ran for the front door. Sliding on the Persian carpet, she grabbed the doorway to stop herself from falling. Stumbling into the back bedroom, she fell to a crouch and stared at the glass scattered across the floor. The window had been smashed from the outside.

She stayed crouched and tried to listen above the noisy pounding of her heart. Either all the noise she'd made sent someone scurrying for cover, or they'd left before she arrived. The house was so silent she could hear the heating system kick on and the distant chug of a boat on the river.

Her heart slowed to its normal rhythm. Inside the house, nothing moved except her, and she retraced her steps to the study.

Don's computer discs lay scattered over the desk. The computer was still on. She grabbed a pencil and used its rubber tip to scroll through his files. He had a backlog of information stored there. When she was just about to give up, a file simply headed *Farrowham* appeared in the computer's recently opened documents. The name was familiar but the file was encoded.

The front door opened, and she jumped to her feet, her eyes sliding wildly across the room for somewhere to hide. She'd only taken a few steps across the room before, DCI Carlisle appeared at the study door, with two other police officers standing behind him.

"Ms. Rowan," he said, his words curt. "I thought I made myself perfectly clear. Do I have to put you behind bars to stop you from interfering in this investigation?"

"I just got here." Casey felt her face grow hot. "The place has been ransacked. A window broken. Why would I do that? I have a key!"

"And how did you come by a key?"

"I borrowed them."

Carlisle's expression didn't change. "And the alarm sequence?"

"Tessa wrote it in my diary when she asked me to house-sit for her." She fumbled in her bag and rifled through the pages. "See for yourself."

He looked at the page she thrust at him but he didn't seem satisfied.

"You're threatening this case, Ms. Rowan. We have a right to know why you're here."

"Looking for anything unusual. I know Don. If something's out of place, I'd know it. I can help." She searched his face. He wasn't buying it.

He walked over to the computer. "That's debatable. So far, you've done nothing but mess up a potential crime scene. What have you touched?"

"I checked the computer files. I used the end of a pencil."

Furious, he motioned to the other two police officers. They left the room, and she listened to them move about the house. "We're going to need to take a trip to the station. You don't seem to realize you're a suspect in a murder enquiry, and now I find you at a crime scene. The Devon police took your fingerprints, didn't they?"

She nodded. "I didn't know it was a crime scene. And I was careful. You won't find my fingerprints here. When did this happen?"

His brows rose slightly. "Friday morning."

"Friday! You might have mentioned it when we spoke earlier."

Carlisle looked tired. He rubbed his hand over the beginnings of a four o'clock shadow, and a muscle worked in his cheek. His tie was loosened at the neck, the top button undone. "I guess I just didn't realize I was supposed to keep you informed. Maybe a night in the cells will cool you down."

"On what charge?" She went to brush past him, but he placed his hand against the wall, blocking her exit.

"Oh, I can come up with a great deal on you, Ms. Rowan. Tampering with a crime scene, for one."

They studied each other. She drew breath, unsettled by his proximity, so close she caught the scent of leather and soap.

A heavy frown lodged between Carlisle's eyebrows, his blue eyes frosty. "I'm still waiting for you to tell me what you're doing here."

"I have to help Tessa find out who killed Don." Her voice shook, more from frustration than distress.

He straightened. "And you don't trust the police to do that?"

"I don't distrust the police, Inspector Carlisle." She clasped her hands together, Don's face swimming again into her vision. "I've lost one of my best friends. I'm frightened I'll lose another."

A long pause followed, and he studied her. Finally, he spoke. "We'll postpone the interview for the moment, but if I find you've messed up, I'll have you into the station faster than you can blink. If you really want this crime solved, don't mess up the evidence—we need to do our job."

He turned to leave. "Inspector Carlisle?"

He spun around and gave an audible sigh. "Yes, Ms. Rowan?"

"Does the word 'Farrowham' mean anything to you?"

"I don't think so. Why?"

"I found it on Don's computer. It's an encoded file. The name sounded familiar, and I think it might be worth looking into."

His eyes widened. "Do you think it's a clue, Ms. Rowan?"

She smiled weakly. "Yes, perhaps."

"We'll see what we can do. Leave it to me." After he left the room, she remembered the notes she'd taken from Tessa's office. What would he have done if she'd told him? Think her mad, most probably, and she would be inclined to agree with him.

❦❧❦

Farrowham. It danced just out of reach, somewhere in the recesses of Casey's mind. Her head began to ache. She needed food—something hot. It was still raining, the traffic was horrendous, and it took her almost an hour to reach

Richmond. She stopped in Richmond Road West at a favourite Indian take-away to pick up a curry and a bottle of wine. She'd come to know the couple who ran the place quite well.

A poster of a graceful, brightly colored dancer performing a Classical Indian dance hung on the wall, and Indian folk music played. Husband and wife greeted her with a smile, and from somewhere down deep, she found the strength to return it. Rani Kaur disappeared into the kitchen, and her husband, Shiblu, and Casey chatted. He expressed concern about another Indian restaurant opening two blocks away.

"You have a great reputation here, Shiblu," she reassured him as Rani appeared and proceeded to put plastic tops on the dishes. "And wonderful food."

The delicious aroma filled the car and made her empty stomach growl the entire drive home.

The rented flat looked dreary and unwelcoming, with all the walls painted a utilitarian gray that lent an arctic feel to the place. Turning on the heat, she huddled on the sofa for a good ten minutes before it felt warm enough to contemplate taking off her clothes. She hopped into the shower and let the hot water run over her neck and shoulders, easing the tension, before towelling and putting on warm pajamas and a robe. While the chicken korma gently heated in the microwave, she popped the cork on the bottle of Napa Valley Chardonnay. She took several sips of fresh, sharp wine to fortify her before ringing the hospital, only to hear the usual reply—no change.

The ding from the microwave made her jump up like a jack-in-the-box. Nerves still strung tight, she retrieved the food, burning her finger, and swore out loud. Wrapping her legs around a kitchen stool, she ate and drank until her headache began to ease.

She opened her bag and pulled out the photocopies of Tessa's case files. She knew Tessa refused to counsel couples if one partner rated less than eight to ten on a scale of agreement. Any less, she said, and her counseling was ineffective. If one partner didn't agree to participate, she would offer the other separation counseling.

The first on her list was a Lebanese Muslim named Bilal Assam, estranged from his English wife, Heather. He had forced her to come to relationship counseling so Tessa could impose his wish for her to return to live with the Muslim family. While living there, she had been beaten and kept a virtual prisoner.

Casey remembered Tessa telling her she'd ordered him out of her rooms by threatening to report him to the police for physical and psychological abuse. She'd then referred the wife to a woman's refuge. This had happened four months ago. She checked the name of the refuge—she might need to find Heather and talk to her.

Next was a company director, Reginald Jamieson, aged forty-two, who assaulted his wife Jennifer both mentally and physically over a period of some years.

Mopping up the last drops of Korma sauce, Casey muttered, "Bastard."

She took another sip of wine, feeling the weight of despair descend and begin to eat into her determination. She prayed forensics would provide a shred of evidence quickly, while Tessa was safe. She turned back to the notes. Jennifer had consulted Tessa during a trial separation of short duration. Reginald had not attended any counseling sessions. They had no children. Casey thought Jamieson would value his reputation. His career might depend on it. Not enough of a motive to kill, though, unless he was mentally unstable—and the file offered no suggestion of that.

Arthur Warren was in the building trade. He was thirty-three years old and in trouble with the law for acting violently towards his girlfriend, Sally Cameron. She'd taken out a restraining order against him after he refused counseling.

Then the brain damage case, Michael Miller, aged twenty-three. His injury was the result of a motorbike accident. Tessa wrote he'd suffered frontal lobe damage. When she'd assessed Miller's personal injury compensation claim, he'd acted threateningly towards her. Casey remembered Tessa telling her sufferers of frontal lobe syndrome had very poor organisational skills, lack goal direction, and had trouble controlling impulses.

A woman Casey found of interest was Maria Bartolomei, an abusive mother Tessa had assessed for the Children's Court clinic in a custody battle. Tessa deemed the mother unfit. Her two daughters were then placed in the custody of their father, who had a new common-law wife. Maria was very jealous and reacted violently towards the ex-husband. Casey put her at the top of her list because the case was relatively new. Secondly, she remembered reading somewhere that a knife was a woman's choice of weapon.

Could any of Tessa's clients be guilty of such a crime? Casey couldn't think any longer. The pages blurred as her lids grew heavy.

She turned off the lights and went to bed, only to dream of Don. He sat in his chair where she'd last seen him, wearing the jacket Tessa always ribbed him about with the worn leather patches on the elbows. He looked directly at Casey, his eyes imploring, and said something—but just at that moment, she woke. She sleepily tried to recall the words he'd spoken, but they were gone.

CHAPTER 6

Rod's police car sped past the River Wey, and he turned to watch children feeding ducks on the bank. A snapshot of a gentle bucolic scene. He took a breath, realizing how intense he'd become of late.

It was still early on Tuesday morning when, a few miles out of Guildford in Surrey, the police car passed through the imposing, ornate gates bearing the family coat of arms of Morris-Smythe and drove down an avenue of beech trees. The voice from the speakerphone informed them they would find his lordship on the putting green. Parking at the end of the long gravel drive, Rod stepped out into the fragile warmth of a sunny winter's day. Singh and Jennings accompanied him. Morris-Smythe's Gothic castle glowered down on them from atop its grassy knoll.

"Not very homey, is it?" Singh observed.

"Haunted is my guess," Jennings answered, gazing up at the gray stone battlements.

Rod checked his notes on Rupert Morris-Smythe. Rupert apparently held only a token interest in his legacy. Since his father's death, he'd not become an active member of the House of Lords. Rod had read a newspaper's recounting of Rupert's brief maiden speech where he deplored the high prices fashionable art brought at auction. He thought Morris-Smythe's position ironic—the paintings from his family's collection, that hadn't been sold over the last century as the family coffers thinned, would now make him one of the richest men in Britain.

It appeared that Rupert's life revolved around sport: cricket, tennis, golf, boating. He played it, and, failing that, flew around the world to watch the best of it.

Rod sent his two colleagues up to the house to talk to the staff while he walked along a path past a croquet lawn and a tennis court. Beyond that lay a swimming pool with a blue cover. Rod wondered how often the cover came off. Morris-Smythe bent over his putter on the pampered green. A caddy solemnly held the flag in the hole. More out of curiosity than politeness, Rod stopped and watched the ball travel a good fifteen feet before it broke, curving in a gentle arc and plopping into the hole. The rich obviously had time to perfect their golf game.

"Nice putt, Lord Morris-Smythe."

Morris-Smythe, a strongly built, fair-haired man with a receding chin, pulled off a golfer's leather glove and offered him a languid hand. "Please join me, Detective Chief Inspector." He strolled to a table with a large striped umbrella. The servant hovered near the pavilion, which resembled a mini-Parthenon. "Can I offer you a drink? No? On duty, eh? What about tea or coffee, perhaps?"

"Tea would be fine, thanks. Just black."

"Tea, and make that a Bloody Mary for me. Thank you, John."

Rod surreptitiously checked his watch. It was just nine o'clock.

The Bloody Mary seemed to energize Morris-Smythe, and he checked his bejeweled gold Rolex and turned back the cuffs of his cashmere sweater. "I'm afraid I have nothing to add to what I told you on the telephone."

"You still haven't given me the exact details of your whereabouts on the night in question."

His sandy eyebrows rose in surprise. "I've no idea why I should. Am I a suspect? Should I call my solicitor?"

Rod sighed. "That won't be necessary at this time. I don't know why you find this question so difficult, Lord Morris-Smythe, unless you have something to hide."

"As I told you, my wife and I went to the opera." He arched a brow. Rod waited, and he continued. "The Covent Garden orchestra and chorus with Antonio Pappano conducting a new staging of Mozart's Le Nozze di Figaro. We left at intermission to attend the Newington's party. We were there until around eleven and then went back to our apartment in St John's Wood. There we stayed the night and arrived back at Penlow Hall around four in the afternoon."

"I'd like to speak to Lady Morris-Smythe, please."

"I'm afraid she left for France last night. She has plans to visit relatives and do a little traveling for a couple of weeks."

"I'll need a number where I can reach her."

"Yes, of course. John?" he called to his man. "Will you get Lady Morris-Smythe's number in Paris and give it to the inspector on his way out?"

"Her mobile number as well, thanks," Rod added.

"I'm afraid she hasn't one."

"Were you aware Donald Broughton was writing his memoirs?"

"No, I can't say I heard about it. It's of no interest to me. I've put that business all behind me. But I must say I'm not surprised someone murdered Broughton." He shook his head. "He poked his inquisitive nose into someone's private business once too often." He polished off the last of his drink and put the glass down purposefully. "Well, if we've covered it, I'm afraid I have business matters to attend to."

You're not above the law, you pompous prick, thought Rod. "I'd like your staff at your St John's Wood home to verify what you've just told me."

Morris-Smythe rose to his feet. "I'm afraid that's not possible. Our live-in staff was absent that night."

He turned away and headed up the path to the house. "Now I'm afraid you'll have to excuse me."

"One more question, Lord Morris-Smythe?" Rod called after him. "I'd also like the color and make of your car."

Morris-Smythe barely paused in his stride. "When I drive myself? A black BMW or the red Porsche. It depends on what mood I'm in."

"And that night, which car did you drive?"

"The BMW," he said over his shoulder.

He watched the man walk away into his fortress of a house. Rod hated the type. Morris-Smythe thought no one could touch him, but did he think that gave him the right to commit murder?

Rod had seen too many like Morris-Smythe get away with white-collar crime and worse. He'd love to slap a murder charge on someone of his kind, not just the young disadvantaged criminals the police dealt with day to day. But he had to admit he was probably wasting valuable time. Too many years had passed since the man had issued his death threat.

CHAPTER 7

Four days had passed since the attack. With the news from the hospital unchanged, Casey poured her nervous energy into cleaning the flat. Emptying her suitcase, she shook sand out of sandals and put her bikini away, and the memory of snorkeling in warm aqua waters returned. She hung and folded summer clothes. Then she scrubbed the bathroom and kitchen and dragged the vacuum around. Earlier, she'd bought the papers. *The Sun* had a picture of Don on the front page and one of Casey on page two, outside the cottage, frowning at the camera. Above her picture, the caption read, *Times Columnist, Donald Broughton Murdered in Devon – Found by American Girlfriend.*

Casey threw it in the bin and arranged some hothouse pink roses in a vase. She put freshly ground coffee on and tried to resist the impulse to call Carlisle about any progress they might have made. Before she'd rinsed her cup, she'd given in, but as she reached for the phone, it rang.

"Ms. Rowan?" Rod Carlisle's voice spread a prickling warmth along her spine.

"Farrowham is a country estate in Wiltshire. It belongs to the Chancellor of the Exchequer, Sir Henry Richardson. Do you know any reason why it would warrant an encoded file on Donald's computer?"

She now remembered where she'd heard of it. "Sir Henry was a friend of Don's, but I don't think he saw much of him, not since he became Chancellor."

"Do you think it's possible he was writing an article about him?"

"Unlikely, but possible, I suppose."

"It's not much to go on, is it?"

He sounded willing to chat, so she ventured a question. "How come the thieves who broke into the Fulham townhouse weren't caught? Didn't they set off the alarm?"

"They did, but due to an in-house security problem, the guards didn't respond until close to twelve. The intruder was in and out very fast. We suspect they came by water."

"No witnesses? It's on such a busy part of the river."

"Nothing's turned up yet." After a pause, he said, "I think we should talk. I have to head back to Devon in a couple of hours, but do you have time for a coffee?"

"Yes."

"A late breakfast in Richmond? I can be there in about twenty-five minutes."

"There's a little place on the river called Sables," she said. "It's right next to the Richmond Bridge. You can't miss it."

"See you there in about half an hour."

She dressed with care, taking a few extra minutes to soften the shadows under her eyes from a restless night. She had no time to wrestle with her hair, so she pulled it back in a ponytail and chose a cream turtleneck sweater with brown pants and boots. Tightening the belt of her tweed wool coat tight around her waist, she felt a welcome kick of adrenaline.

It was still very cold outside. Strong winds whipped the clouds into great drifts across a violet blue backdrop. As she tied her scarf, her mind traveled back to the clear blue skies of the Florida Keys. It struck her again how carefree she'd been, wandering around barefoot, the sun beating down on her head and the raw, salty smell of bait emanating from the fishermen along the wharf.

First to arrive at the Richmond cafe, she chose a table overlooking the river and the diners at the tables on the foreshore. It always amused her how the English seemed determined to eat alfresco, despite the weather. The café was in a picturesque, late seventeenth-century Georgian building. In happier times, she'd enjoyed its ambiance, but today she felt unmoved. Some of the joy had gone from her life with Don's death.

She saw Carlisle come through the door, pulling off his dark gray overcoat. More than one female head turned to follow him as he walked towards her.

"Miss Rowan." He took a seat. "May I call you Casey?"

"Of course."

"Rod."

"Rod," she repeated. "Are the police looking into the possibility that the murderer might be one of Tessa's clients?"

"We haven't discounted it." He leaned back in the chair.

There came a pause she refused to fill.

He angled forward and placed his arms on the table. "Casey, I understand your impatience. The processes of the law can sometimes move slower than you might expect."

"Meanwhile the killer is free to strike again? It doesn't seem right."

"Mrs. Broughton is safe for the moment."

"What are the chances it was Tessa the killer was after?" She halted, the words drying up in her mouth. Even though she'd considered it, to say it made it real, and that was too hard to face.

"Too early to say," he replied gently, reading the panic in her eyes.

She swallowed. "Have you uncovered any evidence at the cottage?"

He seemed to choose his words with care. "If we had, I probably wouldn't tell you about it." He ran his hand through his hair, and an errant lock fell onto his forehead. "Casey, we'd like to wrap this up quickly, too. But the police force is a bureaucracy like any other. Times change, and so do their methods. It's just a myth that one scientist can do everything at a crime scene with instant results— they now farm forensics out to private laboratories. We have to get in a queue."

She looked away from the lock of hair as if she'd seen something intimate. "I would have thought each police station had immediate access to one. Particularly in a murder case."

"Most boroughs have a strict budget—with priorities." Rod looked around. "Where's the waitress?" He raised his arm to get her attention before turning back to Casey. "Any fibers and DNA we find must have something we can compare them with. And we must produce the right stuff in court so a lawyer can sell it to a jury. If we fail in this, the murderers will end up back on the street.

"Ah, here's our coffee." He smiled at the waitress. She tucked her hair behind her ears and a flush crept up her neck.

Casey mentally shook her head. Her first impression had been correct. A man like Rod was used to female attention. He just wasn't her type. Too smart, too good-looking. The mix usually revealed arrogance at a point when it was too late to back away. He was taking time for her now, and she wondered why.

He enfolded his cup, apparently warming his hands. "We try to get digital evidence as soon as we can. Donald's computer was of vital importance to our investigation, as is his mobile, and we can't have you or anyone else blundering in and damaging evidence."

"My private inquiries can't hurt, if I'm careful. There are surely instances where the media has helped in an investigation."

Rod rubbed his chin. "Journalists don't always report evidence accurately."

"I'm aware not everyone is good at their job," she replied. "But I happen to be pretty good at mine. Can you tell me if any of these suspects have alibis?" She pulled out the list she'd made of Tessa's clients and laid it on the table in front of him.

He gazed at her then turned the pages around to face him. "Christ, Casey Rowan!" He shook his head. "Do you think I'm going to give you, a person of interest, this information?"

"You can't believe I'm involved in Don's death."

He huffed out a sigh and looked at her. She thought for a moment he'd laugh, but his face remained steady, expressionless. "I'm going to be honest with you," he said. "The post-mortem report shows the knife thrust that killed Donald and wounded Tessa was probably delivered by a man. You could still be involved, but my gut instinct says not."

"It sounds like your gut instinct was helped along by the forensics department."

He blinked. "Okay, you've got a point. Unfortunately, what I think isn't the issue." He paused. "I want you to promise not to do anything more without checking with me first. Do we have a deal?"

"I don't expect I'll find out much without police assistance." She shrugged.

"I can only feel encouraged by that."

Their full English breakfasts arrived. Guaranteed to warm you up for hours and wreak havoc with your cholesterol level, she thought, suddenly ravenous.

Rod ate quickly with an eye on his watch. He scraped up the last of the egg with his toast, took the last sip of coffee and tossed his napkin aside. Casey, still finishing her toast, noted his eyes on her.

"Casey's an unusual name."

"My Dad was born in Ireland, County Kildare." Feeling awkward under his scrutiny, she touched her lips with her napkin. "He bred racehorses there before he migrated to America. He named me after a bay filly he once had, *Casey's Luck.*"

He laughed. It softened his face and lightened the mood. "A thoroughbred?"

"Dad said she had a big heart and was a fighter."

"And great legs?"

Before she could deliver an apt retort, he drew out his wallet, all business-like again. "I meant what I said before, Casey—don't place yourself in danger. I can't afford another death on my conscience."

Another death? The flash of vulnerability in his eyes would be a siren call to most women, she thought. "You have my promise." She nodded and added, "Tessa's clients?" She'd agreed to his terms, but would he do the same for her?

She counted the beats until he reached for his notebook and flipped through it. "Reginald Jamieson was at home with his wife. The rest couldn't substantiate their alibis at this point. Maria Bartolomei spent the night alone. It seems Mr. Bilal Assam was at a family party, but this needs further investigation. Arthur Warren's had another fight with his de-facto Sally Cameron, and now he's missing. Michael Miller's a piece of work—he doesn't like the police. They were on the verge of taking him in when he admitted he was at a friend's house Thursday night. We're checking on that."

"I'm going to try and talk to Maria Bartolomei and Sally Cameron."

He shrugged. "That can't hurt except to waste your time. We are satisfied there's no connection."

"What about the murderers Gavin Holmes, Cleavy, and Black?"

"Still safely tucked up in jail." He stood and waved away her efforts to contribute. "Holmes has lodged another appeal against his sentence." He gave a wry look. "Use your common sense, Casey—stay out of trouble."

She nodded, already planning her next move.

A sickly row of lime trees grew inside the low wall of Pentonville Prison. Rod crossed the patchy grass and walked along the razor wire to the classical white-painted entrance buildings. Behind them stood taller brick buildings with barred windows—the cells.

A soul-destroying place.

The racket inside hit him like a physical assault—shouting, alarms and slamming gates that echoed down the wings. And the place smelled bad—a dreadful mix of male sweat and desperation.

Gavin Holmes waited in an interview room, bare except for a table and two chairs. A guard stood at the door.

Holmes scowled. Rod pulled out the chair and sat down opposite him, and his pale eyes showed no interest whatsoever. His expression didn't alter when Rod pushed across two packets of cigarettes. He shoved them into his shirt pocket without meeting Rod's gaze.

"I'm investigating a murder," Rod stated.

"Couldn't have been me, could it?" His voice was high pitched, and a bluish bruise circled his chin with a small cut and dried, crusty blood.

"Someone have a go at you?"

"Cut myself shaving." He ran his hands over his face.

"The psychologist at your trial, Tessa Broughton—her husband Donald has been murdered."

Gavin raised his head, and a gleam twinkled in his eye. "Don't tell me."

"And Mrs. Broughton was hurt," Rod continued.

"Great news. So nice of you to come and tell me."

"You have anything to do with it, Holmes?"

"They don't let me out of here at night, don't you know?"

"How do you know the attack was at night?"

"Most are, aren't they?"

"Anyone out there doing jobs for you?"

Holmes shrugged. "Don't have a friend in the world."

Rod studied the small, slightly built man. "Right now, I'd be inclined to believe you," he said. He stood, placed his hands on the back of the chair, and looked down at the surly man. "But if you did have anything to do with it, Holmes, I'll find out. And when I do, you'll see me again."

"What you gonna do, Coppa?" Gavin called after him. "Put me away for life?" He laughed, and it turned into a rattled phlegm, much like a smoker's cough.

"I'd watch that cough," Rod said as the guard opened the door for him. "It might get you before anyone else does. But maybe not, by the look of that bruise."

Gavin snarled but didn't rise. Apparently he didn't have much fight left in him. But then, Rod thought, rape was a grab for power by the powerless.

๛๛

After breakfast, Casey phoned Sally Cameron but got no answer. She didn't hold much hope of enticing Maria Bartolomei to talk to her, but she rang the number Tessa had recorded in her file, and when a female voice answered she launched into her prepared spiel. She told Maria she was from the press, grateful that at least was true, and she was doing an article on the effects of custody battles on estranged couples. She asked her if she could come and see her.

Maria surprised her by agreeing without asking her where she got her information.

"When would be convenient?"

"Any time."

Casey did a quick calculation. At this time of day, she might make Peckham in an hour and a bit, with luck. "I can be there in an hour."

Closer to an hour and a half had passed before she parked in Maria's street. She lived in a housing estate in North Peckham.

"Sorry, I'm a bit late."

Maria merely nodded. Appearing unsteady on her feet, she led Casey inside. The tiny first floor flat was filthy. Dishes in the sink had grown a good crop of mold. Piles of clothes lay strewn about, and Maria shoved them from one place to another, clearing off a chair for Casey to sit on.

Her movements were lethargic. Her hair was dyed orange and gelled into savage spikes, like armour. She had bruised-looking half-moons of fatigue under her eyes and picked nervously at an inflamed scab on her arm.

Even with the knowledge she'd abused her two daughters, Casey felt a rush of sympathy. "I'm sorry things haven't been going so well for you lately."

"Barry and that bitch got my kids."

"Have you been attending regular counseling sessions?"

"It was *because* of a counselor they took my kids away. Tessa-fucking-Broughton—the bitch."

"When was the last time you saw Mrs. Broughton?"

"I haven't seen her since court. I'd kill her if I did." She stumbled over to the refrigerator to drink milk straight from the carton. "Oh, right, the police told me someone's already tried to." She waved the carton around, sloshing milk on the floor.

"Do you have any family?"

She shook her head. She had lovely big green eyes, but the lids were at half-mast, swollen and heavy looking.

How often do you see your counselor?"

"Every week. I'm doing what they tell me—I've got to get my kids back."

Maria picked up a photo of her two little girls in an expensive-looking silver frame and gave it a polish before handing it to Casey. Casey saw the stark pain in her eyes.

She quickly wrapped up the interview as emotion caused a lump to form in her throat. *How does Tessa deal with this stuff?* she wondered, descending the steps to the street reeking of cat urine. Do you become hardened to the suffering after a while, or does the hope of rehabilitation always remain?

Maria may have had the motivation to kill Tessa, but somehow Casey couldn't see her making it to the next street, let alone Devon.

She got back to the car and tried Cameron's number. It rang for some time before a weary female voice answered. "Yeah?"

"Sally Cameron? I'm a journalist."

"No way." She hung up.

Casey dialed again. Just before the call cut out, she answered. "Who is it?"

"I'm an associate of Tessa Broughton," Casey said quickly before the woman hung up again. "I need to speak to you about Arthur. Would you mind answering a couple of questions?"

Sally interrupted her, her voice impatient and anxious. "Tessa? Is she still in hospital? I need to see her."

"I'm afraid Tessa's been hurt pretty badly, Sally. I gather the police have been to see you."

"Uh, yes. Looking for Art. He knocked me around again. They asked me if he was with me Thursday night." Her voice became suspicious. "Who did you say you were?"

"My name's Casey Rowan. I'm a close friend of Tessa's. I'm concerned she may be in danger, and I'm trying to find out what happened. Was Arthur with you that night?"

"No. He didn't come home at all."

"Can you tell me what Arthur thought of you consulting Tessa? Did he mind?"

Her laugh sounded bitter. "He hated it. He's capable of hurting anyone, believe me. I'm saving up to go live with my dad in Leeds. Tessa's going to help me. She promised. Is she going to be back at work soon?"

"Sorry, Sally, it may be quite some time before Tessa's back. If you ring your doctor, I'm sure they can put you on to someone else."

"Someone else? And then tell my story all over again?" Her voice tightened.

"Do you have any idea where Arthur might be?"

"Art hit me because I wouldn't give him any of my dole money. He puts it all on the dogs."

"Where does he go to gamble?"

"Either the betting shop or his favorite pub. The Red Lion in New Cross, his home away from home. You'll find him at the pool table most days. But he hasn't been seen around there for a week. Tell Tessa to give me a ring, will you? As soon as she's feeling better."

"Yes, I will." Casey hung up and grabbed the list, going through it again. Michael Miller and Bilal Assam remained.

She phoned the refuge only to learn Assam's wife, Heather, had gone, not leaving a forwarding address. The social worker told her this was often the case. Bilal Assam lived near the West Dulwich railway station on Thirlow Park Road. He didn't answer his phone.

Casey had planned to return to Exeter in the morning. But after checking Tessa's case notes on Michael Miller, she hesitated, wondering if she should check him out. She tried to ring the number Carlisle had given her and left a message, then rang Miller. He answered on the first ring. He was working at home, he said, and invited her over.

Pleased she could fit him in before heading off to Devon in the morning, Casey made herself a quick sandwich and grabbed a coffee. An hour and a half later, she parked near a nineteen-sixties block of flats in Camberwell. Built of concrete and devoid of color, texture or ornament, the design was guaranteed to kill a person's spirit—but still far better than the housing estate where Maria lived.

Casey climbed the stairs in the poorly lit stairwell. The walls were covered in colorful graffiti and expletives that now failed to shock. Three floors up, she emerged onto an open walkway with a giddy view over the concrete balustrade of the weedy car park below. Apart from pounding rap music coming from one of the neighboring flats and a cavalier black cat sitting atop the balustrade, no one was around.

A powerfully built, stocky young man opened the door to Casey's knock. He had a cropped haircut and small brown eyes so close together they seemed to straddle his beaked nose.

"You're the reporter?" He smiled and stepped backwards. "Hi, call me Mike. Come in."

"No thanks, Mike, I only need to ask you a few questions. This will only take a minute."

Miller frowned and leaned back against the doorjamb, folding his arms. Through the doorway, she could see into the shabby sitting room. It appeared clean and tidy, except for what looked like motorcycle parts lying about on newspaper.

"Bad luck about Tessa Broughton," he said, but there seemed no genuine sympathy in his voice. She guessed with the hard time he'd had lately, the attack on his psychologist wouldn't register much.

"Yes, it is," she replied. "How did you get on with your compensation claim? Did Tessa's assessment help you?"

"I'm getting some money, but it won't exactly compensate for my life being totally stuffed up." He lowered his head and pointed to the bright pink ribbon of scar tissue that bound his shattered scalp together. "Bike accident. I hit a tree with my head." He rubbed his arms. "It's cold out here, why don't you come in?"

Casey looked at her watch. "I only have a minute. Another appointment I'm already late for."

He straightened to reposition himself closer to her. "I was a mechanic before..."

"I'm so sorry." Sensing antagonism, she edged away from him. "You might seek professional advice about how to handle your lump sum payment. They can help you choose a fund to invest in." She began to feel a bit shaky. "When was the last time you saw Tessa?"

He remained silent and continued to stare at her with an expressionless gaze. She barely breathed as his eyes bore into hers. He moved closer, and she stepped back, feeling the rough balustrade press against her spine. With a meow of protest, the cat jumped down and darted away. His breath stirred her hair and made her blink, and he lowered his voice to a whisper. "Do you know I could easily kill you? If I stuck my thumbs into your eye sockets, I could gouge out your brain."

She pushed away from him, wrenched the stairwell door back on its hinges, and leaped down, her feet slipping on the slimy steps. Her ears strained for sounds of him following her.

In the street, she reached her car and searched for her keys. Looking up, she saw Miller leaning over the parapet. He laughed. Her hand shook so much she had trouble unlocking the car door. Cursing, she locked it behind her and drove off, wishing profoundly that she hadn't given up smoking.

CHAPTER 8

Lady Elizabeth Trentham lived in a surprisingly modest apartment in Knightsbridge, but Rod knew it would still be worth a lot of money.

She proved to be different from her brother, Rupert, on many levels. She'd just come in from work, wearing the uniform of a young professional, complete with a fitted black suit and high heels, her glossy, fair hair caught back in a silver clip. She whisked around the room and picked up the toys strewn about, while a young child chattered constantly. A baby lay crying on a blue bunny rug, waving his small fists in the air.

"Sorry, Inspector Carlisle," she called as she disappeared through a doorway. "It's the nanny's afternoon off. Chaos reigns. I'll be with you in a minute."

The minute turned out to be closer to twenty before they settled down on a sofa with coffees. The young child sat watching *Teletubbies,* and the baby, strapped into his highchair, painted the tray and his face with a soggy biscuit.

"Now, we might have a few minutes to talk." She'd taken off her jacket and changed her shoes and looked just like any other young mother. But Rod knew her to be married to an eminent barrister, and she herself had a very influential job as a publicist.

"I had a call from Rupert," she said frankly. "So, I suppose you want to know where he was the night Donald Broughton was killed? He told me he had tickets for the opera. You've probably checked on that anyway, and after a night out in London, he and Claudette always stay at their apartment here in town. I'm afraid I didn't speak to him that night, so I can't really help you. Have you spoken with Claudette?"

"Lady Morris-Smythe is away in France visiting relatives," Rod replied.

Lady Trentham formed a pout with her lips. "Rupert neglected to tell me that."

"You seem surprised."

"It's rather sudden. It wouldn't be filial duty calling her away. Claudette doesn't have much time for her French relatives."

"You don't seem too fond of Lady Morris-Smythe."

"We pretend to get on, but I'll never know why Rupert married her." She grimaced. "Oh, yes, I do. S.E.X. Rupert was never attracted to his own class. Claudette has her hooks into him and spends an unreasonable amount of his money. Rupert acts tough, he thinks he's like our father, but he's not."

"How badly were you both affected by the scandal involving your father and his subsequent death, Lady Trentham?"

"Seems strange to say, but I didn't know him very well. We saw little of him, the *pater familias*, growing up. Of course, what happened affected my life hugely at the time. No one likes the world to learn that their father is a sleazy hypocrite. I lost friends. People can be cruel, Inspector, but I found I couldn't mourn him. It was different for Rupert. He's older than I am and the son and heir. Father's opinion was enormously important to him."

She looked thoughtful. "His pain was intense. Father felt Rupert didn't measure up, you see." She shrugged. "Neither of us did. He always told us we took after our mother, and that wasn't a compliment. Mother had divorced him years before and married an American."

The baby dropped his rusk with a cry of outrage. Lady Elizabeth jumped up and replaced it before sitting down again. She licked a smudge from her finger. "He's tired—it's past his bedtime. So, to the question I know you want to ask me. Could Rupert have killed Donald? He hated him, yes, because he had to blame someone." She looked pensive. "Murder's not necessarily the province of the strong, is it?" Her unwavering, sherry-colored eyes met his. "But you'd have to prove it, wouldn't you?"

Rod didn't know why he still had the capacity to be surprised. People were seldom what they seemed.

CHAPTER 9

Early Wednesday morning, Tessa regained consciousness. When Casey was connected to her room, her mother answered the phone.

"She's going to be just fine." Camilla Huntingdale's said, but Casey detected a fragile tenor to her voice. "We're having her transferred to a private hospital closer to home. Then when she's stronger, she can come home to us."

"Who did this, Camilla—does she know?"

"Some man. Tessa didn't get a good enough look at him, but he wasn't someone she knew. Come and see her, Casey."

"I'm on my way."

On the motorway, she thought how indifferent Camilla had sounded about Don. She was concerned for her own child, of course, but still, Don had been in their lives for many years. She wondered if they'd ever approved of him. His philosophy on life had been so different from theirs.

It always seemed to her that Don and Tessa had dealt with those differences beautifully in their marriage. But what concessions had taken place, and by whom? Did the money for their new home come from Camilla and Roland? Surely, if they had offered it, Don would have refused. He hated being indebted to people. She'd found money often tested a person's principles, especially in families, and even more so if real wealth was involved. Don, she suspected, would have won that fight.

Nothing made sense. She gritted her teeth and kept her unsteady hands on the wheel, feeling terribly alone.

Thinking of the privileged world the wealthy Huntingdales inhabited made her remember Laurence Jason-Leigh—the urbane, sophisticated Laurie. Years had passed since she'd given him a thought. She'd met him at Oxford, and he'd literally knocked her off her feet when he cannoned into her on his bicycle and scattered her assignment all over the road. She'd been furious—it was already overdue—but Laurie took care of everything. He was good at that.

With Laurie, you somehow knew things would run smoothly. He'd taken her for a pub lunch and helped her reprint her work. The relationship had developed into the kind that fulfills a young girl's dreams. Those elegant dinners at his parent's home in Belgravia and weekends at their country house in Gloucestershire. Not to mention the holiday trip to their villa in Tuscany.

Laurie began to organize Casey's life for her, and she saw less and less of Don and Tessa. He told her where to buy her clothes, where to have her hair done, what places to be seen in and with whom. They graced the social pages every other week, and when he asked her to marry him, she didn't hesitate.

It seemed logical, as Casey's mother was dead, that Laurie's mother would plan the wedding. Laurie assured her it would be better this way, for his mother had a great sense of style. "And it's not really your thing, is it, darling?" she remembered him saying.

Don didn't like it. "They'll swallow you up, girl." Casey knew it, too. And three weeks before the wedding, she found the courage to end it. Laurie was now married with two kids, and for a while, she'd see them in *Tatler* and the *Daily Telegraph*—or "Torygraph," as Don called it. Laurie's wife, Cynthia, would be pictured attending some charity function or other, her hair a smooth coiffure.

Casey stopped at a petrol station and grabbed a cup of coffee. With renewed energy, she took off, eager to see Tessa.

She turned on the radio, and the full, majestic tones of Wagnerian opera filled the cabin. She'd never been particularly fond of Wagner in the past, but now she found his music a sumptuous feast. Don hadn't liked Teutonic Wagner either. He'd preferred Beethoven. It was the Romantic view. Don valued the rights of the common man above any government, but his interest was more idealistic than practical.

It occurred to her that he'd listened to Wagner the night he was killed. In the end, he'd had to grow up, just like the rest of them.

Tessa would live. The realization warmed Casey's heart, bringing a sense of jubilation. She wanted to call someone, but none of her other friends had known Don and Tessa. Funnily enough, she wanted to call Carlisle.

She jumped when her mobile rang. His name was on the caller ID. "That's the second time you've done that to me," she said.

"I don't believe I've done anything to you, Casey. Yet."

She blushed—the man was incorrigible. "Rung me, when I was planning to ring you."

"You were, why?"

"Tessa is going to be okay."

"Aye, I know. Great news."

"And she has cleared me."

"As I said, I always knew that."

"Ah, that's right, a cop's intuition."

"I'm a good judge of character, Casey. And right now, you're troubling me. What have you been up to?"

Not wanting to recount the embarrassing scene with Michael Miller, she hesitated. It could wait for a better moment. "I saw Maria and spoke to Sally."

"And?"

"Nothing."

"Anything else planned?"

"No."

"Good. I thought we might have dinner tonight."

Her heartbeat picked up its pace, and she took a steadying breath. *You are not getting involved with this man*, she told herself sternly. "Aren't there rules about that? Cops not fraternizing with the suspects, or witnesses, for that matter?"

"The world is tied up with rules, Casey. You have to eat, don't you?"

"I guess."

"And I have to eat. Is there a rule that states we can't eat at the same place?"

He was right—it was only dinner, and she might learn more.

"As long as we don't discuss the case," he concluded.

Damn. "Where did you have in mind?"

"I know a great restaurant called Milo's. It's a simple place. Are you still at the guesthouse?"

"Yes, but I'll meet you at Milo's. Give me the address."

It would give her plenty of time to talk to Tessa.

⚘⚘⚘

"How are you, Tessa? You're looking much better."

"Oh, God, I can't believe he's gone." Tessa sobbed. "Just like that?"

Casey took a deep breath. "I can't believe it either."

Tessa struggled to sit up in the bed, crying out at the least movement. Casey tried to disengage herself from the emotion she felt at the sight of Tessa's tears, attempting to make her friend more comfortable by putting an extra pillow behind her shoulders. Through the gap in Tessa's gown, she caught sight of thick bandaging. She still had the drip, but at least the monitoring machines had been turned off.

"Can you tell me what you remember?"

Tessa trembled. "It came back to me, in the middle of the night, but I'm still not sure if it really happened that way. I stumbled half-asleep down the stairs and opened the sitting room door, looking for Don."

She rubbed her temples with shaky hands. "The room was dark. Someone had turned off the lamp by Don's chair. Only the hall light shone in. I guess I was thinking the bulb had gone out and Don had dropped off to sleep in the chair. He did that often enough. I was too sleepy to try to find the light switch. I asked him to come to bed, it was late."

She looked up, her face etched with pain. "My final words to him were angry, Casey. You know it always worried me how little sleep he got." Her hands went again to her temples, as if she could rub away the agony. "A man was there, bent over Don's chair. At first, I thought it *was* Don. Then I realized it couldn't be. Don was sitting as I'd left him earlier. He made this odd, gurgling noise in his throat. I must have cried out—or made some kind of noise because the man turned to me, but he didn't speak. He held something in his hand that flashed silver. It must have been the knife."

She started to sob. Casey moved to hold her, but Tessa waved her away. "I don't remember anything after that. It's like a surreal nightmare. You know, one of those dreams where someone's chasing you and you can't open your eyes or run away. I must have turned to run, and he stabbed me."

"Tessa, let it go now. Rest, until you feel better."

She took a shuddering breath. "No. I'm all right, but I can't see the man's face. I've been over and over it. The dark room, him standing there. But I can't see his face!"

"Please, Tessa, this can wait. The police will solve it."

"I wish I could remember more that could help them. I'm so frightened."

A nurse entered the room, checked Tessa's blood pressure, popped a thermometer into her mouth, and took her pulse. "I'll be right back with your medication." She looked pointedly at Casey as she bustled out again.

"Tessa, I'll come back tomorrow."

Her eyes closed. "Yes. And maybe by then..."

Casey walked down the busy hospital corridors, replaying their conversation in her mind. Even if Tessa had seen the murderer's face, she might never remember it, and she would be the first to point out that she'd just described traumatic amnesia.

❧❧❧

The seafood restaurant on Queen Street stood only a few blocks away from the boardinghouse. Casey walked it, enjoying the crisp night air. It was a freshly painted white building with a row of Grecian-style arches across its façade. Inside, the place appeared just as Rod had described—simple, a ceiling decorated in fishing nets, and popular, with the contented hum of people enjoying good food.

She took off her coat and hung it on the rack at the door. She wore her favorite short black skirt, teaming it with a wrap-around black top. Rod had arrived first. He leaned on the bar and smiled at her approach. She felt light-hearted, as if the universe had righted itself a little with Tessa's recovery. Some semblance of order restored.

His lips formed a silent whistle. "You dressed up." He wore jeans and carried a leather biker's jacket.

"Too dressy?" She glanced at the other casually dressed diners.

"I'm sure all the males here are appreciative, particularly Milo. You'll be good for business."

At their table, they ordered a beer for Rod and bourbon for her. She took a hearty swallow, and the alcohol hit her empty stomach with a welcome burn.

They ordered wine while she finished the bourbon and told him about Michael Miller, having decided to clear the air early on in the evening.

Rod put his glass down so suddenly brown froth spilled onto the tablecloth.

"I thought we had a deal."

"I tried to ring you—I left a message."

She could see he struggled to control his temper, his voice steady but brick hard as he glanced away and shook his head. "Not good enough."

An apology at this point seemed half-baked, but she swallowed and gave one anyway.

Rod managed to delay any response by carefully folding a napkin and tucking it under his glass to soak up the spill. "I hope you now realize that police business is dangerous. That guy is bad news—he could have hurt you."

"I doubt he killed Don, though."

He sighed and shook his head.

"Is there anything you can reveal about the investigation?" she asked, trying to move things on.

He took a swig of beer and looked her in the eye again. "No."

She looked down. "I guess I deserve that."

"Casey." Rod paused, and she held her tongue, watching him weigh things up in his mind. "I have a feeling I'm not just breaking the rules, I'm making a colossal mistake in encouraging you." He shrugged. "The murder weapon, a knife, has been found in the woods. And a car reported in the vicinity that night."

"Near the cottage? There are no other houses for miles."

"No, parked on Holly Road, on the far side of the woods. An elderly woman saw it there in the early hours of the morning. There's a decent path through the woods from there. It's a hike, but you can reach the Broughtons' house without being seen."

She remembered those woods, and the thought led her to the cottage. A shiver passed through her body. "What was the car like? Did she say?"

"Only that it was large with a dark paintjob."

"Sounds like something to go on."

He frowned. "We're leaving no stone unturned, Casey."

Wondering why she needed to push this man and spoil a perfectly lovely evening, she asked if they'd found Arthur, the abusive boyfriend of Tessa's client, Sally.

"Not yet, but I'm willing to bet it wasn't him."

"Why not?"

"Warren's a bully, but I doubt he has the killer instinct. He might kill accidentally, but he wouldn't coldly carry out a premeditated, brutal murder like Donald's. A killer like that has the ability to go one step further than the next guy. And we've had no witnesses come forward. It was too late at night."

"And too cold for anyone to be out," Casey added.

Rod leaned on the table. "Do you miss home?"

Where is home? she wondered. "The feet go where the heart wills, I guess. The last trip back was to sell my father's house. It's been tenanted for years—since he died, in fact."

"And did you? Find a buyer?"

"I had a few potential buyers. Most wanted to pull the house down and build something bigger." She looked down at her glass. "I'm having trouble letting it go." On the plane back, her vacillation had annoyed and bewildered her. Instead of reaching some sort of finality, she seemed locked in the past. She just wandered about, drifting from the warm sand to the cool water, unable to galvanize herself into action.

He cocked his head. "Seems like you have a foot in two countries."

"Ask any ex-pat that, and they'll say it's true to some extent. Once you leave your country, you're cursed forever to suffer comparisons."

His eyes searched hers with an intent that made her draw a breath. "But you're not considering going back to live in America, I hope."

Was she? She didn't know for sure. What happened the last ten days had changed everything. "Was it Mark Twain who said you can't go home?"

"Probably." He grinned. "He had rather a lot to say."

"I seem to remember reading somewhere that he said your family home seems to shrink when you return as a grown up. The cottage was always cosy, but now it just seems tiny and oddly quiet. Dad was a noisy person. Always singing along with the radio. He had a good Irish tenor voice. But I spent my adult life here in England. After Dad died, I came over to live with my aunt in Ham. I was fifteen."

"That would have been tough."

She flattened the serviette in her lap with an unsteady hand. So much loss—her mother when she was ten, her father, and now Donald and the deep anxiety she felt for Tessa.

"But you stayed."

"Yes. Maud was a dear. She died when I was twenty." She wanted to add, *And I was alone again*, but bit her tongue instead. The last thing she wanted was for Rod to feel sorry for her. In truth, she hadn't consciously felt this way with Don and Tess around.

He topped up her glass. "You've been on your own for quite a while then," he replied, sensing her thoughts. But maybe she was an easy read.

Casey straightened her shoulders. "It's not all bad." She laughed. "You get to do just what you want."

"What is it about England you prefer to Florida? Don't tell me it's the weather. Englishmen, perhaps?"

She shook her head and smiled. "You ask a lot of questions."

"Sorry—it's my line of work."

"Mmmm. A note for my diary. Men to be avoided as dinner dates—policeman and lawyers."

He grinned. "Not another question. Your turn."

"I don't like the cold much. Love the winter fashions, though." Her stint as a fashion editor in her mid-twenties had been deliciously frivolous. "Seriously? I like the depth of media, the proximity to other countries and cultures. The feeling of being in the thick of it."

"A magazine editor sounds like an interesting career."

"It hasn't quite turned out the way I'd hoped. I guess I was a romantic kid who thought a group of us could achieve something special. In truth, *Hers* is like any magazine, driven by advertising and sales. A few token articles to appease the conscience, some of which I supply, but it survives mainly on the hot stuff."

"Sounds like you're fed up with it."

"Maybe I am." And saying it, she knew that it was true. Three months, and she still wasn't keen to get back. She'd never spent longer than a weekend away from the magazine in the past. She used to live and breathe the place. Was she uncomfortable with becoming just another mag hack?

The Greek proprietor, Milo, brought their meals to the table. "Rod, for you and your lovely lady friend, I have chosen the biggest and the best." He put down the plates with a flamboyant gesture. "Enjoy."

With a sense of relief at the interruption to Rod's interrogation, she tucked into the buttery lobster. While they ate, she filled Rod in on her conversations with Maria Bartolomei and Sally Cameron, admiring his dexterity at drawing out the meat from his lobster claw. A skill she'd never managed to master.

She snapped a lobster claw with her fingers. "My dad used to say the world could be divided into two groups—those who liked to eat seafood with their fingers and those who didn't."

Rod raised the lobster piece he held in approval.

She found herself relaxing into the meal. The food tasted delicious, and the wine had softened any anxiety about being on a date. Was it a date? Well, what else was she doing here, enjoying herself far too much? Initially, she'd come to glean more information from him—but now? Tessa would warn her that she was looking for connections in a strange place as a form of escape. God, she hoped Tessa would be all right.

"How long have you lived in England, Rod? You still have a strong accent."

"Perhaps it's harder to lose than an American accent. I left Scotland years ago, but I haven't been in Devon long. I was working with Scotland Yard. SO13. I needed a change after a police operation went badly awry."

"Do you want to talk about it?"

"My division was investigating the bomb outside Waterloo Station that killed three people. Peter Johnson was a good policeman and a good mate. We were following a lead, but when we received new information, we made an unscheduled stop on the way. We were shorthanded due to a spate of flu—" He took a deep breath. "We agreed to check it out, while this latest lead was still hot, but when we got to the squat..."

His eyes suddenly took on a far-off look, and Casey wondered how often he relived it.

"Pete was right behind me. I entered, took cover and he followed me into a hallway. He took one room while I took the other. Mine was empty, but I heard a shot." He paused and pushed his plate away. "Pete took a bullet in the throat. The bastards got away."

"I'm sorry," she said softly.

He topped up her glass, which was almost full, and she noticed his hand shook slightly.

"I've blamed myself for Pete's death, but he knew the score. We all do. I went up before the board. They cleared me, but I wanted to get away for a while. I had the Detective Superintendent's job in my sights. Won't happen now."

He took a sip of wine, and she noticed he'd actually drunk very little.

"What attracted you to the police force?"

"I guess I like to have some control over things. When Pete died, I felt like someone had taken the lid off life and let me glimpse the chaos beneath."

Casey shivered. "So we tiptoe through life, not walking under ladders?"

He smiled. "That doesn't always work."

She thought bitterly of Don. "No."

"Sometimes a risk is worth taking."

A long pause followed. He looked at her, and she met his gaze.

"Have you checked with Sir Henry Richardson about Farrowham, his country home?"

"We've been in touch. Donald wasn't writing an article on either Richardson or Farrowham," he spoke, his eyes growing wary. "Casey, what are you up to now?"

The wine had oiled the wheels of her determination. "I'm planning to go on a little trip."

"Not Farrowham?"

"Why not?"

He reached across and took her hand in his. His touch felt warm and strong, but he quickly let her go. "Now, what do you believe you'll find up there? You can't believe the Chancellor of the Exchequer is involved in this."

She shrugged. "I haven't a clue." She found it hard to put into words that she was just doing what she thought Don would want. "Don't you think it significant that Don's autobiography is missing?"

"Of course. We've checked with his publishers, but apparently little was discussed about content."

She fiddled with her bracelet. "I just have to *do* something."

"You're letting your emotions get the better of you. That's just illogical. And dangerous."

"Some things defy logic. I hope you're not suggesting we women are governed by our emotions." She had to agree that, in this case, he had a point, although she wouldn't admit it.

Rod shook his head, the movement slow and deliberate, and a smile hovered about his mouth. He signaled for the bill.

"Would you like to come to my place for a drink?"

"And see your etchings?"

He laughed. "Prints at best."

"Not tonight, thank you, Carlisle. I think I'll take a rain check."

"I'll drive you home."

"Under no circumstances could that place be called home, but thank you."

She followed him as he hooked his finger in his leather jacket and swung it over his shoulder. She expected to find a car waiting, but he led her to a motor bike parked at the curb.

He reached over the bike and produced an extra helmet. "I can't have you walking home alone."

"How thoughtful," she said uneasily, tugging down her short skirt.

He waited for her to don the helmet. "You have been on a bike before?"

"Living with Aunty Maud?" She strapped the helmet under her chin.

"No time like the present."

He helped her into his leather jacket, moving his hands over her breasts without hesitation, and zipped it up to her chin.

She worried she might not be able to hold on, but her head quickly cleared as she hugged his narrow waist. The chill of the wind whipped her hair about, and she pressed her cheek against his shoulder, breathing in his male smell. Leather, cigarettes, and something else, intangibly him.

Protected from the cold, she could enjoy the sensation of the powerful bike travelling fast under the moon through the quiet streets. She felt disembodied and free and found herself enjoying it even more knowing that tomorrow she'd lose it again.

They pulled up outside the guesthouse, and he killed the engine.

Casey climbed off quickly. "Thank you for dinner." She turned to face him.

In the light from a street lamp, his blue eyes studied her. "The best laid plans don't always work out, do they?"

"No," she agreed, unsure where this was leading.

"Should we live in the moment? Act on one's impulses?"

Before she could comment, he drew her to him and kissed her. It was a lovely kiss, but her heart and mind already had too much to deal with. She pushed him gently away.

"Do you have a man in your life?"

"Not right now."

"That's surprising."

"There was someone. A brief romance, but it ended when I left America."

"The tyranny of distance?"

She gave a short laugh. "He dumped me, actually."

He grinned. "I'll bet that's the first time that's happened."

"Uh huh." It seemed so trivial now. She realized that only her ego had been involved. "And you?"

"Am I involved with anyone? No."

"No. Have you been dumped?"

A shadow passed over his face. "Yes, actually. Unceremoniously."

"I didn't mean to rub salt in."

"I was accused of cruel neglect. The job got in the way. It happens to cops."

"Was it a long relationship?"

"We were married five years."

"I didn't mean to pry," she said, feeling the conversation had taken a turn for the worst.

"It was years ago. I'm over it now." He shivered slightly, and that naked, vulnerable look appeared in his eyes again. Now that she knew the reasons for it, it became harder to resist the urge to reach out and comfort him.

She peeled off his jacket and handed it to him. "I'd better go in—it's cold."

He gently tweaked one of her curls, an incredibly intimate gesture that left her breathless. "Let me know how you do tomorrow?"

"I will."

She watched his bike roar away down the road. *Down, girl*, she thought and turned away.

CHAPTER 10

Thursday morning, Casey returned to the hospital with an armful of creamy roses
Promising the nurse she'd keep it short, she slipped into Tessa's room and asked gently, "Tessa? Where did Don keep his notes on his autobiography?"

Tessa pushed away her breakfast tray.

"I'm not sure. He kept hard copies in the study in Fulham, but he could have taken them with him to Devon. He did take his briefcase."

"I looked for them in Fulham. Did he save it all on his computer?"

She nodded. "About ten chapters. On his computer and laptop. Backed it all up on disc."

"What had he covered?"

"The police asked me the same question. A first draft of the early years of his career, and I believe it was all taken."

"It seems so. Did he keep anything in Devon?"

"No. He always took his laptop with him."

"Do you think Don could have written or been planning to write about someone who would want to harm him?"

Her hand shaking, Tessa reached for the glass of water from the bedside table. "I didn't read what he'd written, but no, I doubt that."

"Didn't he always discuss his work with you?"

"We'd both been so busy. I know he planned to. Can you think of anything?"

"Only the sex scandal involving the politician, remember? Lord Harold Morris-Smythe. He committed suicide."

"How could I forget? Don felt awful about it. You remember, Casey. He'd gone after that call-girl business because they were employing underage girls, using drugs to get them caught up in it. He had no idea Morris-Smythe was involved. When he infiltrated the firm run by organized crime, he put his life on the line."

"Did you ever meet the son, Rupert, or see a picture of him?"

"No, never wanted to. I just remember the foul threat."

"I never saw the letter. What did it say?"

"It said something like, *this time you've gone too far, Broughton. The Bible says an eye for an eye.*"

"Don didn't contact the police, did he?

"No."

"Did he try to talk to Morris-Smythe about it?"

Tessa closed her eyes and nodded. "But he wouldn't speak to Don. We looked over our shoulders for a while, but nothing further happened. Can't be him, not now, it doesn't make sense."

"I guess not." Casey paused, trying to find the right words to ask Tessa about their obvious newfound wealth. In the end, she just came straight out with it.

Tessa shrugged. "Don received the inheritance a couple of weeks after you left for Florida. I planned to ring you straight away, but he said to wait until you came back. He wanted to enjoy your reaction when you saw the new house for the first time."

She widened her eyes, raising her brows, and Tessa rushed on. "I *know* it's hard to believe that Don, who was an orphan, was bequeathed a lot of money by someone who wished to remain anonymous. But it's true."

"That's so strange. He must have attempted to find out who it was."

"You know he'd been endeavoring to trace his family for years—we just didn't have anything to go on. The solicitors handling the bequest received instructions not to reveal the benefactor's name."

"Would you mind if I saw the solicitor's letter?"

"What do you mean? You think Don was lying?" Tessa asked heatedly.

"No, of course not. The police will want to contact them."

"It should be somewhere in his study. The letter arrived just after we'd sold our house, and Don came home and told me he'd fallen in love with the one in Fulham." Tessa sighed. "I won't want to live there now. It was all Don's idea from the beginning. He was the one interested in decorating it."

"He would have considered that trivial, once."

"Yes, but you know how passionate he'd become about art. He wanted to become an investor, a serious collector. I just didn't want things to change."

Now they've changed utterly, Casey thought.

"You know Rod Carlisle, the policeman working on your case?"

"Yes, of course."

"I had dinner with him last night."

Tessa's eyes widened. "You did? Was that wise?"

Casey felt her cheeks grow warm. "Probably not."

"Did anything happen?"

"You mean sex? No." Casey suddenly felt exposed—she'd enjoyed Rod's kiss, his arms around her.

Tessa's face grew pale, but she smiled. "Life seems so short, Casey. We all need to be a little reckless sometimes."

"Tessa, you should rest now."

"Yes, in a bit."

"Do you know if Don wrote something on Farrowham?"

"Farrowham?" She rubbed her forehead.

"That's Sir Henry Richardson's country seat in Wiltshire."

"Don was invited there for a weekend, a few months ago. I didn't go—I had a cold." Her words sounded strained.

"Did he tell you anything about it?"

She closed her eyes. "He didn't stay, came back the same day. Sir Henry wasn't there—some crisis in London."

"There's one more thing I have to ask you. Did you close my door when you went to bed?

Tessa opened her eyes. "I don't remember. No. Why would I?"

Casey left the hospital and pulled out her phone. "Why has the police guard been removed from Tessa's room?" she asked the moment Rod answered.

"We don't have the resources to keep someone there all the time, especially now she's out of danger."

"And you're confident she is."

"She's given her statement. There's nothing more to nail the murderer."

"You don't believe she was the target, then?"

"We can't watch over her for the rest of her life. Come on, Casey, she's being transferred to a London hospital soon."

He paused, and she considered whether she should fight the issue. Then he said, "Are you still heading up to Farrowham?"

"Yes. I'm just about to leave."

"It's a nice day for a drive. Ring me when you get back."

Don's pampered old sports car awaited her in the hospital parking lot. She pulled a map from the glove box and spread it over the bonnet, tracing the way via the A303 to Andover, where she planned to stop for a coffee break. It would be early afternoon before she arrived in Bilbury. She tugged a knitted cap down over her hair and slipped on leather driving gloves. This time, although it remained cold, there was no sign of rain, and she'd decided to drive with the top down.

☙❧

Shortly after two o'clock, Casey came to the charming little town of Bilbury. With no sign of twenty-first century intrusion apart from motorcars, the town was a tourist haven. She stopped at a busy hotel and ordered a chicken pie, which turned out to be homemade, crusty and delicious. She washed it down with a lager.

At the register, she asked the publican the directions to Farrowham.

"You can't miss it," he said while ringing the cash register. "Just head on up the main road 'til you see the signs. You won't be disappointed. It's a grand old place."

In the Farrowham car park, a large group of tourists spilled from their coach and stood about on the muddy ground. Casey followed the arrows to the ticket booth. An ignominious entrance for so grand a house. Following a path around a hedge, she found herself facing the southern approach to the mansion. The publican had been right—she saw the delicate Ionic columns and the pyramidal roof of neo-Palladian architecture, its classic proportions perfect.

She read the plaque on the wall beside the front door: *Inspired by the sixteenth-century Italian architect Andrea Palladio (1508-80) and revived in the eighteenth century by Inigo Jones, Farrowham has been home to the Richardson family since the nineteenth century and now houses an important collection of furniture and paintings.* Formal gardens dotted with statuary stretched away, and in the distance, sunlight flashed, reflected on the waters of an ornamental lake.

The tourists arrived—a mix of German, American and Japanese, and noisily filed into the Grand Hall. The guide gathered them together to prepare for a tour of the house, so she slipped in with the group. They trooped into the dining parlor, and she only half-listened to the tour guide's enraptured description of "egg and dart" molding and its motif of Thyrusus and Bacchus intertwined with vine leaves.

They moved on through the house. The guide began to talk about the head of Apollo on the marble chimneypiece, and Casey took the chance to slip away. His voice dwindled to a murmur while she studied the magnificent paintings—Rubens, Panini, and Van Dyke among them.

When the guide led the way up the stairs, Casey fell further behind as they wandered noisily along the portrait gallery.

She began to wonder what to do next when a tall, fair-haired man appeared out of a door marked 'Private' and disappeared down the stairs, leaving the door ajar. Before she could allow nerves to dissuade her, she slipped through into what appeared to be part of the family's living quarters.

Moving silently in her rubber-soled boots along a hallway, she came to an empty office and ducked inside. It was a large, airy room filled with shelves and filing cabinets. A computer and printer sat on an antique desk covered in papers. She shuffled through invoices and bills of sale, with one eye on the door. Cabinet drawers contained more of the same—nothing but correspondence with galleries and auction houses.

Casey knew Sir Henry's family had been in the art and antique business for over a hundred years, from the time they lost most of their land and their tenant farmers and became forced to work for a living. Nothing out of the ordinary leapt out at her. Rod had been right—she was wasting her time, and if caught, she'd be charged with breaking and entering. Apparently, she had no shame, for she opened another drawer or two before she left.

She retreated to the now-empty portrait gallery and hurried along it. A man and a woman came up the stairs towards her—the same man she'd seen before, dressed in a superb gray suit. Relief filled her, but at the same time, curiosity drew her gaze in his direction. There was something about him. Up close, she knew she'd never met him. The iris of one of his eyes was a deep brown, the other an amaurotic pale blue.

The woman stopped. "Can I help you?"

"Wouldn't you just know it," Casey said. "I went looking for the toilet and now I've lost my group. I just hope they don't leave without me."

Without a word, the man went on through the door she'd just exited, while the woman turned and pointed down the hall. "I think you'll find them in the souvenir shop. Turn right at the bottom of the stairs. You'll find the toilets there, also."

Her group was enjoying Devonshire teas. She took one look at the brittle yellow scones heated in the microwave and just ordered coffee. They then shopped for souvenirs and made their way to the bus.

Casey strolled purposely back to her car. She'd made it out of the car park and was on the road home before the bus engine turned over.

෴

Casey had driven through the quiet country lane that fed into a slip road some miles further on when, suddenly, the engine spluttered and misfired. Hoping it was nothing more than a hiccup, she tried to nurse it along. No such luck. It gave a couple of heaves then cut out altogether, leaving her to maneuver over to the side of the road.

She phoned for help and waited ten minutes before a melodious hum caused her to look up. Down the road, a large Mercedes Benz advanced at a slow speed, its iridescent-blue paintwork glowing in the sun.

As it came closer, Casey stepped back into the trees. The car pulled in behind Don's car, and the fair-headed, aloof man in a suit—the same man she'd seen at Farrowham—emerged from its interior.

He walked along the road and peered into the trees where she stood. She deliberated whether to blow her cover before he saw her, but then a loud rattling heralded the arrival of the tow-truck. The man walked quickly to his car and drove off before the truck stopped.

The mechanic took a look under the hood and peered in at the dashboard. "You're out of petrol, Miss."

"But that's impossible. I filled up just outside Andover."

"Well, take a look for yourself."

The gauge read empty.

He checked under the car and straightened. "No sign of a leak. I can give you enough to get to the station down the road. Keep an eye on it in future."

CHAPTER 11

Casey drove back to Devon and, on impulse, headed for the cottage. The street was quiet, as if nothing bad had ever happened there. As she sat chewing a fingernail, questioning whether she could face going in there alone, she reached for her phone and dialed Rod.

"What did you find up there in Wiltshire?" he asked.

"A lovely old house."

"I'm glad you got something out of the trip."

He politely passed up the opportunity to say, *I told you so*, and she couldn't help but smile.

"Something odd happened on my way home, though." She went on to describe running out of petrol and how the man from Farrowham had appeared to follow her.

"Could have been just passing by and stopped to help," he said.

"But—yes, I guess that was it. Funny about the petrol, though."

"Those old cars are heavy on fuel. I'll take a modern one any day. Where are you?"

"I'm outside the cottage. I'd like to go inside if I may. The police seem to have finished here."

"No. It's still a crime scene."

"Haven't the crime scene guys done their work?"

His only response was to ask a question. "You collected your things, didn't you?"

"Yes. I just wanted to check out a few things."

A pause followed. "You remove anything from there, I want to know about it."

"Okay."

The central heating had been turned off, and the air was frigid, smelling faintly of mold. She passed the sitting room door, this time without looking inside, and headed for the cubbyhole that served as their study. The thought that Tessa would have to return and deal with it made her breath catch in her throat. Death was so final. It changed every aspect of one's life in one cruel blow.

Bleak daylight stole through the study window, tinting the walls a chilly mauve. An inhospitable, wintry draft crept in through the cracks. Shivering, she tugged the plum-colored curtains across the window and put on both the ceiling light and the desk lamp. Its golden glow gave at least an illusion of warmth. She rubbed the circulation back in her hands and surveyed the bookshelves completely covering two of the walls, stacked high with books and mementos.

An hour later, she'd found nothing. Disappointed, she spun around on the swivel chair. Arranged on a shelf above her were Don and Tessa's awards. Most were from Tessa's childhood, showcasing her tennis and music trophies. Front and center sat Don's artificially bronzed writing award from school.

Shaped like a triangle, it had Don's name and the year printed on it—nineteen seventy-five. She picked it up and swallowed against the lump in her throat. It was so typical of him—he'd considered small things like this important. Casey remembered telling him he was like the late actor, Richard Burton, who apparently never bothered with reviews and kept only one from a small local newspaper in Wales that proclaimed proudly, "Young Richard Jenkins promises fair to be the next Welsh fly-half."

Odd, how much-loved possessions survive people. She reached up to replace it. A flash of white inside the hollow bottom caught her eye. Turning it upside down, she used an opened out paperclip to pry a paper loose from where it was jammed up into the center.

She spread it out on the desk. It was a computer printout of a list of paintings. But they weren't artworks you'd find in any gallery or museum.

Flower Girl by Renoir
A Portrait of a Lady by Jan Mostaert
Falling Angel by Marc Chagall
Sleeping Child by Van der Helst
Landscape with Haystacks by Monet
Girl in a Blue Chair by Picasso
Retribution by George Gross
Spoils of War by Max Beckmann

She knew the Mostaert to be a four-hundred-year-old painting, missing since the Second World War. The rest she had never heard of.

The floor above her creaked. She panicked and shoved the list into her bag. Closing the front door behind her, she bolted down the steps.

❧❧❧

The next morning, Casey went to Middlemore.

"This is a nice surprise," Rod said. "Come into my office and have coffee."

He shut the door after her and cleared a place on his desk for the coffee, throwing empty cartons from the local Chinese place into the bin.

"Late night?" she asked, pulling the list out of her bag and handing it to him.

He nodded, his eyes on the page. As he read, she told him where she'd found it.

"This will have to be submitted as evidence. I'll refer it to the Art & Antiques Unit."

"You don't think it's important."

"There's a lot emerging about the art that the Nazis appropriated during the war. It's definitely worth checking, and the unit has an extensive database, but there's always the possibility it might have been there a long time. Donald could simply have been after a story at some stage."

"What if they all prove to be Nazi art spoils? It would be a fairly sensational one," she said dryly. "And why hide it?"

"Was it hidden? Or just put there quite innocently, to make the thing stand up better? It could be nothing."

She studied him from across his desk. Did he really believe that? Later, she planned to contact the Art Loss Register in New York.

"There's something else I need to know. Was my doorknob fingerprinted?"

He met her gaze. "Yes."

"Are you going to tell me?" she asked impatiently.

"Only your prints were found on it."

"I didn't close it."

"When you went back up to your room with the police officer to get your bag, did you—"

She nodded despondently. "I probably did." She shuddered. "He must have come up the stairs. He would know I was there."

"If it didn't just blow shut," he said.

Rod's effort to calm her failed miserably. She just felt angrier, more fearful, and violated somehow.

"I'm going home to Richmond today."

His eyes searched hers. "But you'll be coming down again? Soon?"

"Yes, of course, to see Tessa."

"Call me?"

❧❧❧

After checking through the Interpol Stolen Works of Art site on the net and finding nothing, Casey got onto Mary-Anne Louis at the Art Loss Register in New York.

She was clearly interested, but cautious, more disposed to obtaining information than giving it out.

"Where did you find it?"

"At the scene of a murder."

Mary-Anne hesitated. "Just so I'm clear on it, you're not with the police. You're a reporter, right?"

"I am a journalist. But it's not as simple as that. Someone murdered my friend, and this list is connected to it somehow. Your help would be invaluable."

"I expect the police will pursue this themselves."

"Yes, but that will take time, and another friend of mine is in real danger, which is my reason for ringing. She was stabbed, and I just want to make sure whoever did it doesn't get another chance."

"I'm sorry." She paused. "Only two of those paintings have been registered as lost. *A Portrait of a Lady* by Jan Mostaert and *Flower Girl*. The others aren't on the register. I guess I can tell you something about *Flower Girl*."

"I've never heard of it," Casey said. "Do you know where it is now?"

"In this case we do. Often we don't. Even the auction houses don't always know who the real buyers are, and if they do, their lips are sealed. We believe *Flower Girl* has found its way into a private collection, and the original owner, a Polish prince, is trying to get it back. When the Nazis invaded Poland in nineteen thirty-nine, they confiscated thousands of priceless paintings, of which *Flower Girl* was one. An American family business named Chandlers bought it. They have galleries in New York and London and have been among the biggest buyers at auction for years now. In fact, they almost sustained the sagging art market singlehandedly through the seventies and eighties."

"Can you tell me who they bought it from?"

"Hang on." Casey heard the rattle of computer keys. "It's been traced to a Reinhardt's gallery in Munich."

"Do you know where the gallery acquired it?"

"I can't answer that. Reinhardt's is an old and reputable business."

"Is there anything else you can tell me?"

"No. The trail stops there, I'm afraid."

"That's frustrating." Casey rubbed her temple. "Do you know who might have the authority to disclose this information?"

"There's a lot of secrecy in the business, but we're working on it. These problems are widespread. There are stolen artworks hanging in the Louvre and many other art galleries."

"Is that so?"

"Yeah. *And* the Tate."

"Extraordinary. Tell me what you think. Is it odd someone should compile a list of this sort?"

"It's very odd. We'd love to find even a whiff of any of those paintings on that list. It could be they're about to enter the market. It's always a delicate situation. We don't want the press until the paintings are located. If they find their way into private collections, we might never hear of them again." She cleared her throat, and Casey imagined her choosing her words carefully. The woman clearly knew a lot more than she'd told her, but Casey could understand her reticence. It was a delicate business, as she'd said.

Caution came with the job. "And you say the person who had this list is dead?"

Casey explained, and the question of why Donald hid the list hit her again. Where had he come across it?

"The conspiracies involving the art world are endless, Casey," Mary-Anne continued. "From fakes to price fixing, to smuggling old masters and illegally excavated antiquities out of Italy, India, and elsewhere. One huge scam involved staff of a top British auction house. Several of them went to jail because of it. And, of course, stories abound about the sales of Nazi loot."

"Have you had much luck with important artworks?" Casey asked.

"Oh, we're much better at it these days. Criminals are now aware it's very hard to successfully re-sell stolen art. Well-publicized loot is impossible to sell on the legal market, but as for the black market, we never know. We've had some great successes. We recovered Paul Cezanne's *Still Life with Fruit and a Jug*, which was stolen in nineteen seventy-eight. And Edouard Manet's *Still life with Peaches*, stolen back in 'seventy-seven.

"You might try the Lost Art Internet Database. It contains data on cultural objects which were seized from their owners, particularly Jews during the Second World War. I'm not sure they'll release information to you, though. It's mainly for the owners and custodians checking the provenance of their artwork."

She paused a moment as if in thought. "Jean-Paul Legrand is an expert in Interpol's stolen art section. He may know something of the other works on your list. Mention my name."

"Great," Casey said, writing furiously.

"If I were you, I'd keep an eye out for Chandlers. They have regular auctions in London. Have a chat with them—you never know."

Casey thanked her and disconnected. She needed to know more about Reinhardt's gallery. Turning on her computer, she e-mailed a journalist friend—Will Shealey, whom she knew was in Bavaria—and grabbed her coat. Tonight she would treat herself to a vindaloo.

There was no sign of Shiblu at the Indian restaurant. His wife Rani took her order quietly, head down.

"That's a beautiful sari you're wearing, Rani," Casey said, eyeing the delicate, pastel green silk when she reappeared from the small kitchen in the back. "Where's Shiblu tonight?"

"He's been called away to Manchester. His cousin died."

"I'm so sorry. Was it sudden?"

Her face crumpled, and her words tumbled out. "He was murdered by a gang. They hijacked him in his cab. They beat him and ran over him in his own cab!" She wiped at her eyes. "A witness told the police they spat on him, abused him. Surjit was a good man, much loved by his family."

Casey ran behind the counter and threw her arms around Rani's shoulders. "Is there anything I can do to help?"

"No. No. Thank you, Casey. My sister is coming to help in the restaurant." Her fingers shaking, she placed the plastic containers into a bag.

Casey drove home in a dark mood. Racially motivated attacks constantly filled the news. Politicians would always talk up anything that encouraged the view of racial difference. The government now seemed to have taken the view that multi-ethnic societies didn't work.

Once she got home, she opened *The Guardian* and searched for Chandlers among the art auctions, but found nothing.

❧❧❧

After breakfast the next day, Casey spent hours on the computer. The databank proved useless. She doubted she'd have much luck contacting Mr. Legrand but was pleased to find, after mentioning Mary-Anne Louis's name, his secretary put her straight through to him.

A charming Frenchman, he had no knowledge of the paintings on the list. "You might need to consult an art historian," he said. "That's not my field. Stolen art can take thirty years or longer to emerge. A stolen Cezanne was kept in a bank vault for twenty years. Someone may hold on to them because they like them, but eventually they'll get found out. Criminals sometimes use them for ransom or to trade for drugs. But we'd have gotten a whiff of that and we've heard nothing." She heard him tap the desk with a pen. "Sorry I can't help you. Good luck with it."

❧❧❧

Casey crossed to Trafalgar Square from Charing Cross tube station. It was close to lunchtime. People strolled about and tourists illegally fed the greatly diminished flock of pigeons fluttering around Nelson's column.

Don would have been pleased to see them disappearing. Flying rats, he called them. She didn't share his opinion but was glad to see the Square almost free of them, nevertheless. She approached the south corner with its statues of James II and George Washington, the latter a gift from the state of Virginia, and climbed the stairs to the piazza in front of the National Gallery. The gallery's library was not open to the public, but she knew it covered painters and paintings in the western tradition. The gallery was busy, filled with tourists and students queuing up for a tour. Casey approached the counter and asked a woman if she might speak to a librarian or art historian. Minutes later, a short man in his early forties with glasses came to the desk—John Follet, according to his name tag. "May I help you?"

Casey showed him her press card. "My name's Casey Rowan. I have a list of artworks here," she said, pushing it forward. "I believe they were stolen during the war, and I'm trying to find some record of them ever existing."

He bent his head over the list, and she glimpsed a bare round patch at the crown. "Can you leave this with me?"

"Sure, it's a copy."

He picked up a pen. "Give me your number, Casey. I'll check this out when things have quieted down around here. It's a mad house this time of day."

"Thanks, John."

"May not be for a few days," he called after her.

She nodded and left the building. The scene in the square had radically changed. Dark clouds had gathered, robbing the day of its light. Suddenly, rain started pelting down and people rushed about like a disturbed nest of ants, the lucky ones under umbrellas. Casey ran down steps slick with water, a magazine held over her head. It would be a long, damp trip home, but at least she felt hopeful.

CHAPTER 12

Casey came home from a solid workout at the gym Monday morning to find what she'd waited for—Chandler's advertisement in *The Guardian*. A special auction would take place the following Thursday at Claridges hotel. Vlaminck, Matisse, and Pissarro numbered among a breathtaking list of paintings to be sold. She ripped the announcement out of the paper and headed out.

At Brook Street, she smiled at the doorman, entered the elegant, art-deco world of Claridges with its columns and mirrors, and signed herself in as a member of the press. Accepting a glass of champagne from a waiter, she followed the collectors, dealers, and journalists into the mirrored ballroom.

She took her seat among the well-dressed crowd with their oval-shaped, bright-blue numbered paddles. Security guards moved into position, silence descended, and the auctioneer with a clipped tone of voice took the podium, tugging at his cuffs. For a moment, she felt like a kid again, standing at the races with her dad and picking up vibrations of high hopes from the expectant crowd—but this was far more genteel.

The lack of emotion displayed around her surprised her. She'd expected art to inspire passion, but apparently, the tension of possibly acquiring great work turned that emotion into anxiety for some, with the rest of a cooler, poker-faced breed.

Two men carefully placed a painting on an easel, and the auctioneer called the lot number. An untitled work by Camille Pissarro. It depicted a wooded scene near Pontoise from eighteen seventy-seven. The auctioneer's voice droned on, informing them of Pissarro's supreme technical skills, and Casey felt a pang of regret. She would never acquire the wealth to own such a painting.

"In its concern for the evanescent effect of light, it is characteristically Impressionist," the auctioneer said.

Casey's gaze traveled through the painting's woods, but the strong vertical tree trunks concealed most of a cluster of whitewashed farmhouses. The village remained beyond her reach, seducing her with the play of light and shadow on the houses' creamy walls, their glowing red roofs outlined against an azure sky.

The bidding started at four million pounds. Barely detectable jerks of heads or paddles sent the figure spiralling upwards. Telephone bidders talked into their mobiles and gestured rapidly in the front row. A buyer soon claimed the painting for eight million pounds.

More works of equal magnificence followed. A few were passed in review, and many of the paintings sold over their reserve. Casey moved through the crowd, recognizing

Bunty Chandler, the doyen of the family enterprise, by her nametag as she posed for photographs.

Bunty's hair formed a smooth blonde chignon, and she wore a silky black suit cut to the curves of her trim body. From a distance, she looked quite young, but up close, Casey adjusted her guess to late forties or possibly older. She was the product of the glossy agelessness that some wealthy American women achieved.

Casey flashed her press card, and Bunty smiled in response.

"Reporters are most welcome."

"Overall, a very successful result," Casey prompted, notebook and pen poised.

"Do I detect an American accent?"

"Yes. Florida."

"But you've been here a while, huh?"

Casey nodded, and Bunty gave her a rundown on the paintings that had passed expectations. She took it down in shorthand, verbatim, though she'd never use it.

"I believe your family company purchased Renoir's *Flower Girl* from Reinhardt's gallery in Munich?"

Bunty's pale eyes took on a wary expression, and she hesitated. Looking about her, she took Casey's arm and drew her away from the crowd to a quiet corner.

"Where did you get that information?" She'd begun to look at Casey as if she'd suddenly developed an infectious rash.

"Are you saying my information is incorrect, Ms. Chandler?"

"I didn't catch who you work for."

"*Hers.*" Casey showed Bunty her press card again.

"That's not an art magazine."

"It's a women's monthly."

Casey watched, fascinated as Bunty apparently tried to think on her feet.

"Uh huh. Uh huh. What's your angle for a story? Not who bought *Flower Girl*, surely?"

"To be honest with you, Ms. Chandler, I'm not interested in who is the genuine owner of *Flower Girl*. But I am trying to find out where it came from before Reinhardt's obtained it." Casey tucked her notebook in her bag. "Off the record?"

She couldn't blame Bunty for her skepticism.

"You're hoping for a much bigger story, of course," she said, nodding sagely. "You think it's going to be *the* story. The one that gets your career off the ground."

"I'm investigating a murder."

"A murder?" Bunty fingered her expensive top button with nervous fingers.

"It's just a lead I want to follow."

Bunty shook her head. "We don't have that information." She wrestled with the button again. "We bought the painting despite there being some doubt to its authenticity."

"Is that customary?"

She looked at Casey, clearly annoyed. "If you were involved in the art world—" she peered at the nametag, "Miz Rowan, you'd know that is often the case."

"Have you reached a decision on its authenticity?"

"Our experts are quite sure it *is* a genuine Renoir."

"If you can just tell me what you know about its past, I promise you won't hear another peep out of me."

Bunty lowered her head and spoke quietly. Although her expression remained one of annoyance, an edge of intimacy crept in. "In a private collection in Europe for almost sixty years, we believe."

"Can you narrow that down to the country, city?" She wasn't sure why Bunty confided in her. Perhaps she had warmed to the suggestion that Casey would then disappear.

"Berlin, I believe."

"I've heard a Polish prince, who claims he lost it to the Nazis during the war, wants it back."

Bunty looked surprised, although she must have heard of it. "Right of ownership's a difficult thing to establish after all this time. I can't comment on that. I must get your magazine," she said suddenly, straightening and looking around her. "I've never read it."

"I could send you a copy, Ms. Chandler."

"Don't bother. I'll pick one up myself." She turned away and began to slip through the chairs.

"Oh, and Ms. Chandler?" Casey called. "I do hope you plan to release *Flower Girl* for exhibitions occasionally, so the public can enjoy it."

Bunty hurried away, her stiletto heels clicking rapier-like on the marble floor. Casey shook her head—she couldn't help but admire the woman. She managed to be both sexy and formidable at fiftyish. Casey wanted to call her back and ask her how she did it, but it probably entailed far too many trips to the gym.

∽∾∽

Almost a week had passed and John Follet from the National Gallery still hadn't rung. Pondering what she'd learned from the Art Loss Register and Bunty Chandler, Casey left the train station and walked down into the busy retail area of Richmond. She bought a snack at Tesco's and settled down for an afternoon in the library on Hill Street.

Several hours later, she'd turned up some dismal facts. Although the art world had decided to get serious about tracking down art stolen by the Nazis in World War II, only a few paintings had been reunited with the heirs of the original owners.

British museums had compiled a list of three hundred and fifty artworks whose whereabouts during the war could not be accounted for and placed it on the Internet with little response.

In Russia, a museum had acquired over three hundred important paintings stolen in nineteen forty-five from a German gallery. The Russians now claimed ownership by virtue of the length of time that had elapsed. Understandably, the gallery in Germany wanted the collection back, claiming its value to be over three billion American dollars.

She knew the paintings on Don's list would be worth a fortune. If he were onto a story, it would have been huge. Had he inadvertently placed himself in danger because of it?

Tomorrow, Don's funeral would be held in Fulham. The police had finally released his body, but Tessa wouldn't be there to see him into his final resting place.

∽∾∽

At the churchyard in Fulham, a rare snowfall dusted the trees. It was bitterly cold, and the crowd gathered in the church entrance, leaving a few photographers stamping their feet in the street.

Observing the police presence, Casey hurried through the impressive group warmed by bodies and straining heaters to slip into a pew beside Tessa's father, a middle-aged man with thinning, ginger hair.

"Hello, Roland," she whispered, noting the absence of Tessa's mother, Camilla.

Roland kissed her cheek. He looked bewildered. His green eyes, the same color as Tessa's, appeared puffy and red. Casey squeezed his hand.

A couple of rows ahead of them sat the silver head of the man who'd caused a stir earlier. The Chancellor of the Exchequer, Sir Henry Richardson. A prominent news reporter had situated herself forward to get a glimpse of him, momentarily stealing attention away from the bleak reason for the gathering. The Prime Minister's deteriorating health had become a major concern for the government, and Sir Henry was his obvious replacement. The news had been full of it for weeks.

After the ceremony, Casey watched Don's coffin lowered into the frozen earth, feeling overwhelmed with claustrophobia. The same helpless sensation she'd had as a child when her dad had taken her on holidays and they'd visited some underground caves in Virginia. She'd wandered away, distracted by the crystal blossoms adorning the ceiling and the rock floors. Then she found the walls starting to close in and couldn't breathe. It was the first time she'd realized life wouldn't always be safe, and her dad would not always be there to make it so.

When the coffin was settled in the grave, Casey stepped forward, fighting to stay calm. She tossed in a small bunch of white snowdrops, adding to the pile of extravagant wreaths. She wondered who among those surrounding her really knew and loved him.

"Rest peacefully, my friend," she murmured. "With angels and archangels and with all the company of heaven." She said this for herself as much as for Don.

An atheist, he'd believed funerals were just for the living. In the end, she didn't know for sure, so here she stood, despite her desire to stay true to his memory, wishing him faith and comfort in a place he'd never believed in. Did she know him any better than those around her, or had Don become more of a mystery in death than he was in life?

Feeling shaky with grief, she drove back to Exeter in her rental car to visit Tessa. Casey found her friend propped up in bed and bent to kiss her. Tessa seemed in an odd state of calm, her eyes red but quite dry of tears. It occurred to Casey that she could still be suffering from shock.

"So it was you there in the end, Casey. I couldn't even manage that."

Disconcerted, Casey squeezed her hand. "Don would understand."

"Did they give him a good send-off?"

She nodded and went into a detailed list of who had been there. "And, of course, Sir Henry Richardson."

An aide came in with a cup of milky tea for Tessa and an arm full of flowers. More bouquets already filled the room, their perfume cloying. Casey tried to occupy herself by arranging them around the room.

She fussed, chatting mindlessly while Tessa remained silent. Tweaking a daffodil's golden head, so beautiful and optimistic for life and sun, she felt aware of how fragile and brief life was.

"I sat with your Dad in the church," Casey said after she'd run out of distractions, but Tessa merely pleated the sheet and nodded.

Casey took her copy of the list of artworks from her bag. "Have you ever seen this before?" she asked, placing it on Tessa's tray. "I found it in Devon jammed up inside Don's writing award from school."

"I've no idea what it is," Tessa said, barely looking at it. "He didn't tell me everything."

"Surely you and he—" Casey began but then saw her friend's face was bleak, exhausted. "I'm sorry, darling, it's just that you seemed so close."

Tessa shook her head slowly. "I wonder..." She sat silently, staring at the wall, before she seemed to collect herself, pulling herself higher onto the pillows. "The police told me this morning that they believe he knew his attacker. He let the man into the house. Why didn't he tell me about *him*?" She pushed away the tray, spilling tea into the saucer.

Casey sat down on the edge of the bed, her heart racing at the news, and put her hand over Tessa's.

"God, he was a great man, but we're all flawed, aren't we?" She looked at Casey in desperation, as if she had the answer. Tessa continued to talk, half-complaint, half-miserable, and her voice became so soft Casey had to lean forward to hear her.

"Some women want a man to control them. Maybe I did in the beginning, I don't know. I guess I agreed, but I outgrew it, and I couldn't make him understand that." She pulled her hand from Casey's and pressed it to her eyes. Casey swallowed, trying to read her mood. Tessa seemed so alone, so far from her now.

"To be honest, in a way I did like being the child-bride. Do you realize that to him, I would always have seemed young?" Her pale face still looked young, even without makeup. "Well, I have my independence now, haven't I?"

"Don't worry about that now," Casey said gently.

"Don became far too involved in your life, too."

Casey sat back, dazed, feeling like she'd been struck. "That's not true."

"I didn't agree with him when he interfered in your first serious love affair. You would have married Laurie but for him."

"Laurie wasn't right for me, Tessa. I decided that, not Don."

"You might think you're smart, Casey—but not about men. I have a mother who taught my sister and me how to manage them. While you debated with Don in Oxford, I seduced him."

Casey opened her mouth to protest, then noticed for the first time that Tessa's eyes had turned almost black, the green diminished by pupils blown large with medication.

"And you haven't formed any lasting relationships since Laurie, have you?" she went on ruthlessly.

"I just haven't met anyone special, that's all."

Casey began to feel leaden with exhaustion. Tessa's words hemmed her in. She needed desperately to get away but felt she shouldn't leave her.

"I know of two possible reasons for a gorgeous woman like you not to have a partner in your life. One is you loved Don, and I honestly don't mind if you did. That I could understand. The other is that a painful experience has turned you into an emotional coward who's afraid—to commit. Which—" Her voice began to falter, and her eyelids drooped. "Oh, God, I feel so..."

Casey sat and watched Tessa sleep until a nurse came. Then she grabbed her bag and left, feeling weak, confused, and so very tired.

Tessa's words rang like a bell in her head. That summer in Florida, Jake had dropped her, saying she would only hurt him down the track when she refused to let any commitment pin her down. She stood at the door of the hospital and pulled out her phone, sensing her past suddenly rendered empty and meaningless. She needed a drink. No, several. And some good company.

∽ↄↄↄ

Rod's place was just one room with partitioned-off kitchen and a bathroom. It was neater than she'd managed. The kitchen was spotless, clothes and linen folded on open shelves. It occurred to her that his neatness came from police training, but she dismissed the thought. She doubted it was something that could be taught.

"You were never in the army, were you?" she asked, sitting on his sofa.

Rod poured her a glass of wine and came to join her. "No, why?"

"You're so tidy."

He smiled. "You'd go mad in a wee place like this if you weren't."

At dinner at a local Chinese place, they'd avoided any mention of the case, probably for different reasons. Casey wanted to put the horror of it aside for a while and enjoy the sense of freedom his company gave her.

She glanced at the clichéd pastoral prints hanging on the walls.

"I rent it furnished," he said, following her gaze.

She laughed, disconcerted. "Where did you live before you came here?"

"I have a big mortgage on a small place in Kingston I've rented out."

"Any family?"

"Mmmm." He put his arms around her, his eyes on her mouth.

"I'd like to know more about you." Her head had begun to swim. She put her glass down carefully on the coffee table.

He straightened with a serious expression, but his eyes remained bright with amusement. "My mum and my sister live in Edinburgh. My ex-wife, Sylvie, does too. We keep in touch." He reached for her again.

"No children?"

He shook his head. "But the breakup was sad, confusing, and unsettling. It's why I left Scotland. I'm still fond of Sylvie. We go back a long way. Sometimes she needs my help. She has a bairn, but he's not mine. She's sick—she has hepatitis."

"Oh God, that's bad luck."

"Aye, it's rough. Life is rough. Casey, do you really want to be here? Is it too soon?"

"For what?" she asked, leaning back, succumbing to the pleasurable sensation of his body pressing against hers.

"This," he said, with a gesture that took them both in. "You and me. I don't want this to be just an episode when you drank too much."

She sat up straight. "Who's drunk too much?"

He pulled away from her. Moving to the table, he waved a bottle of wine at her, almost empty.

She screwed up her nose. "That's not very gallant of you, Carlisle."

He grinned. "You want coffee?"

"Sounds good."

She rose and went on a walk-about of Rod's flat. There were few personal items to tell her anything about him, except for his expensive music system.

"Oh, you have some old LPs."

"They were my father's old 'swing' records from the late forties and early fifties," he said, moving towards her. "These old seventy-eight's were designed to be played in tandem with film, but they only went for four to five minutes. Then in nineteen forty-eight, Columbia Records developed the long play format when they brought in the thirty-three-and-a-third rpm LP, to last as long as a film reel—eleven minutes."

He handed her a mug of coffee. She took a sip, hoping it would make little difference to her pleasant state of inebriety. At the moment, she floated nicely, all fears kept at a safe distance. It was a perilous state, she knew. If she drank more, she'd become an unattractive, weeping drunk incapable of making decisions.

Feeling him brush her shoulder, she searched through the pile full of musicians she didn't recognize. She had trouble concentrating on his words.

His breath feathered the hair on the nape of her neck. "I'll play one for you if you like."

She felt her pulse rise and her senses go on full alert. "Yes, please."

While she watched, amused, he tenderly cleaned the old record before placing it on the turntable and lowering the stylus. He'd chosen *Lady Be Good,* and soon the bright upbeat rhythm of swing filled the room. Gershwin and the Benny Goodman Trio.

"Dance with me?" Rod asked.

Turning, she fitted into his arms. She could always tell by dancing with a man whether they would be good together in bed. And she and Rod danced well together, somehow knowing each other's moves. He swung her around the small room until the music ended and they collapsed onto the sofa.

She was breathless, but not from exertion and felt suddenly unsure. "How about something more contemporary?" she asked.

He took her face in both his hands and touched his lips to hers, so softly that she opened her mouth automatically. He tasted of wine and cigarettes. Her hands tangled in his thick, straight hair.

"You're really something, Casey Rowan." He pulled her down, and she slipped her hand into the neck of his shirt, finding his chest smooth and almost hairless. Unbuttoning his top button, she moved her hand lower. The muscles of his stomach felt taut and strong.

She sensed a puckering of the skin and pulled at his shirt. On his abdomen was a large purple scar shaped like a crescent moon. "What's this?"

Rod sat up.

"I didn't mean to pry."

"The night Pete was killed. I was shot."

She put her hands on his shoulders. "Come here." Pulling him down with her, she gave into a swift, fierce longing.

He let his breath out with a gasp and kissed her, their tongues exploring as their bodies moved together, almost trying to fuse through their clothes. They drew apart reluctantly and hastened to undress. Then he moved on top of her again.

She welcomed his delicious weight. The feeling of his hard cock pressed up against her stomach, toying with the swollen, needy nub of her core, drove her mad.

"Fuck me," she whispered in his ear.

He met her gaze with a naked, raw desire that made her groan. She was glad when he entered her quickly. She wanted it hard, she wanted it now. Somehow, she hoped, filling her body would fill the cold vacuum that had occupied it since that morning. A soft moan escaped her lips, her hands moved to his buttocks to pull him closer, as if that were possible, and her hips rose to meet his thrusts, urging him on.

She hovered on the brink when he paused and tenderly kissed her face, his mouth moving down her neck to kiss each of her breasts.

She didn't want tender. She moved, and they rolled over, narrowly escaping an undignified fall to the floor. Climbing to sit astride him, she leaned over, his hands caressing her breasts. She began to move to some inner rhythm, orchestrating her fast approaching orgasm, taking him with her.

☙❧☙

Casey woke from a brief, exhausted sleep to the sound of a kettle whistling and pulled the sheet up over her naked body. Just then, Rod came around the corner holding two steaming mugs.

He'd already dressed in his suit. "Good morning. Tea?"

"Oh, great, thanks." She took the mug, feeling disappointment and a pang of yearning. He had to leave. He sat down beside her on the sofa bed, a frown forming between his brows. By staying over, she had broken one of her cardinal rules. This was a time to stay calm and rational. She was anything but that and drank her tea so fast it burned her throat.

"I'll be off when I finish this," she said in a strangled voice.

"I just had a call from Middlemoor. My super's getting restless."

"Any new developments?"

"No. That's the trouble." He changed his mug of tea to his left hand and, with his right, traced an imaginary line from below her ear down to where she held the sheet up to her chest. "You were wonderful last night. And I don't just mean—" He paused and indicated the bed behind her. "—all this."

"You were very nice yourself, but surely it's not playing fair when you're dressed and I'm caught like this," she protested. "Why didn't you wake me?"

"I liked watching you sleep. You do wonders for my dreary flat."

"I'll get dressed." She put down the mug and released a leg from its entrapment in the folds of the sheet, trying for a dignified exit to the bathroom.

"Jesus, Casey Rowan, those legs." Rod put down his mug with a clatter and reached for her, his eyes passionate and urgent, just as his mobile rang.

"I'll be there in ten," he said into his phone. Throwing it onto the bed, he said, "*Damn.* Can I see you tonight?"

Casey shook her head. In her fragile state, she could very quickly become overwhelmed by him. She needed space, time to consider her actions, before this man became too important to her. "I'm getting the train back to Richmond. I have to pick up the threads."

Rod groaned. "I'll be stuck down here for a while. Call me when you're back again, and make that soon."

"You'd better go—no sense in putting your gov offside. Don't worry—I'll see myself out."

She kissed him and noticed he didn't seem to want to leave any more than she wanted him to. That felt good, in her heart and under her hand. Finally, he forced himself off the bed and out the door.

CHAPTER 13

Christ, this makes us look bad," Tom Kennerton railed at Rod while waving the newspaper about. His goodwill had run out. *The Mirror* had somehow acquired details of the Broughton murder the police planned to keep hidden. Facts regarding the murder weapon and injuries to Donald Broughton were now displayed in gory detail on its front page. Knowing a colleague had leaked that information made everyone edgy.

"What's the latest on that stabbing in Exeter, Danny?" Rod asked as he and Tom entered the briefing room.

"A domestic. Ex stabbed new hubby in the arm and stole the DVD player."

Someone laughed and whispered, "It was the love of his life."

"Okay." Rod approached the whiteboard and prepared to go over everything again. "The good news is that Tessa Broughton has been moved to a London hospital and is expected to make a full recovery."

A cheer went round the room.

"Donald knew his attacker," he continued, after the murmur of voices had subsided. "That rules out Gavin Holmes' involvement. This is not a break and enter. And there's no word on the street that a contract was out on Tessa."

"Gavin Holmes couldn't afford it," Danny Singh said.

"It was Tessa's routine to lock all the doors before she went to bed," Rod said. "If the murderer had come to the front door, at least one of the women would have heard him—their bedrooms are directly above. Traces of mud were found on the mat and the kitchen floor, due to the rain earlier, so we conclude that Donald let the murderer in through the back door. Then there's the phone call." He pointed to a new member of his team. "DI Wilberforce?"

With a swipe at his wispy, fair goatee Wilberforce shuffled to his feet. "Tessa thought she heard her husband's mobile but she drifted off to sleep before coming downstairs. A trace was put on all the calls made to Donald's mobile that night and found our murderer had rung from a public phone only two miles away at two a.m. Whoever called him could have received an invitation to come to his house or merely wanted to know that he was there."

Rod nodded. "That partial print outside the sitting-room doors is of a size twelve shoe—an expensive one. He's six foot plus. This fits with the autopsy and the little Tessa can tell us about him. Lab is working on the shoe type, but generally, we're not looking for your garden-variety robber. The murderer had his own transport. No way could he get to the house and away without it—he didn't pick up a local cab. Then there's the car parked in

Holly Road. No one appears to have been visiting in the general area. A Mrs. Harrison from number six looked out of her window and saw it was still there about quarter to three, but gone in the morning. It appears the murderer entered the Broughton's property from the rear of the block and left the same way. The footprint and the knife confirm this."

"He must be familiar with the area," said Danny Singh.

"Not necessarily. A street directory and a torch would have done it." Rod made another heading on the board. "The knife—now splashed on the front page of *The Mirror*—is uncommon." He turned to pick up the weapon, with its long, honed blade, lying tagged on the table in front of him. "It's a German make, not legally available here. Except for an aging laptop and a briefcase, nothing of value was taken. He wasn't after money. Ditto, Fulham."

"The two are connected. I don't believe in synchronicity," Tom Kennerton interjected, drawing up a chair.

"As the profiler said," Rod went on, "these attacks appear to have been premeditated. He was organized and arrogant. He brought that knife with him with the full intention of using it. He did so in a controlled mood. He killed first, then headed for the woods, wiped the knife clean and buried it under loose soil and leaves. He was there for some time—the undergrowth's been flattened at one spot, and he may well have changed his clothes before he returned to his car. He must have had blood on him— he couldn't risk anyone seeing him that way. And he didn't want to take the knife with him, so he may not live alone."

"He had to know the police would find it," Barry said.

"So maybe he planted it," suggested Singh.

"I'm with the profiler on this—he wanted done with the whole business there and then," Rod said. "Neatly tidied away. And as he took his time, he was obviously unaware that Ms. Rowan was in the house and could call the police. He might have known it was the Broughtons' habit to spend most weekends there alone and assumed that this would be the same as usual. Ms. Rowan had been away for three months, remember."

"Rowan might be his accomplice."

"Not one of your better theories, Danny," Rod said, and Singh flushed. "What could possibly be her motive?"

"She would have finished off Tessa before calling for help, or waited for her to die," said Anita Jennings. "It wouldn't have taken long."

"Well, I've always suspected more going on between Rowan and Broughton," Tom said.

"Let's move on," said Rod impatiently.

"He poured the man a glass of his best Scotch," added Singh.

"Aye, it wasn't there when Tessa went to bed. There are no prints on the glass. He knew what he was doing. He attacked Tessa in the same ruthless manner—struck her down from behind. This was not a frenzied or passionate attack. If she hadn't come downstairs, he may well have gone to look for her."

"It's lucky for Casey Rowan that he didn't have to," said Jennings.

"Someone shut Rowan's door, remember," Barry said.

"We can assume that he came to the house with the intention of killing Donald Broughton." Rod perched on the corner of the desk. "And here's where we come up against our thick brick wall. So far, we've turned up no one in the Broughtons' lives that fits this profile." He picked up a piece of paper. "This credit slip from Donald's wallet shows he had lunch at Gorky's Restaurant three days before he died. The proprietor said he dined with two men. Perhaps we can get him to expand on that. Have you been able to pin down the proprietor, Danny? If he hasn't made himself available for tomorrow, we'll go after him."

"He assured me he'll be there, gov."

"We can't ignore the autobiography and the possibility that the killer feared something incriminating would appear in its publication and, acting on information Donald gave him, headed straight up to Fulham." Rod shook his head. "It doesn't sit right with me, but we can't ignore the fact that Donald's computer and all his notes and computer disks on his biography were taken—and nothing else."

Tom drew a cigarette out of a crumpled packet with his teeth. He lit up, but exasperated sighs from the group were the most anyone would comment. Someone stared hopefully at the smoke alarm on the ceiling. "Let's look at what we've got on Rupert Morris-Smythe." He forced the words out, grimacing through the exhalation of smoke.

"There's nothing to add to what I've already covered. Morris-Smythe certainly fits the arrogant profile." Rod slid off the desk and walked back to the white board. "They left halfway through the opera—"

"Understandable," a young male PC commented, and several others laughed.

Rod ignored it, knowing they used humor to diffuse the tension they were under. "—and after that attended a party in Belgravia where they stayed for one drink. Witnesses say the pair argued and left well before midnight. After that, Morris-Smythe maintains he remained with his wife in St John's Wood before returning to their country home in Hampshire around four o'clock the next day. His secretary has confirmed the time of their arrival. Claudette Morris-Smythe is in France, and we haven't been able to make contact with her. Rupert drives a black BMW. I've checked with his sister, Elizabeth Trentham. She couldn't tell me much beyond suggesting that he *is* capable of murder."

"Close family," Barry commented, shaking his head.

Rod waved a drift of smoke from his eyes. "He could have made it to Devon in time, with the roads light on traffic."

"Why wait until now to act?" asked Singh. "The guy's father committed suicide years ago."

"There's been some publicity about Donald's autobiography. Morris-Smythe hated Broughton. It might have been festering. And then there's this list of paintings Casey Rowan turned up. The Art & Antiques Unit has been looking into it. They confirm Renoir's *Flower Girl* appeared out of nowhere. The other paintings are still missing."

Tom's mobile rang. "I intend to find the source of that leak," he said, "Anyone who talks to the press will come to regret it, understand?" He threw back his chair and left the room.

Rod frowned. Tom's threat was bad for morale. "So," he said, tossing the marker down, ready to sum it up. "We've looked into Donald's past, and his wife has been helpful in outlining what he planned for the book, but apart from Morris-Smythe, we haven't yet found anyone who would want to go to such drastic lengths to stop him from writing it."

They all hated it when a case seemed to dry up. Rod had watched the enthusiasm of the murder team fade as time went by and no new leads turned up. He was determined to keep the investigation moving. Something had to break soon.

"Colin, you and your team can continue checking every issue Donald took up with in the last, say, nine months. There's a lot—he was a powerhouse when it came to his work. He tackled several contentious issues on his radio show. Euthanasia, fox hunting, and environmental concerns among them. And consequently, he got some heated e-mail.

"There's one particular matter Donald took up I want to check on. The residents of Bishop's Walton near Ringwood Forest in Dorset are in arms over an asbestos dump. A demolition company, employed in its safe removal, dumped it in the woods instead of getting it treated and buried. The local children were found playing in it. For those who don't know, asbestos was used in the building of houses until it was found to cause mesothelioma—a fatal cancer. Apparently, Donald had become a spokesperson for their cause."

"Ringwood Forest? That's a grand place, makes me want to murder 'em myself," said DI Lawson, a new member of the team.

"Well, you can come with me," Rod said. "I'll join you for a drink at the pub, and then I'd advise everyone to go home and have an early night. Tomorrow we'll get stuck into it."

As the room emptied, DC Allen Botham, a young constable recently assigned and still wet behind the ears, lagged behind. "Gov, it was me that let that detail slip," he said, shuffling his feet.

Rod frowned. "How did that happen?"

"The journalist bought me a couple of drinks. We got to talking and I thought anything I said would be in confidence."

Rod ground his teeth. "Let it be a lesson to you, DC. You don't get friendly with the press. Understand?"

"Yes sir. Am I in trouble, gov?"

"I'll let you off this time, but make sure we don't have a conversation like this again."

"No, gov," Botham's face sagged with relief. "I'll see you at the pub, gov."

"No drinking for you while on this case. I can't afford another slip up and neither can you."

"Right gov."

Rod took a deep breath and headed for Tom's office. "I would prefer you not to interfere in my enquiry, Tom," he said. "It undermines my authority with the murder team, and it's not your job."

The older man's eyes narrowed. "You answer to me, laddie," he said. "But I have to answer to everyone else. And they are constantly breathing down my neck."

"Allow me to get on with it, then," Rod said. He turned and left the room.

CHAPTER 14

A week remained before Casey had to return to work, but she couldn't relax. Her thoughts strayed constantly to Rod. They had been so good together, but she found herself dismissing it as a one-night stand. She couldn't dismiss Tessa's words, however—they held enough truth to stir things up, bring all the mud to the surface.

Perhaps she was a coward, fearing the pain when love ended, that agonising sense of loss. And watching Tessa suffer now only made that clearer.

She forced her mind back to the day she met Don, back to that first impression—always the one to stay with you—before their relationship had formed and set into one of friendship.

She and Tessa were having a drink in a smoky Oxford pub when Don came in with a camera crew. They'd been filming a documentary on university life. The crew, a lively bunch, sat down at the table next to theirs. Tessa leaned over and whispered to Casey, "Do you know who that is?"

She knew, of course. She'd watched him on the BBC. He was intelligent and funny, and the mix appealed, on camera and off, it seemed. Tessa was transfixed.

The crew drew them into their conversation, and they turned their chairs around to join the other table. Don talked, and Casey had to concentrate to follow his line of thinking. His mind worked so quickly.

By the time they went back to their rooms later that evening, Casey suspected both of them were a little besotted. But she asked what Tessa thought of Don, and the look on her face signaled something far stronger than the mere admiration she herself felt.

They saw a lot of Don during the next couple of weeks, and once he'd completed the documentary, it didn't stop there. Whenever he could escape from London, the three would meet to go for a bike ride or picnic by the river if the weather was fine. They were sublime days.

A particularly warm day swept into Casey's consciousness. Tessa had a lecture, and Don and she were left alone on the grassy bank, soaking up a sudden bout of sunshine. He was on his stomach, reading aloud excerpts from a book about the Englishmen from Cambridge who became Russian spies, Burgess and MacLean. He seemed caught up in it. To her, the men were just traitors to their country. She lay on her back, her arm propping up her head to watch the ducks making muddy eddies in the water, her thoughts drifting. As he turned a page, she put a hand out, whipping off his glasses and rolling away with them. "Can't you read without these?"

"That's why I wear them. Give them back, pest." Don leaned over her to grab them and hovered there too long.

With his face so close to hers, she realized with a jolt he was about to kiss her.

"Don't!" she said suddenly, pushing up and free of him, almost throwing him back against the grass. A duck took to the air, quacking, and she sat there, breathing quickly, her heart pounding. By the time she turned back, Don had picked up his glasses from the grass where she'd flung them and returned to his book, this time reading to himself. When the sun disappeared behind clouds, they were both ready to leave.

Afterwards, she wondered why she'd reacted so strongly. She hadn't been repulsed by the idea—but she'd liked the way things were, and in the corner of her mind, she knew how much Tessa wanted him. Soon afterwards, Don and Tessa became a couple, and Laurie appeared on the scene to distract her.

Romance between Don and her would have been too volatile to last. As a friend, she thought she had the best aspects of him.

The years passed and the friendship between the three of them became forged like components of a piece of machinery, each with something important to contribute. Like family.

Can a friendship exist without an underlying sexual tension between a man and a woman? Casey never felt it, but she was aware that men operated differently to women. She never sensed it from Don, however. If she had, she wouldn't or couldn't have hung around. They never crossed that line, which made what happened at his fortieth birthday so surprising.

It was the day before she left for America. They dined at a favorite restaurant. Tessa danced with Casey's friend, George, while Don and she sat and watched them.

"I'm forty, Casey," Don said, slurring his words slightly. "I'm that much closer to death."

He was a bit drunk, but Casey felt he was entitled.

"Forty's the new thirty," she said half-jokingly. She watched George and Tessa make a passable attempt at a tango.

"I liked the old thirty better. I need a kiss."

She turned away from the dance floor and, laughingly, put her arms around him, kissing his cheek loudly.

"On the lips."

She pulled back. How drunk was he?

Don threw down the pen he'd been fiddling with. He'd scribbled notes—thoughts for his column, no doubt—on a paper serviette. She watched the pen bounce off the table and roll against a chair leg. Suddenly, she wanted to leave. She pushed back her chair, uncomfortable and shaky at the same time. She was probably a bit smashed, too, but knew this wasn't right. She needed fresh air. He took off his glasses and looked at her. In the flickering candle light, his eyes looked naked and vulnerable. Shaking his head, he said, "Okay. *Don't.*"

Casey wasn't sure if he was trying to hurt or embarrass her, but it seemed he intended to push the point, reminding her of that time by the river, and she felt a surge of anger. They were friends of long standing. And what did he think Tessa would do if she turned and saw them kissing? Or didn't he care?

Casey felt quite sure he hadn't harbored any passionate longings for her over the years. He was drunk and easily distracted. She decided a trip to the bathroom would break this up and give her time to deal with her disappointment in him.

Rising, she gestured towards Tessa and said, "Your wife is a great dancer. George can cut the rug too, can't he?"

Don didn't follow her gaze or her words. He stared at her with an odd expression. "I need to talk to you. Alone."

"Can't you tell me now?"

He watched Tessa for a moment before turning back to her. "No, not here. Not now."

You know I'm flying out to America tomorrow," she said. "Can it wait?"

He didn't answer at first. Then he seemed to make up his mind. "Sure, it'll keep. Have a great time over there in the sun, you lucky bugger."

When Don picked her up from the station, the night he died, he made no mention of what he'd said, and neither did his e-mails to her in Florida. She remembered feeling uneasy but thinking she'd have time to approach him about it. She wondered, if she'd spoken to him at the restaurant, would he have told her what she was now so desperate to find out? The thought rolled around in her mind for some time that night, and she couldn't sleep for hours.

CHAPTER 15

Will Shealey had finally answered Casey's e-mail with a surprising piece of news. Heinrich Reinhardt, the owner of Reinhardt's gallery in Munich that had sold *Flower Girl* to Chandlers, was the uncle of the Chancellor of the Exchequer, Sir Henry Richardson.

She immediately tried to ring Rod, but he didn't answer his phone, so she texted the message to him.

She'd watched Sir Henry on a news program recently, speaking about the up-coming budget. He could make even the budget exciting and had the press, who followed as he walked his schnauzer terrier, hanging on his every word. He was at ease with journalists and known to communicate difficult policies with simplicity to the public. Now he was poised to take over one of the most powerful jobs in the world.

She leapt out of her chair. An idea had come to her that would cure her restlessness. She would go to Munich and visit Richardson's uncle Heinrich. Will wrote that Sir Henry attended university there, living with his uncle in his early twenties. Perhaps she could do a piece on him, something that would certainly prove useful in the future if Sir Henry became Prime Minister.

Casey called the magazine. Hugh sounded harassed, last-minute stress before they went to press. She suspected he agreed to the article just to get her off the phone and felt unaccountably guilty that she wasn't there to help.

She found *Herr* Reinhardt's home phone number on the gallery's website, hoping he spoke English. Her smattering of German wouldn't get her far.

A brusque male voice said, *"Hullo, haben Sie Sprosse das Haus von Heinrich Reinhardt. Wer ist es bitte?*

She grimaced. *"Sprechen sie Englisch?"*

"Yes, may I help you?"

"Guten abend, Herr Reinhardt," she said with relief. "My name is Casey Rowan. I'm a journalist working for *Hers* magazine in London. I'd very much like to do an article about the time Sir Henry spent with you, his university years. It won't take much of your time. Perhaps some photographs. Would that be possible?"

His voice came over the line, polite, reluctant. 'I'm afraid that would not be possible. I'm sorry."

"*Herr* Reinhardt, I was a good friend of Donald Broughton, I'm not sure you ever met him. He was a friend of Henry's."

"Donald Broughton? He came here several times with Henry. A nice man. Do you know who killed him?"

"No, unfortunately, the police are investigating—"

"Well, *Fräulein* Rowan, a friend of Donald's, I am not sure, perhaps I should consult first with my nephew on this matter. You will please ring me—in the morning, yes?"

"Yes, I will. *Danke. Gute nacht.*"

∾∾∾

Casey stepped out of the taxi into the damp chill of dusk in Munich. Street lamps appeared out of the darkness like fairy lights up and down the *strasse*. She entered the *Bayerischer Hof*, having decided on a bit of necessary pampering at an expensive hotel. Her spirits lifted merely from the acres of gleaming marble floor in the foyer, and she realized how much she needed this.

From the window of her room, she glimpsed a crowded square and recognized it as the Marienplatz, the ancient heart of Munich.

She filled in the room service voucher for breakfast the next morning. The words swam before her eyes, she was so bone weary. She had been, really, since this all began, but she fought the urge to lie down.

Studying her map of the city, she noted that Reinhardt lived near the lake at Starnberg. She checked her travel guide and found it was about thirty minutes from here— four strips of a *streifenkarte*.

She briefly considered going down to the restaurant for dinner but gave into exhaustion and soon climbed under the foot-thick duvet.

Waking to the knock of room service at the door, she found daylight creeping between the cracks in the curtains. She ate quickly, delighting in the fresh figs and feather-light omelet. She finished up with rich, strong coffee.

Scraping up the last crumbs with her finger, she rang to confirm the time of her interview with Reinhardt.

It was arranged. She leapt out of bed and headed for the shower.

⌀⌀⌀⌀

"Please enter, *Fräulein* Rowan."

Heinrich Reinhardt lived in a large, dark brick house with a steeply sloping roof from which rose several smoking chimneys. Through the open door, Casey caught sight of walls lined with warm timber. She shook the large, dry hand attached to a big man with a full head of snowy white hair. She knew he had to be at least eighty, but his posture was straight, and his smooth, golden skin bore very few lines. His fingers resting lightly on her back, he led her through his home, and she could sense his pride.

They entered a handsome room with a marble fireplace, deep crimson carpet and floor-to-ceiling windows looking out over the garden. Photographs and glass display cases crammed with artifacts took up every available space. He made coffee, and she studied the photographs. In one, Heinrich wore his German army uniform during World War II, an easily recognizable version of the man who returned with a tray of coffee held high.

"You have the Iron Cross, *Herr* Reinhardt." She smiled at him. "I've never had the pleasure of meeting anyone awarded it. Will you tell me how you came by it?"

"A long time ago now. It was not so noble. I was just doing my job. A man confronted with fighting a war either breaks down in fear or becomes like a machine, you understand." He shrugged. "I had my orders and I carried them out."

Framed pictures of his family clustered about on tabletops. She found some of a young Sir Henry among them. He had inherited his good looks from the German side.

"Yes," Heinrich said, picking up a photograph of Henry posing with a group of solemn-looking students. He seemed to be the only one smiling. "That's Henry. He was not a good scholar, you know."

Casey laughed. "He wouldn't like you saying that to me."

He looked impish. "I can trust a charming girl like you, *Fräulein*, not to put it in your magazine, yes? Henry, he was into scams. I know of an English expression—he flies by the bottom of his pants. Yes, that's it. He never studied, he liked sports, you know? But he was always passing his exams."

"He's known to have been quite a scholar, *Herr* Reinhardt." She picked up another rather faded picture of a young woman with her fair hair parted in the middle and plaited into tight buns on either side of her head like a character from *Heidi*. A plump, flaxen-haired child sat in her lap. "It's Sir Henry's mother who is German, isn't it? Your sister?"

"Yes, that is Anna. It's years ago she died. She was married to an Englishman, Charles. She met him here in Munich just before the war. Henry spent his childhood in England. He is *very* English. I scold him sometimes. I say, Henry, you are an anglophile, what about your Germanic roots?

He arranged the picture frames on the table. "He just laughs at me, you know. He wants to be Prime Minister of

Britain, and I say to him, the English people will never accept him. He tells me I am old-fashioned, that German blood runs in the veins of the royal family. Perhaps he's right. Time changes everything. I know he thinks I should retire. It's true I live in the past, but there's not much future ahead for me, is there? I'm an old man now."

His eyes twinkled at her, vibrant blue and full of mischief, but she thought she detected a trace of hurt behind the words.

"Henry wants to meet you, my dear. When I rang him, he asked me all about you. You'll be hearing from him."

Well, if nothing else, there's a scoop in it, she reasoned, picking up another picture of Heinrich in his uniform with a group of men. Only one wore an *SS* uniform. "Who is this man, *Herr* Reinhardt?"

He took the picture from her and glanced at it. "A fool." He replaced it on the table. She waited for him to elaborate, but he merely said, "They were all fools."

They finished their coffee, and Heinrich showed Casey around. She took shots of Sir Henry's old bedroom, where some of his keepsakes still remained. Finally, they walked over the sweeping lawns on which he used to play football.

They returned to the house, and she asked, "I wonder if you can tell me anything about the painting, *Flower Girl*, by Renoir."

Light seemed to disappear from his eyes. "So, you are here about that painting. Yes?"

"No, I swear to you that I'm not after a story," she insisted, "but I do want to know who killed Donald Broughton."

"Oh? I can't see how I can help you with that. Henry rang me when it happened, and I felt much shocked and saddened, but I haven't seen Donald for a long time. He was here covering a story some years ago. I remember it was some demonstration." He gave her a shrewd glance. "You aren't going to write about that painting, are you? We've had enough bad publicity. It was merely a slip-up by my man, that's all," he went on. "There's some doubt to its authenticity, you know."

"Do you think it's genuine?" she asked him.

He shrugged. "There's often doubt with such paintings."

"What is your opinion, though?"

"They have their experts studying it."

"I won't put any of this in print," Casey repeated, sensing she'd come close to something. Excitement and tension made her steps quicken as they reached the driveway. He spoke, and she held her breath.

"Karl discovered *Flower Girl* in Berlin—a deceased estate. He bought it without consulting me. I was angry with him because I knew its history—the Nazis confiscated it. I sold it for exactly the same money and made no profit on that painting, *Fräulein* Rowan. Nor did I wish to. I was amazed that Karl would do such a thing. I let him go, of course."

"Do you know where he is now?"

"Henry took him on for some reason. I advised him against it, but—" He gave another of his expressive shrugs.

"Karl works in London?"

Heinrich frowned. "No, he's at Farrowham."

Casey handed him a copy of the list of artworks from her bag. "Have you ever come across any of these, aside from the *Flower Girl*?"

Studying it, he shook his head and gave it back without comment, a wary look in his eyes.

"Could you tell me Karl's surname, *Herr* Reinhardt?"

Heinrich opened the front gate. "I think I've given you enough of my time, *Fräulein. Auf wiedersehen.*"

ℰↄℰↄ

On the way back to the hotel, Casey remembered what Heinrich had said about the neo-Nazi march Don had come here to cover. She grabbed a quick lunch in a coffee shop in the hotel and, after looking up the address of *The Munich Times*, headed out the door again.

In the newspaper's morgue, she searched through microfiche copies of 'ninety-five editions. She remembered how Don had come back, fired up to write that award-winning piece. Cursing her limited German, she studied headings, looking for any relevant ones, not even sure what she was after, perhaps only a better understanding of what had taken place here.

She needn't have worried. She couldn't have missed the two-page spread on it, containing several photographs. Judging by the extent of the violence, it had to be the neo-Nazi march Don had witnessed. Her hand fumbled for the switch, and a face in a photograph caught her eye—a man standing at the front of the crowd with his fist raised. She adjusted the picture to make it clearer, and the fervor of his expression, turned to the camera, emerged.

"It can't be!" she said aloud before the librarian quickly hushed her. She sat back in the chair, barely breathing. It was the man she'd seen at Farrowham, no question. Despite the poor quality of the picture, his disparate eyes were unmistakable.

❧❦❧

Back at the hotel, Casey picked up the ringing phone.

"Where are you?" asked Rod, the reception bad, but his voice still giving her goose bumps on her arms. She rubbed them, irritated by how easily she could get distracted. "I'm in Munich."

"Women," he muttered, his tone light. "Always running off when the dynamics get good."

She paused. His jokey tone belied something. She didn't know him well enough and she didn't want to risk taking his words seriously.

A roar came through the line. "Are you at a bar?" she asked.

"I wish. Still stuck in the thick of it. Can't see myself being free to come to London any time soon. I suppose now Tessa's been moved, you won't be coming down? Devon's a great place to rest."

She laughed. "Rest?"

"I'm a reasonable man."

"I've been very busy, Rod. I just interviewed Heinrich Reinhardt for *Hers*." She went on to tell him what she'd found out. "This guy, Karl, the employee of Reinhardt's gallery, has to be the one who bought the *Flower Girl*. It smells bad, if you ask me."

"If you'd asked me, Casey, I could have prevented you running round like a blue arse fly. Interpol checked out Reinhardt and cleared him."

"But would you have told me?"

"I seem to be revealing more and more to you. If my superior gets wind of it, I may have to immigrate."

She laughed. "Anything else?"

"You can forget chasing Arthur Warren, Sally Cameron's boyfriend. He turned up at a betting shop."

"What did Arthur have to say?"

"He got drunk and spent the night with a woman he picked up in the Red Lion. Some of the locals confirm he did leave with someone, but no one seems to know her. I showed Warren's photo to Tessa. Nothing. But I can't count her as a valuable witness, I'm afraid."

"I have a photocopy of this newspaper article. I'll fax it to you. I'm taking it to show Tessa."

"Give me this Karl's full name."

"*Herr* Reinhardt wouldn't tell me his surname. I'm afraid I pushed him too hard."

"You're losing your touch. It shouldn't be too difficult to find out. Have a good flight."

The flight back to London was full, and the meal unappetizing. The man sitting next to her tried a well-used pick-up line, but after several monosyllabic replies, he trailed off into silence. She needed time to think about what she'd found out in Munich. But her mind, annoyingly, kept returning to Rod.

❧❧

Rod and Danny arrived at Gorky's restaurant late in the morning and found it closed. "He'd better be here," Rod murmured.

"I think he will be, gov. He promised. Particularly when I told him we'd pull him in if he didn't."

They pushed the door open to the roar of a vacuum cleaner, which an old woman, listening to headphones, guided absently around the dusty carpet. Heavy red velvet curtains drawn across the windows made the interior dim and heightened the stale scent of cooking, causing Rod to wince.

The restaurant had a reputation for good quality, hearty Russian cuisine and, situated in the West End of London, it drew customers from the tourist trade and the theaters nearby.

Stepan, the owner, a thickset man with a rusty-blond mustache, looked up briefly at their entrance before returning to his pile of papers. "This damn paperwork, it drives me crazy!" he said to no one in particular. He reached for the bottle of vodka at his elbow and filled a glass.

Rod placed the credit slip and a photograph of Donald in front of him on the table. "Do you recall anything about the day this man ate here?"

Stepan tapped the photograph and nodded. "Don, he was a very good man. I remember. It was just before he was killed." He gave a heavy sigh. "Tragedy." He rolled the words on his tongue in a parody of Russian melancholy. "Only the good die young, eh?" He poured another shot and offered the bottle to Rod.

Rod shook his head. "Do you remember the two other men he dined with?"

The grooves on the man's forehead deepened in thought, and he merely stared into the distance for several minutes.

"Their appearance?" Rod prompted.

"We have so many customers." He pushed the papers away and leaned back. Rod despaired of him recalling anything through the haze of time and alcohol, but Stepan surprised him. "I remember one was a very skinny man. The other, an aristocrat." He pulled at a long-lobed ear, his expression seeming to hold generations of disdain—Karl Marx would have approved of it.

"And neither of them paid by credit card?" Rod persisted.

"I told the police that. Cash, both of them."

"I'd like to speak to the person who served them."

"My wife, Zoya, waits that table."

"Is she here?"

Stepan pushed back his chair and yelled, "Zoya! Come out here." After his second booming call, a short, dark-haired woman scuttled from the kitchen. "What d'you want? I have my work to do." She wiped her hands on her apron.

Stepan spoke to her in Russian.

"I remember, because they have big argument." She smoothed her apron. "Donald, he was very, very angry." Her dark, expressive eyes grew wider. "I think he want to slay one of those men. He walk out without he finish his meal. Donald always enjoy our food." She shrugged.

As Rod left the restaurant, he silently cursed. There was only time to grab a bite to eat with Danny before heading back down south. What had possessed him to ask for a transfer? He found himself wishing he were back in his snug apartment in Kingston. It was quite close to Richmond.

He must be feeling better.

CHAPTER 16

The pillared entranceway of the private hospital in St John's Wood looked more like a five-star hotel. Casey entered Tessa's room, unsure about the reception she'd get after their last meeting. She needn't have worried. As she approached the bed, Tessa reached forward, her face brightening.

"I'm so glad to see you."

They hugged, and she felt Tessa's bones and muscle through her nightdress. Her thin, pale face alarmed Casey, but her mood was good and her eyes clear.

"Casey, I'd like you to have Don's car. It's no good to me, and I know he'd want you to have it." She smiled. "It suits you."

She felt tears form in the corners of her eyes. "I'd love it, thank you."

It felt wonderful having Tessa back, someone so anchored in her history they had no pretense between them. Don's death sat heavily upon Casey still, but somehow it allowed her a greater appreciation of what she did have, of the days she had, that he did not. She felt guilty, but it was real nonetheless.

She pulled a chair up close to the bed. "You look so much better."

"Physically stronger. Mentally, I'm still pretty shaky. I know that when I get back out there, it's going to be very hard without Don."

Casey squeezed her hand.

"I spoke to Rod Carlisle. He tells me you've been to Munich."

She showed Tessa the photocopy and explained the reason for her trip.

"Tessa," she began slowly as Tessa peered at the photograph, clearly bemused. "I found this in the Munich library, I—" She paused, and Tessa looked up at her, concern in her eyes. "This could be the picture of the man who killed Don."

Tessa's face blanched, and she stared back down at the image. "This man looks a bit like Don," she said. "It's not in his features exactly, but in the shape of his face, the way his hair grows—that widow's peak, slightly off center." She looked up again, puzzled. "His build, too, and the way his shoulders are set, Casey, don't you think so?" She peered closer. "Who *is* he?"

"He works for Sir Henry Richardson at Farrowham." Casey had rung Farrowham that morning and asked the name of the art curator. "A German, Karl Baumann." Her chest felt tight. "Could it be, do you think, Don's killer?"

Tessa had shut her eyes and leaned back against the pillows. Casey despaired at the sudden change in her. Her breath came quickly, and her hands shook.

"It was dark. I don't know for sure. It's possible," she said. "You know how I said my first thought was that it was Don standing there? This man's a stranger to me. If it was him, then why? I have to know *why*." She balled her hands into fists and put them against her chest. "Then maybe I'd lose this fear."

"I think we're closer to finding out."

౯౩౯౩

As Casey walked to the station, her mobile rang. She reefed it out of her bag and opened it. "Casey Rowan."

"It's John Follet here, Casey. I bet you thought I'd forgotten you."

"Not at all," she murmured, remembering the uncharitable thoughts that had crossed her mind.

"We've been very busy at the Gallery, and it took me a while to chase these up."

Casey held her breath. "You found them?"

"I found out something about two of them. *Retribution* by George Gross and *Spoils of War* by Max Beckmann. Gross and Beckmann's paintings were part of a traveling exhibition that began in Munich towards the end of the war. It was called *The Intartete Kunst.* The artists were branded enemies of the state and a threat to German culture, their art labeled degenerate. Beckman fled to Amsterdam on the opening day of the exhibit." A shiver ran up Casey's spine as he continued. "The only thing I can say about the rest, is that they are genuine artworks probably removed from wealthy Jewish families by the Nazis."

"Do you know what happened to them after that?"

"We know that after the exhibit, paintings were sold in Switzerland at auction, some acquired by museums, others by private collectors. Hermann Goering took fourteen valuable pieces, including a Van Gogh and a Cezanne. The Nazis destroyed many fine artworks they didn't approve of. In nineteen thirty-nine the Berlin Fire Brigade burned four thousand paintings. For all we know the Beckman, Gross, and Chagall could have been among those destroyed. Others were stored underground and ended up in the Hermitage Museum in Saint Petersburg, where they remain."

Destroyed. Casey's spirits dropped momentarily before she pulled herself up. This list led her to believe they hadn't been. "That's very helpful, John. I'm grateful to you."

"Took me quite a while, I can tell you," he said.

"Yes, I'm sure."

"Perhaps we can have a coffee. I can tell you more about the exhibition."

Casey drew a deep breath. With the discovery of Karl's photo, she felt more confident she was getting somewhere. "That would be great."

"There's a coffee shop near the Gallery. Just pop in sometime around two."

"I will."

Casey headed into the Tube and dialed Rod. He didn't answer his mobile.

෨෨෨

Casey's inquires at Middlemoor only seemed to provoke more questions, and by the next day, she still hadn't managed to raise Rod. Finally, he answered his mobile, and she quickly told him about Tessa's reaction to the picture in the newspaper.

"She's not positive though, Casey?" His voice sounded hollow, as if he were on the other side of the world. "I'm in Wiltshire now."

"Have you spoken to Karl?" she asked. "What has he told you?"

"He can't tell me anything, I'm afraid. He's dead."

"Dead!"

"Aye. His body was found this morning in his burnt-out Mercedes, about six miles from Farrowham. He was heading north on a business trip. It appears he was driving too fast and failed to take a bend. His car plunged off the road, rolled several times and caught fire. I'm sorry, Casey."

She mumbled something and put down the phone. Turning, she wiped the table clean of her notes with one sweep of her arm and sank into a chair.

๛๛๛

Casey rang John Follet and returned to Trafalgar Square. She waited for him in the café near the Gallery. He was late, and she had far too much time to think about the dead end caused by Karl's accident. Finally, John walked across the piazza and waved when he saw her.

He entered the café and drew out a chair. "So nice to see you again, Casey."

"I'm very grateful for your help, John," she said. "Can I get you a coffee?"

"Allow me."

She motioned to her cup. "I still have some here. This is my third."

He shook his head ruefully. "I'm sorry I was late. Please don't think ill of me if you lie awake tonight."

She smiled. "That would be most unfair of me."

After he ordered coffee, Casey leaned her elbows on the table. "What do you have for me?"

"The avant-garde German artists who took part in the *Entartete Kunst* were branded enemies of the state and a threat to German culture," he said, nodding to the waitress as she placed his espresso on the table. He paused to stir two sugars into his coffee. "The exhibit was intended to incite loathing against the 'perverse Jewish spirit.' Their art was labeled degenerate, and slogans denigrating them were painted on the walls. Beckman fled to Amsterdam on the opening day of the exhibit." A shiver ran up Casey's spine as he added, "The only thing I can say about the older paintings on this list is that they are genuine artworks, probably removed from wealthy Jewish families by the Nazis."

"Do you have any idea what happened to them after the war?"

"We know that after the exhibit the paintings were sold in Switzerland at auction. Some were acquired by museums, others by private collectors. Hermann Goering took fourteen valuable pieces, including a Van Gogh and a Cezanne.

"The Nazis destroyed many fine artworks they didn't approve of. In nineteen thirty-nine, the Berlin Fire Brigade burned four thousand. For all we know the Beckman, Gross, and Chagall could have been among them. Others were stored underground and ended up in the Hermitage Museum in Saint Petersburg, where they remain today."

Destroyed. Casey's spirits dropped momentarily before she pulled herself up. This list led her to believe they hadn't been. "Might the Hermitage have any of these paintings listed?"

John shook his head. "I checked. That's not to say they haven't stored them in their vault. Who knows what they've got down there?

"Where did you find this list, Casey?"

"A journalist friend of mine had it. He was murdered."

"Murdered?"

"Donald Broughton, have you heard of him?"

John's brown eyes widened behind his glasses. "I used to listen to his radio show. I read about his death in the paper. I hope you're not getting involved in anything dangerous."

Casey shrugged. "This probably doesn't have anything to do with his death."

"Probably not. Those paintings have been missing a long time." He looked sympathetic and reached across the table to pat her hand. "I'm sorry about your friend."

Feelings of grief and anger at the futility of Don's death struck her afresh, forming a tight knot in her stomach. "Thank you."

"I wish I had time to hear it all." He put down his cup and glanced at his watch. "But I have to get back to work."

"This has been great, John," she said.

John pushed back his chair and reached in his jacket for his wallet.

"Let me get it, John," Casey said, grabbing for her bag.

He hovered, fiddling with his tie. "If you'd ever like to learn more about art...or take in a movie."

She slid to her feet and shook his hand. "Thank you. But right now—"

"I know." He grimaced. "You have a mystery to solve."

She nodded gratefully.

As he turned to leave, he said, "Let me know if you uncover anything, will you."

"You'll be on the top of my list."

Descending the steps, Casey reached for her phone. She listened to Rod's recorded request for her to leave a message and debated whether to tell him what she'd learned from John Follet.

It suddenly seemed like nothing—the artwork could have been destroyed over half a century ago and, not wanting to distract him from the very real work of policing, she hung up.

ఴఴఴ

Rod cringed as DI Lawson drove down a steep cobbled road lined with old cottages and then parked the car in the main street of Bishop's Walton, alongside the village green. He climbed out with relief. Some might label golf a boring sport, but if DI Lawson was anything to go by, some pretty obsessive people played it. Across from the general store was a sign. Stretching his legs, Rod went to read it. It was the forest code for those about to enter the pine forest.

Guard against all risk of fire.
Protect trees, plants and wildlife.
Leave things as you find them, take nothing away.
Keep dogs under control.
Avoid damaging buildings, fences, hedges, walls and signs.
Leave no litter.

Simon Lawson came to stand beside him. He scratched his thinning brown hair. "*Leave no litter.* Makes you want to throw up, doesn't it?"

"Aye," Rod said. "But Donald was on the side of the righteous. He would have made a lot of friends here. The man I want to talk to is the owner of the building company, Justin Sorensen.

"We'll check up on what the local guys know," he added. Then grab some lunch at that pub." He gestured at the tiny half-timbered pub with thatched roof and a sign reading, *The Royal Oak welcomes walkers and their dogs.* "After that, I'll leave you to wander about and have a chat with some of the villagers while I drive the few blocks to the building company's office."

They headed over to the police station, a small, red brick building, quaint like the rest of the village—and, Rod suspected, understaffed.

As Rod had already gleaned by phone, the police had little to add. He and Lawson enjoyed a steak and chip lunch, and then Rod left to drive to Justin Sorensen's building company office. It was further out of town than he'd thought. The temperature had dropped several degrees during the day, and the road was icy. He turned off the bitumen road onto an unpaved one. Avoiding pot holes, he drove on for a mile or two before he came to Sorensen's. It proved to be a cluster of prefabricated buildings and a stockpile of building materials and machinery on a weedy acre of ground, surrounded by a high wire fence.

Rod stepped from the car, and one foot sunk into a puddle. Icy water seeped into his shoe. He cursed out loud. A few flakes of snow floated down. It could soon snow in earnest, and he didn't want to be here when it did. Negotiating that road without four-wheel drive was tough enough, even without the snow.

The wire gate was padlocked shut. Rod could see why—the outbuildings had been spray-painted with expletives and abusive comments in red paint. A writ had been slapped on Sorensen, and he was unable to operate— the company had, in effect, closed down—but Rod had arranged to meet him here on site. It appeared that Sorensen was present, for smoke rose from a metal flue in the roof of the small timber building that bore the sign, *Office*.

Rod yelled through the wire and waited, watching a large bird swoop and soar overhead. He became so caught up by it that he failed to notice Sorensen's approach until he heard the rattle of the chain.

"It's a Tawny Owl. Something's disturbed it. They're night birds. Beautiful, isn't it?" Sorensen was a giant of a man, solid through, with white-blond hair and icy-blue eyes. Rod knew that he was forty-one, recently divorced, and had two kids living with him. "Their numbers are in decline, like a lot of other woodland species."

"It's magnificent," Rod said. "Mr. Sorensen? DCI Carlisle."

The man nodded and bent his white head to his task of pulling off the padlock. Then he opened the wire gate wide enough for Rod to pass through.

Rod followed him across the muddy ground to the office, wondering how someone with an appreciation and knowledge of nature could have permitted such desecration to the forest. And not just any forest, one so carefully preserved and protected. It would rob him of his livelihood, and possibly his liberty for some time, but his self-respect in the community was gone forever.

Rod watched Sorensen duck his head at the doorway. Unnecessarily, for it wasn't particularly low.

Sorensen caught Rod's expression and shrugged. "Force of habit." Inside, he signaled for Rod to take the spare chair. The hut was warm, and Rod moved his wet and frozen feet closer to the wood stove.

"Can I get you a coffee?"

"Thank you."

Sorensen took two cups down from a shelf, then removed a coffee pot from the stove. "Milk? Sugar?" When Rod declined, he poured strong black liquid into a cup and handed it to him.

Rod took a grateful sip. It thawed his insides. "It's good, thanks."

"You're here about the asbestos." Sorensen turned back to pour his own cup.

Rod waited for Sorensen to settle himself in the chair behind a desk covered in papers and folders. Then he told him about Broughton's murder.

Sorensen's white eyebrows rose in surprise. "Donald Broughton has been here to the village. I knew he'd taken up the cause and was giving it a good airing on the radio, but I never met him." A flush, high on his cheekbones, warmed his sallow skin. "As a journalist, I felt he should have come and met me." His mouth formed a hard line. "Heard my side of things."

"Perhaps you'd like to tell me your side of things now."

"It won't help me."

Rod put his cup down on the desk. "Nevertheless, Mr. Sorensen, I want to hear it."

"I've been in this business all my life. And I've seen some pretty shabby things done in the industry. But not by me." He shrugged again, a gesture he used a lot, Rod noted—not an apologetic shrug, more a comment on the randomness of life. "It's a simple tale and a sorry one. When the scare about asbestos took off, I got very busy and eventually had to bring in extra help. Hired a guy named Shaklehurst, Harry Shaklehurst, to take up some of the slack. He cut a lot of corners, I found out later, the worst of which was dumping the asbestos in the forest. Something I knew nothing about," he said firmly. "Now, he's disappeared and I'm left to cop the flack."

"And you wanted to tell this to Broughton? Why didn't you?"

"I tried to ring him on his show. They hung up on me."

"Broughton hung up on you?"

Another shrug. "Never got to him. Someone at the radio station."

"You didn't try to ring again? Write him a letter?"

"Didn't seem much point."

Rod studied the man's face. The muscles around his mouth had tightened, as if he was clenching his teeth. Their eyes met briefly. Sorensen's seemed clouded before he glanced away. Rod got the impression of a dam with cracks spreading across its surface. "So, you've never met Donald Broughton?"

"No. I told you, I never met him."

"Where were you on Thursday night, the Twentieth February, and early Friday morning?"

"At home with my kids. I have a girl, ten, and a boy, eight. I'm not about to leave them alone. Certainly not now they're copping such a lot at school."

"Anyone else with you?"

Sorensen shook his head.

"No neighbors see you. No one phone you?"

He shook his head again.

Rod found himself wanting to believe him. "Did you watch television?"

"Might have been the night I watched a James Bond movie. Came on at ten-thirty. One with Roger Moore in it. Think I dropped off. I like Connery better."

It was no alibi. Rod left the site as the snowflakes thickened into a flurry. He drove back along the rough road, ice cracking beneath his wheels. Snow began to pile up on his windscreen. He put on the wipers, and they labored, giving him a small window of vision in which to view the road ahead as he tried to put his thoughts in order.

Sorensen had reason to feel animosity towards Broughton, certainly. Enough to want to kill him, though? Only if he wasn't wrongly accused, Rod decided. But if he was innocent of this crime, he made a very unlikely murderer.

On the other hand, murderers were often an unfathomable lot. Sorensen had come across as an outraged, but principled man. Perhaps he'd intended to give that impression. But Broughton was not murdered by enraged killer, Rod reminded himself. The murderer had carried off a detailed, well-thought-out plan.

Deep in thought, Rod came to the bitumen road without noticing. As he turned right, the car wheels struck an icy patch on the road, and the car lost traction. Cursing, he spun the wheel, going with the skid. The car revolved in an almost three-sixty degree arc. He eased on the brake and pulled to a stop, ending up halfway into the other lane. The engine stalled.

Rod turned the key, threw the car in reverse, and accelerated slowly, more slowly than he wanted to, out of respect for the icy road. A blast of a horn sounded, loud and long. Rod pumped the accelerator hard, and the car reversed onto the far verge. It rocked as a truck loaded with livestock flew past with another angry blast and slapped a spray of sleet and snow onto Rod's windscreen. Heart pumping, he cursed again.

He drove through the village and spied Lawson doing something akin to star jumps on the pavement. He pulled up beside him.

Lawson wrenched open the door and jumped inside. "Brrr, it's bloody cold." He settled on his seat and grabbed the seatbelt, and Rod took off again.

"What did you find out?" Rod asked.

"Sorensen was well liked around here before the asbestos dump was discovered." He took off his gloves and gingerly rubbed at his fingers before drawing out his notebook. "He was the local scout master."

He sneezed. "Don't like his chances of restoring his reputation around here," he said, echoing Rod's thoughts. "It takes a lifetime to obtain it, and probably a generation to get it back."

To Rod's relief, it stopped snowing.

"Apparently, he's taken to drinking alone in the Royal Oak, the publican said," Lawson continued. "A Mrs. Swan from the grocery store told me he leaves the kids on their own." Lawson swiveled in his seat and whistled. "Looks like a great golf course they've got here. What did you find out, gov?"

While Rod went over his conversation with Sorensen, he drove along the road bordered by golf greens now under a blanket of white. A misty dark green haze of pines lay ahead in the distance.

CHAPTER 17

Almost two weeks had passed since Casey had returned from Munich. During that time, she'd tried to establish some order, burying herself in work. An enormous amount of reading had piled up on her desk, plus phone and e-mail correspondence she needed to deal with.

In a subconscious apology for her declining interest, she worked late, zealously tackling tasks usually allotted to others, booking photographers, proofreading, and going over layouts. Still, while sipping coffee in an editorial meeting, she found her mind wandering. Even in death, Karl Baumann was never far from her thoughts. Neither was her next assignment.

She'd interviewed actors and pop idols for the magazine in the past but saw Sir Henry Richardson as the highlight of her career. Landing such a big name at this point gained some much-needed accolades from Geraldine and Hugh.

Casey had hoped to see Sir Henry at Westminster, but he invited her to dine at The Ivy, a celebrity friendly restaurant.

She made her way through the door with a growing sense of anticipation, past a bunch of photographers who quickly dismissed her. The photographers' patience had already been rewarded tonight. Apart from Sir Henry, show business royalty had arrived—Vanessa Redgrave, dining with her daughter, Joely Richardson.

Sir Henry stood at Casey's approach. The muscles around her solar plexus tightened, and she took a deep breath, letting it out slowly. Another man, security, perhaps, left the table as Casey shook the hand of the man most favored to become the next Prime Minister of Britain.

Close up, he looked younger, his silvery-blond hair thick and vigorous, his light olive skin smooth. He had a fine-boned symmetrical face, but when he smiled his slightly crooked smile, it took on an expression of boyishness and complicity. She sat down, and his mobile rang. He held up a hand in apology. "Sorry, I need to take this."

She observed him, thinking he had that indefinable quality that makes people defer to a leader. But she knew his meteoric rise from MP to member of the Treasury Select Committee, to minister, then to chancellor was due more to his intellect. When he disconnected, he put his phone down on the table and focused on her with eyes as blue as his Uncle Heinrich's. "You're an American?"

"Yes, but my father was Irish."

"You were a friend of Don's, but somehow we never met. It's sad that it has to be under these circumstances. I miss him."

"Me, too, very much."

"The police seem no closer to solving it. Strange that he should admit someone into his home at that time of night, but he was an insomniac—did some of his best thinking at night, I remember him telling me," Sir Henry said.

"Yes, he seldom managed more than four hours."

"I deeply regret that I didn't get to see Don when he came to Farrowham a few months ago."

"I have quite a few regrets of my own," Casey replied, her voice husky.

"We're not to know these things, are we? Tell me something about your magazine."

She gave him a rundown on *Hers*: their success in the marketplace and the triumphs over the past few years. She'd outlined what she wished to cover in this interview to the member of his staff who'd rung her.

Sir Henry made an excellent subject by any standards, an attractive, childless widower who would appeal to their readers not just because of his highly successful career. She found herself enjoying the convivial setting and, excepting the brief mention of Don, the conversation had only been as serious as dishes on the menu and the weather.

At the moment, in fact, Europe was suffering through the worst winter for over a decade. Extremely low temperatures and roads heavy with ice had caused many accidents on the motorways.

Rod hadn't come up to London, and she hadn't suggested going down there, but it wasn't the weather that stopped her. Though she wanted to see him again, something held her back. Whenever she tried to predict where her life might go, the effort left her feeling wobbly and stressed—and from what he'd told her, and the tone he used, she suspected he was having a tough time of it at Middlemoor.

She and Sir Henry continued to talk of generalities while she finished her Scottish salmon and he his steak. She refused dessert, and they ordered coffee.

She drained the last of the superb Sauvignon Blanc from her glass, and he told her an amusing story from his childhood at Farrowham. He drew her in, and her carefully prepared questions deserted her. He had authority, control, influence, and a wickedly dry wit. Society loves and forgives those with good looks and sex appeal, and Sir Henry would go far. The only reason Clinton rose above his dishonesty and adultery was because he had been so charismatic.

"I wonder if you are aware that your employee, Karl Baumann, attended a neo-Nazi rally in Munich back in ninety-five?"

Sir Henry sat back, eyes widening in surprise. "I don't examine the politics of my staff—that's not my business. Only that they perform their job to my satisfaction— although I'd like them all to be Tories, naturally," he added, smiling.

She remembered a quote from Disraeli: *Damn your principles, stick to your party.* "But, Sir Henry," she protested, "does that mean you'd be willing to employ a neo-Nazi?"

"It means nothing of the sort," he replied. A pale, pinched look to his nostrils made his face appear rather delicate. "Where's your proof? I simply don't believe it."

She pulled the photocopy of Karl from her purse and showed him.

"So?"

"You must come to the conclusion from this photo that he was not indifferent to the neo-Nazi cause," she said, unable to resist the irony.

"Was Karl dressed in combat fatigues, marching with the rest? You don't understand the circumstances or the feelings of the German people. These matters are never simple." He pushed the photocopy away. "You journalists rely so much on labels. Karl might have hated the effect the influx of Turkish migrants had on his country and its culture. Does that mean he's a neo-Nazi? I saw Karl at that rally—he was merely observing, as I was. In fact—" Sir Henry leaned across the table to make his point, his eyes now silvery-gray. "Don and I were there with Karl at the rally."

She looked down at the picture again. "I knew Don was there."

"We ran into Karl, and he joined us for a drink after the rally. I remember I was taken by the fact that Karl was Don's doppelganger. The likeness was remarkable. Perhaps we all have one somewhere?"

He was another who found a resemblance between them? She searched for a likeness in Karl's odd, cold eyes.

"Can you tell me anything more about it, Sir Henry?"

"I thought we were here to do a follow-up article for your magazine," he said, eyebrows raised.

She wondered how long he would tolerate her questions. She took a breath. "You employed Karl Baumann although he was dismissed by your uncle for purchasing a painting known to have been stolen by the Nazis. That can't have been prudent."

He stirred his coffee with a steady hand, a flash of annoyance crossing his face. "Karl took the opportunity to buy a valuable painting at a good price. A mistake, certainly, but he didn't steal it. My uncle is old-fashioned. Karl was an excellent art historian, and I was in need of one. So?"

Which wasn't meant to come out in the press, she thought. Or didn't he care? Perhaps he considered himself untouchable.

"Why did you really visit my uncle? Were you after a story on the *Flower Girl*? A little late, I think, Casey—it was sold a year ago. Digging it all up now can only hurt my uncle—no one else."

She had no wish to hurt Heinrich but she didn't say so. She waited, hoping he would offer her more off his own bat.

But Sir Henry pocketed his phone, and she knew she'd gone too far.

"To be honest with you—and I will state this publicly, if need be—if Karl were involved in anything scurrilous, I would have sacked him immediately. I never saw evidence of that. Now he's dead. Let him rest in peace. Whatever secret longings he had should be buried with him, surely."

"I wondered if he might have had a reason to kill Don."

He looked incredulous and laughed. "Now you are being fanciful. What reason could there be? You're way out of line. Anyway, he couldn't have done it."

"How can you be so sure?"

"Because he was with me."

She felt her face begin to burn. "Until what time?"

He looked into her eyes. "You should get your facts straight, Casey. Karl and I had dinner together at Farrowham and discussed business. I know he sat up late working on that business, because he presented the work to me at breakfast. I left him there when I returned to London later that morning." He patted her hand and rose.

She cursed under her breath. She'd lost him.

"I can see you're upset, but he hardly knew Don." A spasm crossed Sir Henry's face, making him appear suddenly sadder and older, robbing him of his quixotic charm. "Forget these fanciful notions, Casey. I'd like to know who killed Don, too, very much, but it wasn't Karl." He beckoned to his man. "You've lost a friend, my dear, and I understand your grief, believe me. I have lost two."

She watched him stride out of the restaurant, feeling disheartened. She'd made a hash of it. She'd had an audience with the Chancellor of the Exchequer, a man whose hard decisions had taken the UK from the threshold of recession to one of the fastest growing economies in Europe, with unemployment falling to the lowest level of any major country, and inflation below four percent. She should have been searching for her lead, getting her story set, focusing on the essentials. Instead of listening for quotes, she'd been intent on proving Karl's guilt.

Now she would have to spend more hours researching, working the story out, finding its center, padding it to the right length, and she had wanted this to be her *coup de grâce*, the jumping off point for a change of career.

She walked out into the street. In truth, the article could never have been great. Her colleagues at *Hers* felt she should focus on Lady Felicity Markham, the earl's daughter dating Sir Henry. Some of the more malicious tabloids described her as "horsy" and always photographed her riding in Rotten Row dressed in jodhpurs, or at the family's country seat in Surrey, in her tweeds. Now Casey would have to call in a favor or two to interview her.

She hailed a black cab. The driver refused to take her to Richmond and, too tired to fight him, she alighted at Victoria Station. She managed to find a seat, and the train pulled away, heading for Richmond, while exhaustion settled on her like a heavy coat.

ↄↄↄↄ

Casey spent an hour on the phone trying to contact Felicity Markham and in the end had to resort to an old university chum, an unabashed Sloanie, Sarah Windham-Castle, who knew Felicity well.

Casey rang Rod in the evening, finding him at home. She could hear one of his old jazz recordings playing in the background and wondered if the music took him on a nostalgic trip back to when his father was alive.

"You might have let me know that Karl was with Sir Henry the night of Don's murder *and* the following morning."

"Should I have?"

Disconcerted by his sharp response, she went on quickly. "Would it have caused that much harm to tell me? I felt like a fool."

"All hell's broken loose down here. There's been a damnable cock-up with Interpol. The Chief Constable has called for an update. We could lose half our team."

"You sound as if you're ready to throw in the towel."

He laughed, but probably only at her boxing parlance. "Hardly that. This case is growing colder every day. If we don't find the answers quickly, sometimes we never find them. I may be assigned to another case. If it happens, I'll give serious consideration to returning to Edinburgh."

"I'm sorry things are so tough." Casey felt a surprisingly strong sense of disappointment at the thought of him disappearing from her life.

"What was your opinion of Sir Henry?"

"Impressive, actually."

"Aye," he said. "A popular choice for prime minister. One political pundit has compared him with Clinton."

"Superficially, perhaps. Clinton wanted people to know about his weaknesses and to love him despite them. Sir Henry would keep his weaknesses to himself." She still couldn't let go. "So Karl was definitely at Farrowham all of that night?"

"Casey." He groaned. "Karl and Sir Henry did dine together, and they were there the next morning at the time of the Fulham robbery. If there's a link between the murder and the break-in, and most of my team believes there is, it cancels Karl out. And what about motive?"

"Any feedback on the list of artworks?"

"Not a whisper. What are you doing with yourself apart from interviewing potential prime ministers?"

She found herself longing to be there, listening to music with him. Her mind formed the picture, but she asked herself some painful questions. Did he look as tired as he sounded? Was he alone? "I've made a mess of this interview with Sir Henry. Now I need to interview Felicity Markham or the magazine will have my head on a stick. She has a horse running next Saturday. She's promised me a few minutes of her time."

"Ascot?"

"Yes, as a matter of fact." She waited, counting the beats.

"Want some company?"

"Love it."

"I'll have to head back to Exeter late in the afternoon, I'm afraid. My super's retiring. There's a dinner for him."

"I see."

"It's not what I want."

A thrill passed through her at the passionate note in his voice. She wondered if he regretted as much as she did the few short hours they'd have together. He sighed. "Not much chance of being alone at Ascot is there?"

She laughed. "Felicity's horse is named Dark Dancer. It's running in the Maiden Fillies Charity Stakes at two ten. I'll make a booking for The Old Paddock Restaurant. Shall I meet you there? I can slip down to see Felicity after the race."

"Make that booking for twelve," he said. "We'll eat oysters and drink champagne and inspect our bets in the pre-parade ring."

"And play footsie under the table?"

"Ms. Rowan!"

Despite her earlier fears about him getting too close, she found herself falling for him. She'd missed him, missed his touch. They may not have a chance to make love before he left, but Casey was determined Rod would return to Devon wishing fervently that they had.

❧❧❧

Casey fixed her hair in an elegant twist but made no other concession to classic styling. This was not Royal Ascot, just a weekly race meeting. And it remained far too chilly for chiffon and feathers. She chose a short, black, wrap dress with a deep V neckline and added a cropped black velvet jacket, tied at the waist. She teamed it with high-heeled black boots and a vintage, silver-sequined newsboy cap hat she'd found in the Richmond markets.

The day began with a cold wind, making her glad of her choice of outfits. Parking the MG in the car park, she made her way through the gates to the restaurant. It was early, and the races had yet to begin, but already the place burst with life.

The Old Paddock restaurant was all starched white tablecloths, crystal flutes, and silverware. It overlooked the pre-parade ring, saddling boxes, and the beautiful paddock. Down below stretched the lawn enclosure. Hopefully, she would have time to gather enough information after the race to pad out her article.

She waited at the table until Rod appeared at the door, carrying his leather jacket. He'd obviously ridden his bike, but he'd respected the dress code by wearing a shirt and tie. Their eyes met, and she took in a breath. She'd almost forgotten how good-looking he was.

He came to the table and bent over her, his lips brushing her cheek. "Hello, Casey. My, but you look nice."

Sitting down beside her, he unfurled the *Guardian's* racing page.

"Feeling lucky?" she asked him.

He reached forward and took her hand. "I'm here with you, aren't I?"

"That's a corny line, Carlisle. Can't you do better?"

"A lot better, but look around. People would disapprove."

She laughed. "What price is Dark Dancer?"

He glanced through the racing form. "Four to one in here."

They searched for the latest price on the television monitor. "Three to one," he said. "It's been backed in, but that's still good odds. Did Lady Felicity offer any tips—is the horse ready to win?"

"She told me to put a bet on it, but can owners be that objective?"

"That's good enough for me." He ran his finger down the page. "There's a horse in the next race I like—Sleek Lover."

"Any particular reason?"

He looked up, his eyes full of laughter. "I like its form."

The waiter appeared, and they ordered seafood and champagne. Sleek Lover's jockey paraded him around the ring, so they took the opportunity to study the horse—

powerful chestnut with a magnificent mane. Their oysters arrived, and the race appeared on the screen. Sleek Lover missed the jump and came in next to last.

"Just goes to show you can't go by appearances," Casey concluded.

"I'm unlucky at cards, too," Rod said, shaking his head. "But love..."

Casey felt suddenly awkward. She was so much at home with this man, and yet she knew so little about him. "Dark Dancer's race is up next. Shall we go down and watch it? Then I'll have to leave you for a while."

After placing their bets, they made their way down onto the lawn and joined the crowd. The horses had jumped by the time she and Rod had found a spot on the fence. She moved to gain a better view while people continued to close in on their space. The field was near the sweeping Ascot home turn, with the long straight in front of them.

A deafening roar went up once the field had turned for home. Casey could see Dark Dancer's jockey attempting to move out wide. Halfway down the straight, she watched the pink and black silks dart through an opening and race clear. She found herself hanging onto Rod's arm to stop her heels sinking into the grass, barracking loudly as Dark Dancer went on to win easing up. She turned to Rod and threw herself into his arms.

People around them dispersed, intent on claiming money or laying more on the next race. Rod took the opportunity to kiss her.

"Wow," Casey said.

"I'm that good a kisser?"

She laughed. "You are. And I just won a hundred pounds."

Reaching into her bag, she drew out a lipstick and a compact to repair the damage. "I have to go and do this interview now."

"Before you do—" He kissed her again, a long hungry one that left her breathless and wanting more.

Casey made her way to the race stalls, where she spied a tall blonde woman talking to the jockey and a gray-haired man. She waited for their conversation to finish.

A strapper hosed down Dark Dancer in front of her stall. She was a nondescript, small brown horse. A plodder, some had said. Casey remembered her father's response to such an accusation of one of his horses, "Some plod faster than others."

Felicity ended her conversation and turned to acknowledge Casey. Close up, she had wary, green eyes— the caution no doubt the result of a healthy dislike of the press—an aquiline nose, a full-lipped mouth that suggested passion, and a rather strong chin.

"*Hers* magazine, I'm told," Felicity said coolly.

Casey nodded. "Congratulations. You have a fine filly there. My father bred racehorses in Ireland years ago. He would have loved to own her."

"Really?" Felicity's eyes softened. "She is my favorite."

"With me as well. I just won a hundred pounds on her."

"Well done," she said, smiling warmly.

Casey was relieved that her initial frostiness had melted. "My readers would like to know a bit about you," she explained. Certainly true if she married Sir Henry. "Perhaps some romantic angle on how you met Sir Henry."

The corners of Felicity's mouth turned up, and an impish light appeared in her eyes. "Across a crowded room, that sort of thing?"

"That would be perfect."

"Not true, unfortunately. I met him at one of my father's political soirées. I'm a very determined person. I pursued him."

"He seems to have been a very willing victim," Casey suggested.

"I do hope so. It's no secret that I adore him." She sighed. "But I sometimes think he loves his little schnauzer more than people. His father was a cruel man. He had Henry's pet dog put down while he was away at school. Can you believe that?"

"Sounds like he had a sad childhood."

"Oh, absolutely. He didn't see much of his mother as a child either, particularly after the divorce. It was bitterly contested."

They continued to talk while watching Dark Dancer being rubbed down. Felicity had relaxed into the conversation—Sir Henry was obviously her favorite subject—but Casey came away dissatisfied. The information had proved too personal and too one-sided for a newsworthy story.

She decided she needed to do more work to get a realistic view on Sir Henry. Felicity and Sir Henry seemed well suited—Felicity with her own spectacular career rising speedily from gofer to management of Lovelique Cosmetics with no visible signs of assistance. That, in itself, would make a great story. Geraldine would be pleased.

She rejoined Rod at the table, and they ordered coffee.

"Find out anything interesting?" he asked her.

She told him about Sir Henry's unhappy childhood.

"Money doesn't guarantee happiness, does it?" he said.

"No."

After they'd watched another two races, where their choices failed to match the spectacular win of Dark Dancer, Rod checked his watch before glancing up with a regretful expression in his eyes. "I'll have to make tracks."

They walked out to the car park together. Rod swept her behind a concrete pillar and slipped his hands under her jacket, kissing her again. She coiled her arms around his neck.

"I'll try and get up to London next weekend," he said.

"Promises, promises."

"Don't think I don't want to. You feature heavily in my dreams."

She laughed. "Do I? Not nightmares?"

His blue eyes searched hers, half-rueful, half-laughing. "Whenever I get you in my clutches, you disappear."

She watched him ride away. Don's murder still seemed to hang over them like a portent, making everything else appear trivial by comparison. They could forget it for a while, but because they were both so caught up in it, it always crept insidiously back into their consciousness, turning their conversation back to the case and dulling any joy they took in each other.

CHAPTER 18

Rod rang to tell Casey he had to go to Scotland for a few weeks. His ex-wife had died. Concerned about the sadness in his voice, she wondered if connecting with family and friends might make him decide to return there permanently.

A fairly quiet period descended over the magazine before the next panic-filled rush to publication. She drew breath and turned her thoughts again to the police investigation.

She now had to admit to strong doubts about Karl Baumann, but if he hadn't killed Don, who had? She made a cup of tea and sat at the kitchen table with pen and paper, writing down the names of all those connected with the case. The possibility that Tessa was the target was still frighteningly plausible. Leaving Lord Morris-Smythe pending, Casey went back to her original list of Tessa's clients.

Holmes, Cleavy, and Black remained in jail and would for a very long time, the appeal denied. That was all she could glean from Rod. Maria Bartolomei—disqualified by her gender. Bilal Assam—a short, fat, balding man who had been at the wedding of a relative that night. People confirmed his presence there until the early hours of the morning. Reginald Jamieson had only his wife as an alibi. Tessa had ruled out her client, Sally's, de-facto, Arthur Warren, but as Rod had suggested, how reliable a witness was she?

Casey rang Tessa at her office. She'd told Casey that the desperate need to keep busy had driven her back to work.

"Are you free for lunch?" Casey asked. "I'll come your way."

"Lovely. Italian? There's a little place down the road, good regional food, Cucina Romana."

"Sounds great. I'll be at your office at twelve. I'm going to have another look at some of your clients."

"Oh, Casey, you're not still probing? That man Karl is dead. We should let it go."

Casey bit back her surprise. She'd thought Tessa needed to find out the truth as much as she. Or did she just want to put it all behind her—walk away and seek a quiet life? Casey wished she could do the same. It occurred to her that Don's determination to take life by the throat might have made life difficult for Tessa at times.

Tessa was seeing a client out of the door when Casey arrived. She returned to her desk and looked at Casey over the top of a stack of files. Casey thought she still looked fragile.

"I'll deal with these later," Tessa said, dropping the pile on the floor beside her. She fished her makeup from her handbag and glanced warily over the top of her compact. "What are you up to, Casey?"

"I want to recheck a couple of your clients. Those I feel might have had reason to harm you."

"I thought we'd decided that man, Karl Baumann, was the main suspect."

"It's looking increasingly unlikely that it was Karl."

"If it was one of my clients, I'd know, wouldn't I?" A frown emphasized a new maturity in her face.

"Are you sure?" Casey asked gently. "You've counseled their partners, but have you met Reginald Jamieson or Arthur Warren?"

"They showed me a photo of Arthur Warren. I'd have said if I thought it was him." Her voice sounded strained.

"What about Reginald Jamieson? I know you're very good at what you do, but it seems strange to me that the wife of a wealthy company director living in Hampstead Heath would come down to Camberwell to consult you."

"Reginald was an associate of Don's. We went to their house for a dinner party, and his wife, Jennifer, contacted me soon after."

"What interests would Don and a property developer have in common?"

"I think Don met him when he was writing a piece on the re-development of the Docklands."

"They couldn't have been on the same side," Casey protested. "Jamieson would support the demolition of affordable housing and want to turn it into luxury properties for the rich."

Tessa shrugged her shoulders. "They also shared an interest in art."

They walked to the restaurant, and Casey made an effort to lighten things up. They talked about Tessa easing back into life, searching for a new place to live, this time an apartment. Casey felt constantly aware of how delicate Tessa remained. And something else bothered her. The easy rhythm of conversation between them had disappeared. They couldn't connect. She put it down to all that Tessa had been through and still suffered. Still she couldn't help but wonder.

ↂↂↂ

Casey went in search of Arthur Warren, now out on bail. It took several trips to the Red Lion before she finally located him in the back room, a pool cue in his hand. His eyes squinted at her through smoke from a cigarette hanging from his lips. The pub was overheated. She peeled off first her coat and then her jacket and walked towards him. He straightened at her approach and arrogantly looked her up and down.

He removed the cigarette. A white-toothed grin parted his full lips and his good looks appeared, as though the light outside had changed and revealed features previously hidden. Some handsome men could do this, she'd noticed, hide their sexuality until they needed it. She watched him carefully, wondering why he chose to show it to her. His shirtsleeves were rolled up and, still looking at her, he racked the balls.

"I'm here about the murder of Donald Broughton." She waved her press card.

He changed his expression, now looking bored and rubbing chalk into the tip of his cue.

"I've already spoken to the cops about it."

He had big strong-looking hands, the tips of the fingers square. "Have you remembered anything since? Where you spent that night? The name of the woman you were with?"

His eyes slid away from hers. With an expert jab of the cue, he hit the black ball into a side pocket. "Nope."

"No recollection at all? That seems strange." The man was lying, and she needed to know why. He also thought he was doing a good job of it, and so far, he'd kept his defenses down.

He threw the cue down and moved closer. "Perhaps the lady is married and I'm a gentleman. You're much too good-looking to be bothering with all this. How about a drink?"

Her imagination couldn't do the leap required to place Arthur Warren in the role of a gentleman. "No, thanks. How did you feel about Tessa Broughton counseling Sally? Were you angry?"

He stubbed the butt of his cigarette into an ashtray and turned to look at her with narrowed eyes. "You're looking at the wrong guy. I didn't waste Donald Broughton and I wouldn't hurt Tessa."

"So you had no problem with Sally consulting a relationship counselor?"

"I was angry at first."

"What happened to change your mind?"

He grinned. "Tessa persuaded me otherwise."

"Then you've met Mrs. Broughton." She tried to hide her surprise.

"Yeah."

He moved closer. His eyes scanned the open neck of her shirt before moving back to her face. He had black eyes that refracted light and were very hard to read. Fascinated and repelled, she studied the long fringe of coal-black lashes that framed them. He curled his fingers around her bare forearm. They felt rough against her skin. It sent waves of tension through her, but she resisted the urge to pull back. Let him think he had control over her. See what it made him say.

"When was that?"

"Now, why don't you just go and ask her?" he said.

Unnerved by the insinuation in his words, she stared at his hand in distaste. "Take your hand off my arm."

He removed it in mock surrender.

Casey walked away, hearing his hoot of laughter, annoyed that her heart beat too fast.

Just after she left the pub, she rang Tessa. "Arthur Warren says he knows you. Is that true?"

Tessa didn't answer her at first. The long silence made Casey think they'd been disconnected.

"Can you come to my office, Casey? We need to talk about this."

Perplexed, she drove to Tessa's office. When she walked in, Tessa had coffee ready. Casey sat down opposite her.

Tessa's shaky hands spilled sugar as she emptied a sachet into her coffee. "I never wanted you to find out about this."

"About what, Tessa?"

"Arthur Warren came to my office just after Sally's counseling sessions started. He was angry—he felt the police always took Sally's side."

"Why didn't you tell the police about this?"

"Because it's no one's business but mine."

"What happened when he came to see you? Did he frighten you?"

"Initially, but we got to talking...Look, I had sex with him a couple of times."

"You—" Casey looked at her carefully, trying to control her shock. Tessa's eyes flickered with something. Anxiety, guilt, or was it something else entirely? Did she know this woman at all? "You had sex with Arthur Warren?"

"I told Don after it was over. Arthur's strength attracted me. Sometimes men like that can take you into a different place, less cerebral—more primeval."

"You mean he's a stud."

"Well, yes, if you want to put it like that." Tessa looked at her as if she were a toddler behaving badly. "I don't believe I acted unprofessionally. He wasn't my client, and Sally had moved on. You can't tie a man like that down anyway." She fiddled with her hair, platting it loosely and then letting go. "I don't expect you to understand. I have nothing to say in my defence, except...I guess I always felt too safe. Ironic, isn't it?"

Casey tried to analyse the feeling rushing through her—protection of Don, hurt that Tessa had never confided in her. Jealousy, too, perhaps, that she had a life

Casey knew nothing about. Didn't Tessa trust her? "Did it end badly?"

"No. It was casual, recreational sex. It meant nothing to either of us."

An enormous sadness flowed over Casey, and she realized it was for the romantic view she'd cherished of Tessa and Don's marriage, now in tatters. Arthur Warren's blatant sexuality and his arrogance had made *her* shudder. It put her on the defensive. Was she a wimp as well as a prude? "Have you seen Arthur since Don died?"

"I've had no reason to." Tessa looked away, biting her lip.

"Wasn't Don angry when you told him about this?" she persisted.

"We had an understanding, but this time I pushed it too far, and he was furious. You've never needed a part of your life to be secret?" An urgent note had crept into Tessa's voice. "Something you could hold close, all to yourself?" She sighed and shook her head. "Look at you. You don't know what I'm talking about."

"I'm trying to understand. I really am."

Tessa's eyes looked red. She reached over to take Casey's hand. "I hope I'm not going to lose you over this. I can't lose you both."

"No. Of course you won't." Casey spoke firmly, but she was rattled.

Driving home, she thought again about Don's odd behavior on the night of his fortieth birthday. Had he been sad, maybe even heartbroken? Or had something even more disturbing been on his mind? She couldn't go on with this line of thought—it seemed unfair to Tessa, and Casey needed to deal with the living now.

She returned to her sunless flat, which only contributed to her low spirits. Watering her struggling African violets, she decided she needed warmth and sunshine as much as they did. She'd pushed life and change away and didn't want to do so anymore.

CHAPTER 19

Casey turned her attention to the last of Tessa's clients on the list. Tessa had told her Don had known about Reginald Jamieson's spousal abuse. Why, then, would he have associated with this man? Nothing about this association seemed to add up. She decided to set up a meeting with Jamieson, under the guise of a potential buyer.

Ringing his office, she spoke to his secretary, who informed her that Jamieson didn't deal personally with clients. A salesman would see to any requests she had.

"You mean Mr. Jamieson doesn't deal with general inquiries," Casey said. "I've come from America with the express wish to purchase a riverfront property."

"As I said, Miss. Rowan, we have first-rate sales staff working here who can assist you."

"Mr. Jamieson was recommended to me by a mutual friend," Casey said forcefully. "I'm here in London for only a few days, but if that's the way investors are handled by your company, I might be better served to look elsewhere."

It worked. First thing Monday morning, Casey was at the offices of Mayville Holdings, the real estate developers involved in the construction of the latest apartments in the Docklands area and along the banks of the Thames. She dressed in her most extravagant outfit, an Escada soft gray leather pencil skirt, teamed with a caramel pin-cord blazer, both bought in a sale at Harrods. She added high-heeled boots and her vintage Dior coffee leather bag.

"Welcome to Mayville, Miss Rowan." Jamison, a tall, narrow-shouldered man, directed her into his office. His face formed an oddly attractive series of hollows and planes, his cheeks carved out, giving him an almost hungry look. Apt for a developer, she reasoned.

She declined his offer of a drink, and they sat. She detected something not quite natural in his voice—a North Country accent that had all but disappeared, with the speech patterns too carefully modulated and precise. He cleared his throat often before he spoke, and she began to suspect it was a nervous habit. Perhaps he was not quite as pompous or sure of himself as he appeared. She relaxed into her character, becoming aware that he too had created a role for himself, disguising something he didn't want seen by others.

It made her wonder what else he had to hide.

"Thank you for seeing me, Mr. Jamieson. I'm in the process of selling a waterfront property in America. Now I'm looking around London. I checked out your latest development. I like what you're doing there."

His gray eyes brightened. "You won't find a better spot for the price. What exactly are you looking for?"

"A one-bedroom apartment."

Not the right answer. He smiled thinly and shuffled the papers on his desk. "They are very popular these days. So many young people choose to remain single."

He glanced over her shoulder at the building under construction next door, and she realized she needed to get to the point before she lost him. "You were recommended to me by Donald Broughton. I believe you knew him?"

He crossed his arms across his chest as though he too were in danger. "Donald? I was shocked to learn of his death. A thoroughly distressing business."

"Donald was a very close friend of mine, Mr. Jamieson. How did you two meet?"

"Through an acquaintance. Donald was a keen art collector, and I have a gallery in London. He purchased a couple of very fine paintings through me."

"The Kandinsky?"

"Ah, you've seen it. Wonderful, isn't it?"

"Magnificent." She smiled, hoping to keep his attention now she had it, but aware the true reason for her presence could so easily put him on edge. "Who was the acquaintance?" she asked casually, immediately regretting it. "I probably know them, too."

At this point, his eyes went blank, like a pond losing the evening light.

"We share so many friends who love art—it's really a joy." Her smile felt forced now.

He assessed her slowly, his own smile forgotten. "I doubt you would know them," he said. "Now, I'll give you a quick rundown on what one-bedders we have, and then you must excuse me—I'm due for a meeting."

She left feeling she'd accomplished little and irritated with herself for playing her hand too soon. She still had a lot to learn. Reginald was a dissembler who would give little away to anyone. Still, his marriage had been in trouble. Would his wife have given him a false alibi? She would have to talk to her and work out a better strategy than the one she'd just used.

Most likely, Reginald wouldn't have told her anything even if she'd been royalty looking for a six-bedroom penthouse on the Thames, but the fact was he was her last lead, and she had nothing left. It made her mood sour, and she had a sudden urge to give it all up and spend her free time curled up in her favorite spot on the sofa, safe and warm with a hot chocolate and a good read.

She arrived home to a phone call from America, which dashed her plans of a quiet few hours. The agent had a potential buyer for her father's house. She hung up and dug out a photo, sitting down to study it, a lump forming in her throat. Her childhood home. The two-story clapboard waterfront was once part of a community, until most were bought up and turned into luxury million-dollar homes.

Dad was strong to have made a new life for himself in a new country when things went bad for him in Ireland. She hoped she'd inherited his strength, though lately she'd begun to doubt it. The demands at *Hers* for more sensational pieces had not set well with her for some time, and her interview with Sir Henry seemed the last straw. She intended to search for a new home, but first, she had to resign from the magazine and knew this would result in the expenditure of more emotional energy.

The next afternoon, she trudged up the hill from Richmond station, her painful resignation from *Hers* behind her. An uplifting sense of independence and a crippling anxiety at cutting loose fought for dominance in her emotions, making her slightly nauseous.

A sign had appeared on the graceful Victorian church surrounded by magnificent old cedar trees on the corner of her street. It was to be converted into apartments. She'd known attendance was down—they'd hired out the church hall for Spanish dance classes to pay the bills. Given enough time, everything changed.

ɛ⁄ɔɛ⁄ɔ

Casey stood across the street from a semi-detached Late Victorian cottage, only blocks away from her flat. The dainty carved woodwork and bay window charmed her, as did the wisteria covering a pergola over the front path.

When the agent appeared and showed her around, she saw the advantage of being at the end of a row—light shone down into what would otherwise be quite a dark interior. Shabby, it needed new carpet and a coat of paint and was the first house she'd looked at—but she immediately took a lease with an option to buy. It wasn't an old fisherman's cottage by the sea, but it would do.

ɛ⁄ɔɛ⁄ɔ

Soc, Don's cat, approved of his new home. Tessa didn't want him, but Casey was glad to have him, although at times, with him on her knee, painting the walls during the day, or reading until the early hours at night, she wondered if perhaps she'd become too reclusive. She'd begun to feel the life of a free, independent woman was not as exciting as it used to be. Not when you faced a lonely bed every night.

Before she could worry herself further, Rod rang, making her feel wild and young again.

"Your magazine told me you'd resigned and moved house, all in a few weeks. Not one to let the grass grow under your feet, are you?"

"Not once I make up my mind. How are things with you?"

"I just got back from Edinburgh."

"I'm sorry about Sylvie, Rod." She swallowed back the rush of sorrow. So much death...

"Aye. I found myself thinking of our baby—the one Sylvie lost—he or she would be in their teens now."

"She had a little boy, didn't she?"

"The father's family has taken him in. They're nice people. He'll be okay."

"What happened?"

"She had hepatitis, as I told you. She didn't look after herself."

A lot of history lay behind his words. She wondered how much Sylvie's death had hurt him. Your first love always remained special.

"I just got back yesterday to a mile of paperwork. Casey?"

"Yes."

"I'm determined to be free this weekend. Nothing short of the station burning down will keep me in Devon. I'd love to see you."

Her heart did a little flip. "Come for Saturday lunch."

"Will you cook?"

"I promise not to."

He laughed. A sexy sound that set her heart racing.

"Don't you want the address?

"I already have it."

She smiled. "Of course you do."

After she'd hung up, she thought about the fact that she hadn't told him about her investigation of Tessa's clients. No matter. It was proving a waste of time and would spoil their time together. She was determined not to let anything do that.

And she couldn't possibly tell him about Tessa's affair with Arthur.

⧫⧫⧫

As Rod parked his motorbike and walked up the path, Casey admired his graceful stride. He looked great. He'd had a haircut, and it made him look somehow vulnerable—younger, perhaps.

She showed him around. They went upstairs to the bedrooms, and she grew painfully aware of the frilly pillows on the bed. Had she really tucked a teddy bear in among them? Rod looked so out of place, she felt a jolt as it became obvious to her she'd created a girlie space no man would feel at home in. However, he didn't seem to notice her discomfort—or the décor. They stood in her bedroom for a moment too long which turned into an awkward silence. Perhaps, like hers, his thoughts went to the time they were together.

"Lunch?" she suggested, as though her main concern in life was to provide him with nourishment—although, at that moment, food was the last thing on her mind.

She opened a bottle of Chardonnay and kept lunch simple with a leek soup, rare roast beef sliced cold and served with an excellent homemade horseradish she'd found, rolls, salad, cheese, and fruit. The vicious cold had abated, so they sat outdoors. The food settled her nerves, and the wine warmed her insides. She leaned back in her chair and gazed in a lazy stupor at the tiny buds painting a soft green haze over the bare branches of the surrounding shrubs and trees.

As she answered Rod's questions about the causes Don had espoused over the years, he smoothed enough horseradish on his meat to make her wince. She watched in fascination as it went down without a murmur.

His next words jolted her. "You and Donald seemed very close. Like soul mates?"

Choosing her words carefully, she said, "A very close friend. He and Tessa were like family."

Rod didn't comment but he watched her over the top of his wineglass, his eyes the color of some far-off, exotic sea she wanted to dive into.

She crushed a grape with her tongue. It reminded her of warmer climes. She asked the usual question. "How's the investigation going?"

Lines of unease appeared across Rod's forehead. "The forensic report on Karl Baumann has thrown up something strange. They've put the body's height at five feet nine or ten."

"And Karl was well over six foot."

"Six two."

She drew in her breath. "How accurate can they be about the height of a badly burnt body?"

"They can get it pretty close, when the body's still intact, by the use of X-rays, measuring the length of bones in the leg, and good calculations. In this case, though, with the legs pretty smashed up, it has proved difficult. If it hadn't rained, we'd have nothing but a pile of ashes to deal with."

"What about dental records, DNA?"

"No success with those either, but the corpse did have quite a few missing teeth."

She thought of the elegant man she'd met at Farrowham. "He could have worn a plate. Would that burn?"

Rod lay back on the sofa and said wearily, "There'd be some trace of it, and none was found. With DNA, they can take the pulp from a tooth and match it with someone's toothbrush or hair from a comb. There's a problem with that, too."

"What problem?"

"Karl was on an extended business trip, planning to be away for some time. He'd packed just about everything he owned. To obtain DNA, the clothes we use need to have been worn, and those left behind were freshly washed. His bed had been stripped, his towels washed—bleach was added. There was very little to use."

"Devon Police are still investigating Don's case, though?" she asked. "It's still top priority?"

"A high profile murder in Devon? Of course. When we know why it happened, we'll be closer to knowing how, and by whom." He took another sip of wine. "People kill for different reasons. Curiosity—if I do this, what will happen? Will I get the attention I crave? Donald wouldn't be the first celebrity killed for this reason. It could be sexual, or some other perversion. Or maybe to control or to silence."

"The latter, surely," she said, hoping to hear more.

"Possibly." He paused. "What's next for you, Casey?"

She took note of his rapid change of topic. "Freelance work with the *Evening Standard*."

He grinned. "It will prove quite a change from a women's magazine."

She watched a squirrel leap from a branch of a tall Ash. "I do believe you are teasing me, Carlisle."

A pause followed before he said, "I've missed teasing you."

"I've missed it, too."

He put out his cigarette and reached across for her hand. "I picked up the phone to ring you, several times."

She smiled. How many times had she done the same, hung up before the first ring? She relaxed as a rush of something—lost love, pleasure—warmed her.

"I'd have liked that. If you'd actually called." She looked at his mouth, remembering. Pleasure threaded its way through her like hot chocolate. "I've been a bit of a hermit."

Without letting go of her hand, he pulled her to her feet and into his arms. "Come to bed?"

She gave him full brownie points for lowering his voice to a whisper.

ⅇ⌇ⅇ⌇

"What is it you want from life?" Casey lay on her side watching him, not wanting him to retreat from her now. His dark hair was tousled, and her fingers itched to reach out and stroke it back from his forehead.

"You promise not to laugh."

"Of course I won't."

"Of course you won't laugh, or of course you won't promise?"

She smiled, suddenly aware of her nakedness, and pulled the sheet higher. "I won't laugh," she replied but poked him in the side, half in encouragement, but mostly just to feel his warm skin once again.

"I'd like to be a gairner," he said.

"A *what?*"

He grinned. "Have my own bit of ground, where I can see lots of sky. As a kid growing up in Scotland, we ran wild. I miss that."

"So, you are going back."

"Mmmm, one day. Not right now, though." He moved closer and ran his fingers along her spine. She shuddered with pleasure.

"I thought you grew up in Edinburgh?" she asked, mainly to get her mind back on track.

"Further north, just a wee village. Beyond the end of our town, it was all hills and crags. The other local lads and I were gone from morning to night. We used to fish from the Laird's trout stream—sell them, too, if we had a good day."

"Why, Inspector Carlisle. That's stealing."

"Aye, but we didn't see it that way. He had more fish than he could eat."

"Egalitarian, I suppose. What if the law catches up with you now? The trouble you'd be in."

Rod groaned. "I'm in enough trouble, back at Middlemoor and now here with you."

She didn't know what to say to that, so she just watched him, waiting. She hoped he'd confide in her, but he merely stretched as if to cast off his fears. He spoke again with a lighter voice. "When Dad died, Mum was determined that my sister and I become grammar-folk—"

"Grammar-folk?"

Rod laughed, and she knew he teased. "Educated."

"My dad was full of Irish sayings. A favorite was, 'God is good, but never dance in a small boat.'"

He placed his hands each side of her face. "But you didn't listen to him, lass. You've been rocking the boat since I met you." She watched the amusement fade from his eyes.

A while passed before their conversation continued.

"We moved to Edinburgh," he said. "There wasn't much money and even less chance of getting a job. I went to university and worked in a bar at night. That's where I met Sylvie. When she got pregnant, we married. I was twenty-one, and she was nineteen.

Nothing for it then, I had to find a proper job, so I joined the force." Rod took a deep breath and let it out in a sigh. "After Sylvie lost the baby, things went downhill for us. Work took up so much time, and we just sort of drifted apart. I guess she knew it before I did. Women seem quicker to pick up on these things. And they're braver. She found someone else quick enough. I think the whole thing made me a bit wary of being caught up in a relationship for a while." He turned to her. "Now it's your turn," he said, surprising her.

"Oh. I think my life's been affected by a sense of impermanence," she answered vaguely, horror-struck at the thought of listing her relationship failures. "I wanted to keep my options open so I could go back, and when I'm back in the Keys, I'm afraid I'll be trapped into staying." She shrugged, embarrassed. "A bit of a mess, really."

Rod wisely said nothing.

ೕೠೕ

The next morning Rod had to head back to Devon, and it was still dark when the alarm went off. They were both in a dazed state of happy exhaustion, but Casey followed him out of bed and pulled on a robe. He came out of the bathroom smelling of soap and a fresh aftershave and pulled her to him, his hands moving over her body inside her robe. He undid the belt, and she felt that rush of warmth. Memories of their night together made her body respond to his touch.

She kissed him.

"Casey," he groaned, pulling her down with him onto the bed.

He eased up her nightgown, and she wrapped her arms and legs around him.

They made fast, furious love and broke apart, sweaty and gasping.

Rod rolled away and jumped to his feet with a regretful laugh. "If I'm not careful, I'll lose all track of time, and life down at Middlemoor really will get thorny."

She handed him his shirt and jeans. "Your shoes are on the bottom step. Let me make you some coffee." She yawned. "I start my new job today."

"You won't be too sharp," he said, smiling.

She made coffee and wrestled with the toaster that produced toast either limp and pale or burnt. Suddenly she realized, with a jolt, she felt happy. Rod looked up from pouring milk into their coffees. "I'll have a look at that," he said, eyeing the smoke pouring from the toaster.

She sighed. "Go ahead. Otherwise I'll throw it out. Damn thing."

Sipping her coffee, she watched his deft fingers tinkering with the toaster. "This needs a new plug," he said. "I'll fix it next time I come." With his dark hair still wet and brushed back off his face, she could envisage the little boy he used to be, clambering over the moors.

Watching him fiddle with the toaster reminded her of her dad. For a moment, that elusive warm and secure feeling returned. She found it hard to see where this relationship was going. So many things stood in the way of its success. Yet to her surprise, she found she wanted it to succeed—with a sense of commitment entirely new to her.

Watching him roar off into the early morning light, she felt a stab of excitement at the prospect of work. She had time for a couple of hours more sleep, so she crawled up the stairs, fell into bed, and burrowed her nose into Rod's pillow.

CHAPTER 20

Rod watched Claudette Morris-Smythe make her way across the floor to his desk. Though not a tall woman, she was exquisitely put together. She lowered herself into the proffered chair, crossed her legs, tucked a lock of black hair behind her ear, and smiled. She looked like a woman who was used to getting what she wanted in life.

"Lady Morris-Smythe, I've been trying to get hold of you for some time," he said, determined to get the interview onto the right footing. "You didn't respond to any of the messages we left."

She waved in a Gallic gesture. "I'm sorry, but when you are traveling—"

"The message that the police wanted to speak to you didn't reach you?"

"It did, finally, so here I am."

Rod glanced at his file on her. She grew up in Marseilles, one of six siblings from a poor family. Her father left when she was ten. Won a modeling contest that took her to Paris, where she met and married Rupert. Rod remembered what Elizabeth Trentham had said about her brother not liking the women of his own class. Rupert must have married for love. Lust was more easily, and less expensively, satiated.

"You've been informed of what we needed to know from you. I gathered you've now consulted your diary?"

"Yes. That night we went to the opera, then on to a party in Belgravia. I was home before midnight, and the house had been left in a mess. I was angry." She smiled at him conspiratorially, as though he shared her experiences of poor staffing. He attempted to hold his face blank but felt himself smiling back all the same, not because he understood her problems, but because he found her naivety amusing.

"And Lord Rupert spent the whole night there with you?"

She pouted. "No. He did not come home with me."

"He wasn't there at all that night?"

"No."

"Your servants at Penlow Hall told us that you and Lord Rupert arrived around four o'clock the next afternoon."

She nodded. "He came back to the apartment, and we drove down together."

"What time did your husband arrive to collect you, Lady Morris-Smythe?"

"Close to one o'clock. I was prepared, and we left straight away."

"Do you know where he spent the night?"

"He was with his mistress. He always goes to her when we quarrel. He is like a little boy."

Not like any little boy Rod knew. "Do you know who this woman is?"

"Of course."

"You do realize that this differs from the story Lord Morris-Smythe has told us."

"Poor Rupert wanted so to be like his papa," she said inconsequentially.

Rod frowned. "I'm not sure what you mean."

"This mistress, she is a mere status symbol for Rupert, but he will not want it known about Monique now. We are about to divorce."

It certainly fitted Rupert's profile, Rod thought, looking at the trophy wife over the desk. "Can you give me this woman's surname and address?"

"I have it written down for you." She opened her handbag with a click.

"I take it your explanation of your husband's whereabouts is merely an assumption."

She uncrossed her legs and leaned towards him. "One thing I do know, Inspector Carlisle, is my husband—how he thinks. I make it my business to know these things."

Rod found himself almost inclined to believe her.

CHAPTER 21

Casey watched the news on television and considered her next assignment. She had a few things in mind. When a neo-Nazi march came on, she leaned forward. It wasn't unlike the one in Munich but it was in Bradford, where the simmering racial tension had become a powder keg. She watched the crowds lining the street and the skinheads marching with their banners. A simple hunch led her to make up her mind.

She rang the paper and discussed the possibility of doing a piece on Bradford. By the time she hung up, it had been agreed. She would leave in the morning. She checked her case, making sure her digital camera had fresh batteries, her trusty thirty-five millimeter SLR had a roll of black and white film plus six extra rolls, and her handheld tape recorder worked. Then she added a light recorder and flash.

On the way up to Bradford in the train, she phoned Rod.

"Couldn't you cover the Chelsea Flower Show?" he said jokingly. She heard the strain in his voice. He would have to accept her job as she did his, she told herself, wishing she didn't feel guilty. She didn't mention her main reason for choosing this assignment—put into words. It sounded too ridiculous.

She arrived at Bradford railway station at eight o'clock in the evening, having prepared a list of interview questions during the trip. Exhausted and planning an early start in the morning, she piled her overnight bag and camera case into a taxi and went straight to her hotel, which was decorated in thirties grim.

After a breakfast of scrambled eggs and coffee in the hotel dining room the next morning, she felt revived. Skinheads had attacked a young Pakistani man, Tahir Ghazali, at a pub a week ago, and there were rumblings about the police's failure to act. She'd organized an interview with the victim at his house. Afterwards, she hoped to stakeout the city center for a vox pop.

She called a taxi to take her to Tahir's house, a couple of miles from her hotel. As she unloaded her gear from the cab, he answered the door, a sticking plaster across his forehead.

"Come and meet my mother." He led her into the dark hallway. In the tiny sitting room, his small, anxious mother waited. After an hour of interviewing them both, it was clear neither had anything good to say about the state of Bradford society. Mrs. Ghazali told Casey she never left the house. Casey took photos of them both and, downing a quick cup of tea, called a taxi to take her to the town center. She felt empathetic towards Tahir and his mother, who were trying to make a life in a new country as she had. However, the brutal opposition and sense of powerlessness was something she'd never experienced.

The taxi was a block or two from the center of the city when a woman came running around the corner, screaming.

"Can't you stop?" Casey asked the driver, but they were already turning the corner. She craned her neck to see a crowd of people spilling out onto the road behind them.

"I think I'd better take a detour," the driver said.

"No." She gathered her things together. "I'll get out here."

"Could get a bit nasty."

"I'll be okay."

She paid the cabbie and joined the crowd in time to see a youth with bleached dreadlocks throwing bricks systematically through a row of shop windows. As if on cue, several people broke away from the mob and followed the youth into the shops, scrambling over broken shards of glass and grabbing at anything they could lay their hands on. Some ran away with toaster ovens, their cords trailing, while others staggered under the weight of televisions and microwaves. An Asian man stood near Casey, tears streaming from his eyes. Above the uproar, she heard his loud wail. It must have been his shop.

Some skinheads and Asian youths began to fight, and Casey took refuge with a group of frightened bystanders on the far side of the street. She heard the sirens, but the sound appeared to have no impact on the rioters. From the far end of the street, the West Yorkshire police riot squad emerged from vans and formed a line, moving in with batons raised.

Backed up against a brick wall with the rest of the crowd, Casey could only watch as men hurled bricks and firebombs at the police. Several police officers fell, their colleagues dragging them away out of sight. Billowing, black smoke rose like a portent of doom from the next street.

A boy ran up to them, his face streaked with tears. "They're rolling cars, setting fire to them," he said, clinging to a woman beside Casey.

A building near them had been set alight. Casey's eyes burned, and the air she inhaled was hot and smoky. She reefed her Minolta from her bag, uncomfortably aware it would attract attention, and left the relative safety of the crowd. Moving forward cautiously, she took shots of the dazed and angry faces of the bystanders, the set expressions of the looters, and the decimated buildings.

She had landed in the middle of a tragic event and desperately wanted to document all of it.

She had her tape-recorder out, in search of people's reactions, when the back of a curly fair head about fifty feet away caught her eye. For a mad moment, she thought it was Don. She kept her eyes on him, willing him to turn.

He did, and she stopped dead. A woman behind her cannoned into her back. She'd seen those strange eyes before, even stranger now for the fierce kind of pleasure they held. Her hunch had been right. Karl Baumann.

She fumbled for her phone but dismissed the idea. She'd never manage to make herself heard. Shoving her tape-recorder away, she held her camera high above her head, clicking rapidly, but he was leaving, pushing through the throng. Finally, he broke free and hurried up the street. She followed, staying half a block behind, and saw him cross the road and turn the corner. She raced up and peered around it as he entered the Bradford Arms Hotel. She reached the front entrance to see him take the stairs two at a time.

Keeping some distance between them, she began to climb the stairs, but he didn't look back. He went up another flight and opened the door to room 203. Once the door closed behind him, Casey turned and went back down to the front desk.

"I wonder if you could help me. Is a man called Karl Baumann staying here? I believe he's in room 203."

The clerk thumbed the register. "Sorry. We don't have anyone by that name registered here."

"I saw him enter the hotel," Casey said, trying to calm her breath. She tucked her hair behind her ears, adjusted the camera bag that weighed heavily on her shoulder, and smiled at the clerk. "I just missed him. A tall man with fair hair."

"Just went up? That's William Brandt. He's in 203." The clerk looked suspicious. "You have his name wrong, though." He glanced at her again, and belatedly she noticed in the glass behind him a dark smudge across her forehead.

"I heard sirens," he said. "And people running. They tell me there's a riot going on out there."

"A violent riot. Men are robbing shops and burning cars."

His eyes widened, and he gazed towards the door. "Unbelievable."

As the vivid images she'd witnessed flashed through her mind, she felt completely drained. She wanted to sink into a sofa in the foyer and stay huddled there until it was time to go home, but she couldn't. Not yet. "I'm so upset my mind's gone blank," she said. "I've met so many sales representatives this morning. Yes, now I remember, Mr. Brandt."

Back on the street, she rang Rod, but his mobile was busy. She left a message and considered whether she should ring Middlemoor. But then Karl came down the stairs.

He left the hotel, heading off in the opposite direction from which they'd come. He now carried a black bag and had changed into beige chinos and a brown leather jacket. Casey almost sobbed with weariness, but she tucked her mobile away with the camera and tape recorder in her big canvas tote and broke into a run, her new joggers rubbing at her heels.

She positioned herself behind a group of people hurrying away from the violence, but Karl was soon far in front, his long legs widening the distance between them with every stride. Her camera bag banged against her hip. Limping, but grinding her teeth, she kept going, fretting about her deadline.

When she turned a corner, he was gone. The group of people she'd used for cover crossed the street and took another fork in the road. Walking slowly up one side of the dead-end street and down the other, she checked all the doorways. Where could he have disappeared to? She was in a rundown warehouse district, which seemed like a ghost town. Every building she passed was boarded up. Not a soul was around. Feeling defenseless, her skin crawling on the back of her neck, she walked quickly away and returned to Karl's hotel. She sat down in the foyer as rain began to beat against the windows.

The clerk came over to her. His hard, suspicious gaze raked her over. "Mr. Brandt has gone," he said, glancing at her breasts. "Can I help you with anything else?" Maybe he suspected her of soliciting.

She opened her mouth, but her mobile rang. Rod. "I'll have to take this," she said. The man looked annoyed as she moved out of earshot. She quickly outlined to Rod what had happened.

"The man's supposed to be dead. How sure are you?"

"I'm positive, but if he doesn't come back soon, I've got to leave." She eyed the clerk again. "I have a deadline to meet."

"You're in the middle of a war up there. The police are all tied up."

"I know that, Rod."

"Where are you?"

"At Karl's hotel. The Bradford."

"Right. Stay there. It might take a while, but I'll arrange for someone to pick you up. I'll send them a picture of Baumann. Wait until they arrive, Casey. It's too dangerous to be out alone."

She started to protest, but he interrupted her with a voice so tightly controlled, she wondered if he was angry with her—or worried. "Don't fight me on this one. I'd tell anyone the same thing, so don't start accusing me of being chauvinistic. Let someone protect you. There's a riot, for God's sake."

"I think Karl could be involved in what's happening here."

"Leave it to the police."

Casey knew if she caught sight of Karl again, she would follow him. While she deliberated this, Rod said, "We'll talk later," and rang off.

An hour later, just as the front desk clerk came towards her, his face set in distinct lines of disapproval, two men in suits entered the hotel, shaking umbrellas. The bigger of the two approached her. The other man went over to the desk.

"Miss Rowan."

She rose with relief as the thickset police officer flashed a badge at her before thrusting it back into his pocket with his huge paw. Then, fishing around, he pulled out a packet of cigarettes and offered her one. "DC James will remain here." His voice surprised her, a countertenor where she'd expected a baritone. "You'd better come back to the station."

"No, I can't. I haven't the time. I have to get back to my hotel. I've a plane to catch."

He looked her over. "No problem—where are you staying?"

"The Emporium."

She followed him outside, and hovered in the covered entryway as he unfurled his umbrella and leaned down through the car window. He said something to the driver she didn't catch then opened the car door and beckoned to her. She climbed in, icy rain soaking her through. He slid in beside her, sat back, and turned to face her, his look as cold as she now felt.

"You might fill me in on exactly what you know, Miss Rowan."

She told him the whole story. It tumbled out, and when she paused to take breath, she slumped back against the seat, reciting it more slowly, in order. He took out a notepad and started making notes.

"And you believe that person is here in Bradford, even though he was found dead in Wiltshire," he said, not looking at her.

"I'm positive it was him."

He tapped the driver's shoulder, and the car started up.

"There must be some kind of conspiracy that Donald Broughton stumbled onto, and he was killed for it." She knew it sounded bizarre, but she had to tell him everything. She was sure they'd heard it all, but something about the man's slow, calm manner made her hope he'd at least consider her theories. "Why would Karl Baumann fake his own death?"

"Not something that happens every day, is it?" he answered dryly. "They say Lord Lucan did it. Haven't seen him over there in America, have you?"

Casey bit her lip. She couldn't blame him, but maybe he would find something later to confirm her outlandish claims. The car weaved through the narrow streets. Her sense of direction began to fail her, and she thought they headed in the opposite direction from her hotel. With the windscreen wipers bashing back and forth on high, she tried to peer through the fogged up windows, seeing nothing familiar in the dismal, shuttered streets.

"Detective..." In her haste, she hadn't caught his name.

"Detective Sergeant Forster."

"What exactly did Inspector Carlisle tell you?"

"That's confidential police business, Miss Rowan."

His mobile rang. He listened and then emitted a "yeah" and looked at her, raising his eyebrows.

She rubbed at the window, her apprehension growing. It occurred to her his badge could have been a fake. She still saw no sign of her hotel.

"Did Inspector Carlisle fax you information from Plymouth police station?" she said, testing him.

He reached into his suit coat once more. Her mouth dried to the scratchy consistency of a potato chip and swallowing became difficult. He withdrew his hand as the car pulled sharply into the curb, throwing her against him.

"Devon & Cornwall, wasn't it, Miss Rowan?" He showed her a copy of a photo of Karl. It was part of a brochure from Farrowham, small and grainy. "DC James just quizzed the front desk clerk, who swears Brandt was not this man—nothing like him, he says."

"I took a few photos of him on the run." She pulled out her digital camera and began to check the shots she'd taken, but the ones of Karl proved blurry and totally useless. She looked up at him and shrugged.

His impatient expression told her he thought her just another lunatic wasting his valuable time, and her heart sank. Feeling her face burn despite the cold, she clambered out of the police car into the rain. Her shabby hotel stood across the street, and she ran for it. She might have saved herself angst if she'd checked the cops IDs more closely up front, but she hadn't been mistaken about Karl Baumann. She *had* seen him—very much alive.

She was sure of it.

CHAPTER 22

C asey made it to the airport for her one o'clock flight with only a few minutes to spare. As the plane rose in the air, she peered through her window to take one last look at Bradford, but a pall of smoke hid everything from view.

When they served the inflight meal, she quickly drank the orange juice, having gone without food or drink since her morning cup of tea. How maddening it felt to leave now, with Karl and all his secrets lurking somewhere out of sight.

Rod was on his way up to Bradford. The West Yorkshire police would no doubt tell him they thought she was mistaken. She groaned softly. As the plane banked and the drenched, muted moorlands disappeared from view, she pulled her laptop and tape recorder out of her bag, plugged in her earplugs, and began to type, heading the piece, *City in Fear*.

By the time they landed at Heathrow, she had her copy. Leaping into a cab, she headed for the newspaper office in Derry Street, Kensington, where she handed the disk in along with the images from the riot. A crew was up in Bradford now, but Casey had been on the spot and had made the fourth edition.

Once she could at last focus her thoughts beyond the whereabouts of Karl Baumann, she had to admit the article would give a boost to her career.

೮っ೮っ

Casey entered the Tube, thinking she could relax at last and put the extraordinary events of the day into some kind of perspective, but at West Kensington, her train came to a juddering stop. She waited for the dreaded announcement—a breakdown. Everyone would have to disembark, and the claustrophobic tube station was the last place she wanted to be.

Lining up with the rest of the disgruntled crowd, six deep on the platform, she watched a train hiss past like a brightly lit snake. She stood in the first row positioned just behind the safety line. A gust of stale air hit her face, heralding the train's imminent arrival.

They all took an expectant step forward. She felt a thud in her lower back and lost her balance. Throwing herself sideways, she fell hard on one knee as the recorded voice told her to mind the gap. She clutched the edge and stared down at the tracks between the platform and the train, a nerve-wracking few feet below her.

A young black man, his big, dark eyes wide in shock, silver stud lodged in one nostril, stood above her. He extended a hand to pull her to her feet.

"Are you okay, luv?"

"Thank you," she said shakily. The last of the commuters, anxious to make it through the doors before they shut, propelled them into the train. She grabbed hold of a pole and studied the people around her packed in like a Fortnum and Mason's Christmas hamper. Her nose curled involuntarily at the human stench—sweat, perfume, garlic, stale tobacco and the odd whiff of alcohol. Her knee stung, and her heart thudded.

Someone had *pushed* her. She searched the indifferent faces of the weary commuters, all resigned to a period of discomfort until they reached their destination. No one met her eyes, and she recognized no one.

At Richmond Station, she raced up the steps and headed out into the street as if murderous intent lurked behind every face. Once she reached the bus stop, she breathed deeply, both to slow her heart rate and to steady her lightheadedness. She felt disconnected.

Just then, the man with the nose ring walked past her. "I'm sorry luv, my fault. No hard feelings?"

He shot her a wink, and she stared after him until he mingled with people two blocks down and disappeared.

 දංදං

Worn out and dispirited, Rod rubbed the back of his neck. He sat downing a coffee in DS Forster's police station in Bradford's city center. A clearer photo of Karl had made no difference to the young clerk's opinion, and he nervously avowed the occupant of room 203 was a different man. William Brandt had checked out and disappeared, into the post-war zone Bradford had become.

Rod had made the rounds of some of the neo-Nazi haunts with Forster. Swastikas adorned the walls of a hall filled with men stomping to loud music in a kind of frenzied victory dance. Rod saw the violence in their eyes and understood them to be on a bloody path they believed would make their lives significant.

By the time he prepared to leave Bradford, he was deeply troubled.

CHAPTER 23

Shaken by her paranoia, Casey walked into the house, calling Soc. He refused at first to come, hovering just out of reach. She checked that the neighbour had left him food and water and made a mental note to thank him.

She unpacked and searched cupboards and freezer for food, but nothing appealed. She considered going out, but the idea exhausted her. She wondered how Rod was getting on up in Bradford but didn't call him—she felt sure Karl would prove too slippery to catch. If only those shots she'd taken of him had come out.

Pouring herself a glass of white wine, Casey found some stale biscuits and a bit of Stilton, then ran a bath, emptying the remains of a bottle of bath oil into it. She soaked in the dim flickering light of candles, and, slowly, the tension and apprehension melted away. When her phone rang, her wet fingers almost dropped it.

"Casey?"

"Rod. Where are you?"

"I'm still up here. We didn't find a trace of Baumann."

She made a low noise, acceptance mingled with exhaustion. At that point, little mattered to her more than to hear his voice and to stay in this bath forever.

"Are you in the bath? I hear water."

"Hmmm."

Silence unfolded on the line for a moment. "Wish I was there," he said eventually. "When I close my eyes, I can see those two dimples in your lower back."

She laughed. "I wish you were here, too." She told him about the incident on the train.

"Casey..." He said nothing for a long time, but she could hear his heavy, regular breathing. He was tired, too. "I've been worried about the danger you could find in your search. And now I'm even more worried you've found it."

"I'm sure it was merely an accident."

"I wish I shared your optimism. I have to go— Forster's waiting. We'll talk later."

Once she was tucked up in her duvet, trying to concentrate on a novel she'd bought at the airport, Soc hopped up to settle on her feet. Finally, she gave up and turned out the light, but sleep proved impossible. The incident in the Tube station swirled through her mind until she couldn't think straight. At last, exhaustion wiped it all away.

She didn't know how long she slept, but a crash somewhere in the house woke her with a jolt. She lay there listening, every muscle tense, her heart so loud she felt sure it could be heard out in the street. The familiar roar of a motorbike kicking into life broke the silence, and she thought first of Rod. She shook herself awake. It couldn't be him. She clutched the sheets in breathless fear as the bike's roar grew fainter. Then silence.

She crept to the top of the stairs, Soc circling her bare legs. The moon's silvery light threw a ghostly glow about the hall and sitting room below, turning the furniture into unfamiliar shapes crouching by the walls. She stared, and their contours seemed to shift. Was it exhaustion playing tricks, or was something there? It seemed quiet now. She and Soc hovered together while she debated whether she'd been dreaming. Then Soc disappeared in a shadowy blur down the stairs. She heard the cat-door bang and felt strangely deserted.

Returning to her bedroom, she unscrewed the lampshade from its heavy brass base and descended the stairs with the base clutched tightly in her hand. In the hall, the moonlight picked up shards of glass.

Casey turned the light on. A rock lay on the floor. The window beside the solid front door was shattered. Secured to the rock by an elastic band was a piece of paper.

She rang Richmond police station and peered out into the darkness, frightened, but still angry enough to fight if she had to. The street light revealed a shady picture of the deserted road, every tree and shrub a possible hiding place. Racing to the kitchen, she donned rubber gloves and pulled off the note. *Mind your own business or we'll make it ours.* Written with a child's thick red pen.

She curled up in the sitting room, wrapped tightly in a rug from the sofa. Her tired eyes watched the clock, and her ears strained for the police. Twenty minutes later, they arrived.

A gray-haired policeman with an avuncular manner praised her for putting the deadbolt on. "The blighter could have easily reached the latch and come in if you hadn't," he said.

She told them she'd get an alarm installed. To their credit, the police spent a long time checking all the other windows and doors, but when they left, she felt vulnerable and alone. There was no sign of Soc, so she sat up waiting, cold, fearful that something awful had happened to him, and conscious of the fact that only glass and a flimsy piece of wood stood between her and those who wished her harm.

Finally, as the sky lightened to gray, she heard the flap, and in Soc waltzed to lay a dead mouse at her feet. She found it oddly soothing.

౭౩౭౩

Rod came to see Casey the next afternoon. Fortunately, she didn't have work to do and had been able to grab a few hours of fitful sleep. As he took off his suit jacket and hung it over a chair, he looked as tired as she felt, his eyes bloodshot. She had dressed in her comfort clothes, her oldest frayed jeans and a blue wool sweater with long sleeves that curled over her hands. She rolled them back to make him some coffee. Then they sat on the sofa together.

She watched him light a cigarette. "Can I have one?"

"I didn't know you smoked."

"I gave it up four years ago."

"You're vulnerable here." He handed her a lit cigarette, and she drew in deeply. Memories of the past wafted through her with the smoke.

"Not if you find Karl and put him away," she snapped, the lack of sleep making itself known in more than her disheveled appearance.

Rod put down his cup and placed his arm around her shoulders, drawing her protectively against him. "Okay, you say you're positive it was Karl Baumann up in Bradford."

The cigarette made her feel light-headed and slightly unsteady. She stubbed it out in the ashtray.

"Karl's passport wasn't with his possessions, but there's no record of him leaving the country," he continued. "His bank accounts haven't been touched."

"Rod, the note around the rock said 'we.' Is there something you've found out that you're not telling me?"

"You have to be done with this, Casey. Hasn't what's happened been enough to frighten you?"

She wouldn't admit to how she felt, how she kept remembering Karl's eyes, filled with an awful passion. "I was right about Karl Baumann. He's a neo-Nazi."

"Neo-Nazi groups like Combat Eighteen add fuel to the fire of most of these riots."

"I've heard the name. Who are they?"

"A group of right-wing extremists—fascists, basically. Their name is based on Hitler's initials—the first and eighth letters in the alphabet. That's all you need to know."

She moved away from him. "Don't patronize me, Rod. Eighty policemen were hurt in that riot."

He sighed. "Combat Eighteen was originally set up by MI5, to keep a watch on subversives. It's largely been disbanded now. And not all skinheads are neo-Nazis. But in Bradford, you have the National Front and the Anti-Nazi League both pushing their causes, creating racial tension among people dissatisfied with their lives, and it permeates every layer of society, from the grassroots level up."

"It all helps the British National Party perform well at the polls."

Rod nodded. "People resent bureaucracy—sometimes for a very good reason. Many feel they've had a raw deal."

He shifted his position on the sofa, moving slightly away from her. "Surely, you've achieved what you set out to do. Your by-line's in the paper."

"After Don returned from that neo-Nazi rally in Munich, he wrote a prize-winning piece on this very subject."

"Aye...he did," Rod said softly. "Placing yourself in the firing line isn't going to bring him back, is it?"

"Perhaps I could check with the Art Loss Register again. There may be unsubstantiated developments that you wouldn't get to hear of."

A tense pause fell between them, and she held her breath, feeling Rod's body stiffen beside her.

"It seems to me that Donald Broughton is fucking with you more in death than he ever did in life."

She sprung to her feet. "You have no right to say that," she growled, her voice rising in outrage and something very close to hurt. "My being in Bradford had nothing to do with Don."

He rose and followed her across the room. Grabbing her shoulders, he turned her to face him. "Didn't it? You don't think you're still trying to live up to some plan he had for your life?"

Although it had a ring of truth to it, the accusation left her speechless, her breath coming in uneven pants of rage. "Don't you trust my judgment at all?"

"I don't expect you to see life the way I do, through a cop's eyes. But you don't listen to me. You don't even seem to value your life as much as I value it."

She stared at him. He shook his head and turned away to look out the window. "You haven't a clue what you're dealing with, Casey. These guys aren't just a bunch of skinhead boys out to cause a bit of trouble, nor are they simple soccer louts. They're led by small groups of intelligent people, who hold high positions in society—organized, structured groups with a strong commitment to the neo-Nazi cause. And this isn't the safest place you could be."

As he swiveled on his heel, his face expressionless, and gestured around the room, the house suddenly seemed a fragile barrier against the world.

"Look how easy it would be to break in here," he demanded. "They just didn't want to—next time, who knows? It could be a letter bomb exploding in your hall. You were seen documenting the events in Bradford. Now they've warned you. You keep digging, ignore what happened here, and me, then I can't keep you safe."

"I'm already in the firing line, as you say. I wanted to help Tessa, and now I need to keep digging for my own safety."

"No, you don't. You could take a holiday. Go back to America for a while. Just back off, Casey."

Stung that he now wanted to get rid of her, she said bitterly, "Hardly my fault I ended up in the middle of a riot."

"No, that wasn't your fault. Can I trust you to leave things alone from now on?"

"You want me to sit around and wait for someone to..." Her voice trailed off at the horror of it.

"No. Will you go away for a while?"

She frowned and shook her head. "This is my home. What good would running do? I'll have to come back sometime."

He grabbed his jacket and walked to the door. "Well, don't ring asking me for information." He wrenched the door open. "Your obsession with this case just adds to my worries, and it seems to be doing you no good either. Again, I repeat, for Christ's sake have done with it."

She watched him through the window as he left, and then she banged around the kitchen in a clumsy attempt to clean up, her fury mounting when she broke a glass.

She would have loved to replay the last couple of hours, to have him back here with her, on good terms. She should have tried to explain to him that she had to fight. She needed to make sense of it before she could rest.

She narrowly missed chipping a favorite plate, and an idea came to her. She'd follow Rod down to Devon and pay a visit to the elderly woman in Holly Road who'd seen the car. But first she would have to visit a Mercedes-Benz dealer.

Immediately, she felt stronger at the prospect of something to do. She pulled out the phone book and started flicking through it.

❦❧❦

Arriving in Devon in the early afternoon, Casey made her way to Holly Road and parked. The sky was gray, and the wind had sprung up, stirring the trees. Now that she'd calmed down, she had to admit most of her anger was directed towards herself. She hated that Rod was disappointed and exasperated with her, and, at this point, it seemed they couldn't possibly move forward, that their relationship had been blighted from the beginning.

She didn't know the woman's name or the number, so she walked along until she located the path through the trees that led deep into the woods skirting Don and Tessa's cottage. Then she crossed the street to start door knocking.

At the third house, Casey found her—an elderly woman dressed neatly in a sweater and pleated skirt, her hair pulled back into a snow-white bun from which a red knitting needle protruded.

Her name was Cecily Harrison. She courteously looked at the catalogue Casey offered her and invited her in. Cecily perched on the edge of her chair, her body so tiny that her floral-patterned slippers barely touched the floor, and poured tea from a large brown pot. Over tea and biscuits, she talked about her family. A widow with five children and eight grandchildren, Cecily made a good pot of tea.

"Oh, there it is," she said as her hands found the knitting needle she'd stuck in her hair—the one Casey had carefully avoided looking at.

As Casey searched for a polite way of bringing her to the point, the older woman brushed crumbs from her skirt, put on the glasses hanging on a chain around her neck, and examined the catalogue. It pictured a car close in model and color to the one Casey had seen Karl driving.

"I'm sure that's the car. Such a pretty color. I remember the moon came out from behind the clouds, and it just glowed."

"Did you tell the police that?"

"Well, no. I didn't remember until you showed me this picture, dear."

Casey decided against ringing Rod. He would only accuse her of leading the witness. And Mrs. Harrison's wavering opinion would carry little weight. The visit had confirmed Casey's own belief, however, and her sense of frustration lessened.

CHAPTER 24

Rod and DC Anita Jennings arrived at Monique Clement's terrace house in Notting Hill. A dark-haired young woman, looking remarkably like Lady Morris-Smythe, opened the door. Lord Rupert seemed consistent in his taste and choice of women, Rod thought. On closer inspection, however, he found this woman to be quite different. It wasn't just that her hips were rounder and her face softer. It was more the big picture. Her home was comfortably furnished, but not in any way flashy. She sat on a settee covered in a faded, floral fabric with bazaar throw cushions and settled herself across from Rod, her feet tucked beneath her, her long gypsy skirt arranged carefully over her legs. Having done so, she waited for him to speak. She appeared to lack both the feigned hauteur and expensive haute couture of Lady Morris-Smythe, and Rod suspected it had little to do with money.

An hour later, he and Jennings climbed into the late model police sedan with a signed statement declaring Lord Morris-Smythe had arrived at eleven forty-five p.m. on the night in question and stayed until seven the next morning.

Jennings tucked a stray blonde hair under her cap. "You think she's telling the truth?"

"Gut feeling? She'd say whatever he told her to say." Rod paused for a moment, wondering if that was fair. "Trouble is," he muttered, more to himself than to his young colleague. "In this job you get so caught up with base instincts, you forget there's any other sort."

Nevertheless, he wanted to see Lord Rupert Morris-Smythe again. For whatever reason, the man was plainly lying.

಄಄಄

Sarah's cheerful voice on the phone was a gift, lifting Casey out of her dark mood. She seized the opportunity for a night out. She'd stubbornly held to the view that Rod should ring and apologize and grew incensed when he failed to do so. She'd tossed and turned in bed the night before, and after she finally fell into the deep sleep of exhaustion, she'd dreamt of the deer she'd seen in Devon just after finding Don dead. It was as if a switch had been turned on, returning her to that dreadful morning in vivid Technicolor. She had never felt so alone, lacking even the company of Soc, now shut in the kitchen in his basket to avoid setting off the new alarm.

She and Sarah used to meet regularly for a drink on Friday nights. A petite and feminine blonde solicitor, Sarah had an uncomplicated attitude to sex. Casey was in awe of her confidence—for herself, she'd never figured out how to treat sex, or life, it if came to that, so lightly. Sarah always made good company, kind and generous, but rather impatient with anyone too emotional, and Casey now found that attitude curiously restful.

They met in The Mariners, a pub on the Kings Road. Several hours later, they entered an up-market bar, having visited several along the road. Immediately, Sarah spied someone she knew and left Casey to her own devices.

She climbed onto a stool. As if by signal, a man came and sat down next to her and offered to buy her a drink. She refused, but through the smoky haze, his blue eyes looked like Rod's when he smiled.

The bar closed an hour later, and they all emerged into the street. The cold air made Casey feel slightly woozy. Sarah took off with her arm through her chosen victim, leaving Casey with Hugh, the man she'd ended up talking to for most of the evening.

"Care for a coffee at my place?" he asked, pulling on his coat.

Her ears still ringing from the deafening music in the bar, she opened her mouth to refuse, but for some reason not clear to her then or since, instead she nodded in agreement.

Hugh lived in Earl's Court. He was a broker of some sort, with a voice that sounded like Prince Charles might after a few drinks and lovely manners, something that disappeared the moment he shut the door. With no further offer of coffee, he drew her down on the sofa. She barely had time to take in the expensive fittings and impressive disorder before he tried to pull her top over her head. She pushed him lightly away with a laugh, and he stopped, excused himself, and headed for the bathroom.

She sat up and took stock. This would not be the cure for what ailed her. She felt disloyal, although she wasn't at all sure she'd ever see Rod again. She guiltily scribbled "*Sorry*" on the back of a coaster she found in her bag. It had some guy's phone number on it she knew she would never ring. Straightening her top, she left.

Miraculously, she hailed a black cab outside Hugh's apartment almost immediately. Once she'd alighted in Richmond and the taxi's headlights had disappeared around the corner, she realized with a sense of unease that her street now appeared shadowy and altogether too dark. She crossed the road and hesitated at the gate. The bushes in the corner of the garden rustled in the light wind that blew her hair across her face. Heart thumping, she darted up the path and fumbled with her keys. She slammed the door behind her and stood listening for a sound beyond Soc's plaintive greeting. She would never feel safe again until Karl Baumann was behind bars.

CHAPTER 25

Casey received an acceptance to a request for an interview with Reginald Jamieson's wife, Jennifer. She was still interested in the property developer because he was so unlike anyone Don would have associated with, even if they did share a love of art. And the possibility that Jamieson had given the list of Nazi artworks to Don nagged at her.

The girl at the gallery had told her Jamieson would arrive there at ten. Not wishing to run into him again, she arrived early and parked in the street across from his house. Wearing a cap pulled well down over her hair and sunglasses in case he looked her way, she felt sure that, in the old *MG,* she was well beneath his radar.

She whiled away some of the time with a McDonald's breakfast she'd picked up on the way. It promised much but delivered very little. Munching through a muffin with the consistency of a sea sponge, she tried to make out his house through the car window, but it was set too far back from the road. The raked gravel drive curved away out of sight through dense shrubbery and trees. She could just see the crest of its gray-green slate roof.

Jamieson's Bentley cruised out the gates at nine-fifteen. She gave up on the muffin and began eating an apple and listening to the radio. She'd scheduled the interview for ten. She was using a pseudonym she'd adopted before, Catherine Chalmers.

Casey had asked *Hers* if she could write the odd piece, and she'd found it easy to sell them on the idea. Not only was Jennifer the daughter of a High Court Judge and a high profile socialite known for her exhaustive charity work, she had also produced a coffee-table book on orchids that proved a surprisingly good seller. It had caused quite a ripple, and not only in gardening circles. Casey had spent last evening reading it and found it read rather like a crime novel—an intriguing history of passionate and fiercely competitive people, searching remote jungles, some even stooping to acts of violence, to uncover that ultimate prize, a rare orchid. The book was filled with glossy, beautiful prints that provided the icing on the cake. Of course, the proceeds went to charity.

Casey looked forward to meeting Jennifer. Disposing of her apple core, she checked her watch and crossed the road to buzz the intercom. A man's voice answered, and she balked before reason took hold.

"Ms. Chalmers here. Mrs. Jamieson is expecting me."

The gate clicked, and she pushed it open, carrying her camera case up the path through flowerbeds decked out with new spring growth. With closed-circuit cameras watching her progress, she crossed to the columned porte-cochere. The house was the size of a modest hotel, three stories plus attics, built in mellow brickwork, with small-paned windows and large shutters.

A butler opened the door before she'd put a foot on the step. He seemed rather disappointing as butlers go, with an apron tied around his waist, slippers on his feet and a hankie held to his nose.

"Madam will be with you in a minute," he said croakily, the hankie muffling his voice. He ushered her through a lofty marbled hall and into to a long room, quite breathtaking in its proportions and fine furnishings, but empty of habitation.

A row of French windows opened onto a terrace, and one stood open. She sank into the soft down cushions on the sofa enjoying the breeze.

Minutes ticked by as she sat back and surveyed the room. It was a conservative and elegant mix of cream and green. She eyed the paintings around the walls and thought one hanging over the fireplace could be a Constable.

She got up and checked. It was. She began striding restlessly about, examining pieces of antique porcelain in a glass cabinet. Finally, a woman in a loose shirt, black pants, and a large-brimmed straw hat came up onto the terrace and entered through the open door.

Jennifer Jamieson was tall and thin, not pretty, but arresting. Her face formed a long oval, like a Modigliani painting, with brown, almond-shaped eyes—not particularly large but with an attractive upward tilt at the corners—and heavy, straight brows. She'd drawn her ash-brown hair back off her face in a rather severe style, but a surprisingly soft flowery scarf fluttered free when she pulled off her hat. She removed spotless gardening gloves and came towards Casey, extending a slim hand for her to shake.

"I'd offer you some tea," she said. "But I'm afraid I'll have to go and make it. Simon isn't very well at present."

"No, please don't bother. I'm fine."

They sat and discussed her latest successes in her work with disadvantaged children. Jennifer positively glowed while talking about them. Casey had her tape recorder running, and when Jennifer paused to draw breath, Casey suggested some photos. She asked if Jennifer would want to change and do her hair, but she demurred with a quick smile and wave of her hand.

"One of me at my desk, perhaps, in the study. There are photographs there of the children we've been able to help. I have my favourites, I try not to, but you know..." She shrugged helplessly.

"Our readers would enjoy pictures of this beautiful house." Casey began to feel edgy and wanted to wrap it up quickly, but not before she saw more of the house. She needed to learn more about Reginald the pretender.

Jennifer looked doubtful. "Well, to be honest..." she paused and then threw Casey a quick smile. "Reginald would kill me for saying it, he loves it. Obviously he loves property and he found this place for us years ago, but now, I don't know, I guess it's not really what we're about."

"It's beautiful," Casey said. "And it creates a terrific backdrop. Anything that captures the readers' interest will be good advertising for your work. Do you have functions here to raise money?"

"We do." She paused. "Perhaps the conservatory would work? I spend a lot of time there. I like to get my hands in the dirt."

Casey couldn't help but glance down at them, held softly in her lap. The pale oval nails were long and perfectly buffed, the cuticles matching round half-moons that spoke of care. But Casey could visualize Jennifer up to her elbows in compost. There seemed more to this woman than the persona she presented to the world. Another pretender, perhaps? A graceful socialite who didn't quite play the game with that extraordinary exposé she wrote, and her honest appeal to Tessa for help for her troubled marriage.

Casey began to feel nothing here was as it appeared. Jennifer's violent marriage seemed like a canker in a perfect world. She couldn't help wondering afresh why Jennifer had taken Reginald back, and if she had lied to the police to give him an alibi.

Casey took some shots of the sitting room with Jennifer posed against the fireplace, one long, slim leg crossed over the other. Her hand rested on the white marble mantle-piece while Casey angled to get the Constable painting into the background. Then they went to the conservatory filled to overflowing with foliage.

As Jennifer took her for a walk along the rows of potted plants, Casey was struck by their variety—from delicate, pastel blooms to vigorous, brilliantly hued ones.

"They are fabulous." Casey said. She remembered her aunt's pot-bound orchid and its runty spray of greenish flowers.

Jennifer picked up a small potted plant adorned with perfect, shell-like white blooms. "For you," she said, holding it out.

"It's beautiful. Thank you."

They went to her study, and Casey set her camera on its tripod. Glancing around the room, she checked for family snaps that might tell her more about Reginald, but he didn't feature here. Jennifer sat among her many framed photos of little children as Casey clicked away, hoping to catch the expression on her face—her absolute devotion.

They finished up just as voices sounded in the hall. A male voice called, "Jenny?" and Casey froze.

"Why, that's my husband." Jennifer looked startled and hurried to the door.

Casey swallowed hard, her skin prickled with cold and, for a minute, her mind went blank. Her fears were about to be realized. She didn't know what she would say to him. "I'd like to take this opportunity to pop out to the garden," she said, "for some exterior shots."

His presence had a profound effect on Jennifer. She nodded, her gaze vacant, and left the room.

Casey slipped out onto the terrace and sprinted away out of sight round the corner of the house. A truck stood in the driveway beside Jamieson's Bentley, and two men were in the process of extracting a crate from it. It didn't appear to be that heavy, but they handled it with great care. She watched them disappear inside the house and ran to peer into the truck's dark interior. After a quick look around, she climbed onto the back and ventured inside. Two crates remained, each held in special brackets. One corner of a cardboard cover appeared loose, and she worked at it, prising it back. Inside she spied the thick palette-knife strokes of an oil painting. Both paintings had the same German return address. She pushed the flash button on her camera and took a couple of quick, random shots of it. Then she heard men's voices approaching and slipped back into the garden, running between trees like a burglar, her heart thudding as if she had indeed taken something priceless with her.

Taking a path that led her away from the house, she heard her name called faintly behind her but she kept going.

She'd circled around, finding herself close to the road, and heard Jamieson's car. It paused at the gate. He appeared to be looking directly at her where she crouched among the rhododendrons. Her mind filled with hasty excuses, all ridiculous, all iced with the dread she felt at being uncovered as undignified and illegally obtaining information from a woman who had only been gracious and generous with her time. A shaft of sunlight threw the sharp angles of his face into relief so he appeared chiseled in marble, like one of his statues. Then the car took off down the road, and Casey made her way back to the house.

Jennifer stood on the terrace, arms folded, a frown in place. "*Well.* There you are," she said. "I wanted you to meet my husband."

"Oh, I'm so sorry. Has he left?"

She nodded, her expression fixed. The sense of becoming suddenly unwelcome, a source of irritation, sat poorly on Casey. She longed to rectify it—for her own peace of mind and because she'd come to respect Jennifer. She had the urge to reveal the true reason for her visit and sensed she could trust Jennifer, but it was too late.

"That is a shame. I got lost in the gardens," she said with a light laugh, hoping to explain her breathlessness and the grass stains marring the knees of her cream wool trousers. "How glorious they'll be once spring fully takes hold."

The frown left Jennifer's face. "Yes, we'll have a good season this year. We'll have to end this interview now. I have some urgent matters to attend to."

Casey packed away her camera while Jennifer hovered, impatient for her to be gone. The change in atmosphere seemed so profound Casey wondered if her disappearance or the arrival of Jennifer's husband had caused it. "I suppose Mr. Jamieson is caught up in your charity work, too?"

"I'm afraid he's much too busy for that."

"Thanks again for this," Casey said and picked up her potted plant. Slinging her tote bag over her shoulder, she grabbed her camera case, relieved to get going. If those shots she took of the boxes came out, she might well have the lead she'd hoped for. In her quick glance at the address, she'd only remembered the town, Farnberg.

CHAPTER 26

Rod took the call from Bishop's Walton police while he crossed the street. They'd located the man responsible for dumping the asbestos in Ringwood Forest in Wales. Harry Shaklehurst had confessed to acting alone and had cleared Justin Sorensen of all culpability. Rod felt glad for Sorensen—maybe he could get his life back on track after all—but he'd long ago lost interest in him as a suspect. He had much bigger fish to fry.

He entered the interview room at Fulham police station and found Lord Morris-Smythe waiting for him.

"Are you about to charge me?" Morris-Smythe asked.

"No, I'm not charging you at this point, but you were advised to have your solicitor here if you wished," Rod said.

Morris-Smythe shook his head. Rod noticed his face had grown thinner, making him appear years older. He stared moodily into the video camera and ran his hand through his hair to smooth it, but the jerky movement left it standing up on end. A stain spoiled his expensive silk tie.

Rod pressed the button on the tape recorder and stated the date and time, adding his name and Singh's.

"Haven't we sorted all this out?" Morris-Smythe asked. He sat stiffly, his hands clutching the arms of the chair, ready to rise at the slightest suggestion.

"We might have, Lord Morris-Smythe, had you told me the truth."

"I'm in the middle of a very delicate divorce case. I know nothing about the death of Donald Broughton. Why must you persist with something that's grown a beard, eh, Carlisle?"

"Because you continue to equivocate, Lord Morris-Smythe. Why would that be, I wonder? You said you were with your wife the night of Donald Broughton's death, but she denies it. Now, a young woman, Monique Clement, claims you spent the night with her in her house. Her neighbors, however, tell us she was away. Perhaps you have seen Broughton since you made that threat. Perhaps you killed him. I'd like the truth. Where were you that night? Who were you with?"

"The truth never hurts the teller, eh?"

Rod sucked in his breath and waited. He'd thought a man like Morris-Smythe would always give at least the appearance of being in control. Someone or something had pierced his armor—it seemed likely to be Claudette, but Rod suspected there was more to it.

"I could say I was with Monique and leave it to you to prove otherwise." He appeared to make an attempt to gain his composure, but it proved short-lived. "I've been in a pretty delicate financial position for a while," he confessed. "My wife and I enjoy a lifestyle that costs a lot to maintain, and I've been forced to sell some investment properties. One was a warehouse in the Docklands area. I went to a developer chap I knew by the name of Reginald Jamieson. Anyway, to cut a long story short, he bought the thing from me for an acceptable sum, and we lunched together. A disastrous idea, for who else should turn up to lunch but Donald Broughton."

"I find that coincidence hard to believe."

Morris-Smythe shrugged. "The London art scene is an incestuous place. We were bound to meet."

"Where did this lunch take place?"

"Gorky's, a Russian restaurant in the West End."

"Was this the Tuesday before Donald Broughton was killed?"

"Yes."

Rod shifted forward on his seat. "I'd like you to tell me exactly what went on at that lunch."

"It was tempestuous, but not for the reasons you'd imagine. Jamieson's an odd ball—not my type of fellow at all—hasn't a shred of class. The London art scene being what it is, dealers and auction houses are constantly touting for my business. It goes without saying Jamieson's keen to get his hands on my last remaining paintings, those of any real value, particularly now it's a masterpiece market. Sotheby's and Christies are quite aware I still have the Monet. A Monet *Waterlily* sold for twenty million American at Sotheby's just a few weeks ago. Sadly, mine's a less important work—won't bring anywhere near that." He slumped in his chair. "They all keep in close touch. They're a crafty lot, the dealers. Some would take over your affairs and manipulate you into selling short if they could. I'm sure Jamieson has made it his business to find out about my finances. He knows I'm going to have to sell, sooner rather than later."

"The lunch?" Rod prompted.

"I don't go by my title in matters of business. Jamieson introduced me as Alistair Penlow. Broughton didn't twig to it, which surprised me. He seemed distracted, quite nervous, in fact. I recognized him at once, of course—there's a picture of him at the top of his column in *The Times,* and I would never have forgotten his face anyway. I found myself in the curious position of being able to study an enemy at close quarters. So, I sat down and we ordered."

"In what way did he appear nervous to you?"

"Well, the fellow looked like absolute hell. It obviously wasn't going to be a relaxed lunch—that was clear from the outset. He rushed in and said something about wanting to see Jamieson alone—Reginald had been avoiding him, apparently. Broughton barely acknowledged my presence. It suited me. I ventured little to the conversation—I was waiting for my moment." He smiled thinly. "But in the end, I missed it."

"How so?"

"Naturally, the conversation centered on art. Broughton's passion for it was obvious, and I admit his knowledge was impressive. Jamieson and Broughton began to argue about a particular painting, a contemporary piece. I hate the artist's work, grossly overrated in my opinion." He paused. "It was odd. I suddenly found I couldn't follow the conversation at all. It was as if they were talking in some kind of code. Broughton went hammer and tongs at Jamieson about this painting Jamieson had suggested he buy. The price was too high, he kept saying. Then, before I got my chance, the blighter leapt to his feet and left."

Morris-Smythe sighed heavily. "Jamieson, smooth operator that he is, immediately switched into another gear, acting as if nothing had happened. He wants to be a player who can rival the big ones, and maybe one day he will, but he has no real love of art. It's nothing more than money to him."

"Why didn't you tell me about this before?"

"It doesn't look particularly good for me, does it? Some coincidence, that I run into the man I've threatened and blamed for my father's death, three days before he's murdered?"

"And I'm still waiting for that alibi."

"I was watching my wife."

"Go on."

"Claudette. I wanted to see what she would do if I left her alone. I believe she has a lover." He had another go at his hair, smoothing it with his fingers. "I think they were together in Paris."

"And did you confirm your suspicion? Did she leave during the night?"

Morris-Smythe's mouth pulled down at the corners. "She didn't, but I'm sure it's true. She's made a cuckold of me."

"This vigil, it was a stakeout from your black BMW car, I presume?"

"Yes, the Beemer."

"Until what time?"

"It was close to midnight when I dropped her off at the apartment. I stayed in my car for a number of hours and then went to my office in Putney at about five a.m.—stretched out on the chesterfield for a while. Hardly a watertight alibi, eh?" Morris-Smythe shuffled in his seat. "I find I love my wife, Carlisle."

"Love" seemed to Rod so ambiguous a word. A shrewd woman like Claudette would use it to her advantage, and even a selfish man such as Morris-Smythe could find himself dashed on the rocks of emotional need by it.

Rod's thoughts turned again to Casey. He'd hoped she would think things through and ring him. So far, she hadn't. What the devil had made him criticize Donald Broughton in that vicious way? He wasn't usually insensitive and cruel. Could he be jealous of a dead man?

"I believe you own a boat, my lord. A powerboat, moored at Fulham at the Hurlingham Yacht Club, where you are a member. Is that correct?"

A film of sweat had formed on Morris-Smythe's upper lip. "A sports boat, yes."

"Then it wouldn't take long for you to leave your office and be out on the water."

"That was the general idea of it."

"And from there, it's a small trip to the Broughton's Marina." Rod held his patience, sure the man had come close to breaking.

"If it's in Fulham, that's fairly obvious."

"I put it to you that you did take out your boat that morning, Lord Morris-Smythe. There's no point in denying it—we've confirmed it with the club marina." Rod showed him a copy of the page from the marina's register. "You arrived alone and took out your boat at ten-ten a.m., returning at eleven-forty a.m. Is this correct?"

"As you say, no point in denying it, is there?"

"I believe you tied your boat up at the Broughton's marina, broke a window, climbed in and stole their property."

"I just took the boat for a run, Inspector, to clear the cobwebs."

"Another strange coincidence then, Lord Morris-Smythe."

"Indeed."

Rod tried to control his exasperation, his patience close to deserting him. "The police are formulating a case against you. Why delay the inevitable?"

Looking completely exhausted, Morris-Smythe ran his hands over his face. "Time, Inspector." He pinched the bridge of his nose and sighed.

"Time for what, exactly?"

When the man didn't answer, Rod asked. "Do you have anything to add?"

Morris-Smythe didn't look up. He shook his head.

"I think you'd better get in touch with your solicitor, Lord Morris-Smythe. I feel you're going to need him. A policeman will go home with you, and you can surrender your passport to him. We will be in touch." Rod turned off the tape recorder. "Goodbye, for now."

CHAPTER 27

Casey looked over the prints from the photo lab. Most of them had turned out well—those featuring the house and garden, and of Jennifer Jamieson herself, excellent. She sorted out the ones she'd present to *Hers*, working on automatic pilot, her focus still on the paintings in the truck. The address had emerged in clear detail. She located a map of Munich and its surrounds on the Internet. Farnberg was a small town with a population under a thousand. The boxes didn't state whether they'd come from a gallery, and they hadn't included a phone number. It appeared she had only one way to find out.

She rang the paper and told them she was heading over to Munich for a couple of days. Her taxi headed into Heathrow as dusk descended over London, giving it a peculiar yellow haze. By dinnertime, she was in her hotel room in Munich, having passed the Bayerischer Hof with a regretful glance. She'd chosen a much cheaper hotel this time—no mints on the pillow. At the hotel restaurant, she had a hearty, rather stodgy meal of pork covered in gravy, accompanied by an enormous pile of sauerkraut she pushed to the side of the plate.

After dinner, she went back to her room to watch television. Feeling apprehensive and fidgety, she fought with her pillow before finally falling asleep.

Farnberg lay twenty-five kilometers to the north of Munich. She bought her train ticket and waited outside for the train. A bone-chilling wind swept along the platform and wrapped itself around her, causing her eyes to water and her nose to run. She was thoroughly miserable by the time the train finally pulled in.

As she stepped into the carriage, her mobile rang. "Hello, Rod."

She settled herself into a seat by the window and tried to deal with her conflicting emotions. She'd almost convinced herself singledom was her true lifestyle choice, but hearing his voice seemed to make a mockery of all her plans.

"I was hoping we could meet," he said.

It seemed churlish not to tell him where she was and why.

"An art gallery?" He paused, and the tone of his voice altered. "I apologize for what I said about Donald. I've regretted it since. But it worries me that I can't keep you safe."

"I'm used to taking care of myself, Rod. I've been doing it since I was twenty." She didn't add she liked it that way, because she was no longer entirely sure. Since Don's death, she felt she'd lost one layer of her defensive skins, along with the youthful assumption that she was bulletproof.

Rod's laugh sounded strained, and she quickly explained about the boxes. "The paintings in Reginald Jamieson's van looked amateurish—it made me suspicious."

"You'd better explain that."

"I was curious as to what Reginald Jamieson would want with work of such obviously poor quality. He supplied Don with art for his new house, the Kandinsky for one, which is extremely valuable."

"I don't like where this is heading. Jamieson was known to have had a quarrel with Donald about art, three days before he was killed. I'm about to pay him a visit." Abruptly, his tone changed. "Come home—I want to see you."

Suddenly breathless, she said, "I'd like to see you, too."

"Then leave it—come back to London."

"I will. As soon as I'm done here."

After a pause, Rod said, "We're close to wrapping up the burglary at Fulham. It's become pretty clear it was Morris-Smythe."

"Morris-Smythe! You're sure?"

"Aye, but he's not talking. Yet. And we've turned up more on Karl Baumann. He was a bit of a loner, never married, no known girlfriends, or boyfriends for that matter. He inherited a fortune when his mother died earlier this year in Berlin, but his bank accounts contain only a couple of hundred pounds. He must have money stashed away. In Swiss bank accounts more than likely. He might have been aware that Interpol had him on their list of people of interest since the sale of the Renoir. He's certainly kept his nose clean since he came to England."

"If it wasn't his body in that car, then whose was it?"

"We suspect it might be an old tramp who used to hang around the estate. He disappeared at about the same time. We've traced his family and we'll know soon."

"Karl killed him?"

"Aye...it's possible, but the man was in a bad way, apparently—in and out of refuges, health on the decline. He could have died of natural causes, and Karl just found him and decided to put his body to good use. Or maybe something spooked him to take drastic action."

"Could he really have pulled it off—faked his own death?"

"It has happened." He paused. "I can get up to London on Friday."

"How about Sables, Friday at noon?" she suggested, but static broke up their conversation. They traveled out of range, and the phone went dead. She thrust it away in her bag, unsure if he'd heard her.

Farnberg proved a bit of a whistle stop. Leaving the station, Casey paused at a small eatery for a cup of chicken soup and showed the address to the woman serving behind the counter. She directed Casey in halting English—a right turn, a left, another left.

Casey hoped she'd got it straight. She'd worn walking boots over thick socks and decided to keep going on foot. It was certainly a pretty place, in a chocolate-box-quaint kind of way. All it needed was snow to complete the picture, and the rawness in the air suggested it wasn't far off. She trudged along, drinking from her Styrofoam cup, the chill snapping at her fingers.

After hiking for almost an hour, she found herself in a country lane. The community of cottages had gradually diminished, giving way to fields stripped of color by winter frosts. She walked further, and rows of tilled red mud appeared like slashes of blood across the ground where the preparations for spring planting had begun. A fine mist hovered over the ground like steam.

She halted, unsure if she was on the right track, and retraced her steps to a signpost. Pulling off her glove with her teeth, she pulled the address out of her pocket and checked it. She appeared to be going the right way. She stood looking at the road curling away into a distant band of trees, admitting she should have come by taxi—but having committed herself, she might as well keep going.

Reaching the fringe of trees, she saw that the road headed into a dense wood. She pulled the collar of her anorak up around her ears and walked into the semi-darkness. She trudged along for another mile or so without one car passing. The woods were spooky, silent and still—apart from the occasional rustle or birdcall. To her relief, they began to thin to a few straggly trees and became open country again.

She'd expected to find a town, but instead, she saw only one property, with a letterbox bearing the number she sought painted on it in clumsy black letters. A rutted dirt road led to the rundown farmhouse, with nothing but fields for miles around. Smoke drifted from the chimney—someone was home. Had she gotten the address wrong?

A few black and white cows stood in a field beside a tall red barn. Their soppy brown eyes watched her without curiosity while they chewed their cud and flicked their tails.

Casey suddenly felt ridiculous. What could she possibly find here? She tried her mobile again, to no avail. The cold made her nose run, and she scrabbled in her pocket for a tissue. Shrugging off disappointment and weariness, she opened the squeaky gate and walked up through the trees. Close up, the house appeared even more down-at-the-heels, long overdue for a whitewash. The front door, once painted red like the barn, had only a few patches of red paint remaining. It appeared like the rest—sad and neglected. She'd obviously made a mistake. She would find nothing here of interest, but she knocked, hoping they'd have a phone so she could call a taxi.

Karl Baumann opened the door.

CHAPTER 28

Rod watched as Reginald Jamieson, stony-faced, checked the search warrant.

"I don't know what you think you'll find, Detective Chief Inspector," he said, handing it back. They stood at the door of the gallery's storage area, where the police pulled out crates one by one from a stack and jimmied them open. "Be careful with those paintings, you dolts," Jamieson yelled. "They're worth a bloody fortune."

Rod interrupted his tirade. "I think we'd better have a talk, Mr. Jamieson."

"Can't it wait until tomorrow? We're setting up an exhibition."

"Now. Down at the station."

Jamieson tossed his clipboard down and walked stiffly to his office, grabbing his coat from the peg.

❧❧❧

"Water?" Rod asked Jamieson once they'd sat down in the interview room at Fulham police station.

Jamieson shook his head. "Let's just get on with it, can we? I need to get back."

"You had lunch with Donald Broughton three days before his death. An argument erupted between the two of you. What was that about?"

Jamieson shrugged. "It was merely a routine business lunch between a couple of investors—Rupert Morris-Smythe and Donald Broughton."

"Lord Morris-Smythe and Donald Broughton were hardly friends, Mr. Jamieson."

"Rupert asked me to set up a meeting with Donald. Don't know why—it was a strange request, but I've had stranger. I was to use his business name, Penlow. I did as he asked because he has some excellent art that I'm interested in. He didn't get much of a chance to speak to Donald, as it turned out. The lunch fell apart pretty quickly."

"Why was that, exactly?"

"I'd sold Donald a couple of paintings in the past. He was after another, and we disagreed on the price. That was all."

"Broughton was reported to be furious."

"He had his heart set on a painting by Lucian Freud but felt the asking price too high. Freud's works bring large sums these days—he's been called the world's greatest living painter by some."

"I don't doubt it," replied Rod. And he didn't. After all, the man had lived longer than most. He'd seen photos of Freud's work in a recent article—nudes displayed like pale, landed deep-sea creatures, plain and helpless, the women overweight and the men with flaccid penises. The article had stated Freud was a visionary because his work revealed to the viewer that even the unlovely could know love. This may be true, but Rod didn't feel the same urgency to have one hanging on his wall as Broughton apparently had.

DS Burrows stuck his head in the door, saying, "I think you'd better come back to the gallery and take a look, gov, when you've got a minute."

Jamieson clammed up, demanding his solicitor be present. Rod wrapped up the interview, and they drove back to the gallery, parking in the loading dock at the rear of the building. In the storage area, six gaudy paintings lay stacked along the back wall. One of the experts from SO6, the Art & Antiques unit at Scotland Yard, crouched down with a spatula in his hand. He had lifted a layer of canvas away from the corner, exposing blue plastic underneath. He peeled the plastic gently back to reveal another painting, obviously a far superior work.

Casey. Rod pulled out his phone and turned away to ring her number. Maddeningly, it went straight to voicemail. He hoped she was flying home and would meet him for lunch tomorrow. He turned back to Jamieson, his voice calm. "I'm afraid I do doubt the validity of all you've been telling me." He studied the nervous man beside him. "I'd like another chat back at the station."

Jamieson paled, and his eyes looked frightened. "Not without my lawyer," he said, clearing his throat.

CHAPTER 29

For a long moment, Casey looked into Karl's eyes, watching his expression change from incredulity to anger. Caught flatfooted with nowhere to run, she cursed her stupidity. He grabbed her arm and hauled her stumbling into the house.

"You were at Farrowham and again at Bradford. What do you want with me?" he demanded.

"I want to know who killed Don Broughton," she panted, struggling to break free from his grasp.

"You think it was me? I *didn't* kill Donald." He pushed her backwards onto a seat. She perched on the edge with Karl hovering over her, so close to the roaring log fire that it scalded her shins. Easing her legs away, she said, "Then who did? Why was he killed? You know, don't you?"

"I would *never* have harmed Donald. He had the same German blood in his veins as I."

"Don was English."

"He was my half-brother."

She stared at him open-mouthed before finding her voice. "Don was an *orphan*. He didn't know who his parents were." She watched Karl frown. His whole body looked tight, menacing.

"Who sent you?"

"I'm a journalist. The newspaper I work for knows where I am."

"I doubt they know much." He searched through her bag.

"You're lying. Don would have told me if he'd found his family."

Karl had found her wallet and pulled out her press card. Rifling further, he pounced on her passport. "Casey Rowan—American." He began to pace up and down the narrow room. She looked around for possibilities of escape, but she knew she couldn't outrun him.

"You have gone to a lot of trouble to find out what happened to your friend. Such loyalty in the face of danger is impressive—or are you just another nosy journalist?"

He threw another log on the fire, and she began to sweat in her jacket. "Can I move my chair away from the fire?"

"You will stay where you are."

"Where did you meet Don?" she asked, hoping to distract him while she edged her chair away.

"Why do you call him Don?" he asked, frowning. "His name was Donald."

"He was *Don* to his friends."

"I met Donald in Munich in 'ninety-five," he said. "After that, I went home to Berlin to tell *Muti*."

He continued to relate his story, and she felt a chill run through her. This man would not let her go.

"*Muti* had told me she'd left a baby in the Broughton orphanage when she was in England. My father would have killed her had he found out. When Henry mentioned Donald had been placed in that orphanage as a baby, I put two and two together. Then I looked at him, and I saw it made four. We were most alike, don't you think?"

Casey shook her head. Don's kindness showed in his eyes, but she saw something else in Karl's. "Who was Don's father?" She wished she could control the tremor in her voice.

"*Muti* would never tell me that. We had different fathers. My father was the love of *Muti's* life, but she rarely saw him, and sometimes she..." He shrugged. "He made very few secret trips back to Europe. It was too dangerous."

"When did Don find all this out?"

"When *Muti* died, she left him money—a lot of money."

"Is that why you killed him?"

Karl looked at her. There was no compassion in his eyes when he said, "A pity for you, you couldn't mind your own business."

"The police are aware that you're alive. I told them I saw you in Bradford. They know that I've come here."

"You have come here on your own. You are a foolish young woman, and no one will take any notice."

He was uncomfortably close to the truth. Casey knew she had to keep him talking. She'd read somewhere you should become familiar with your attacker, become a person, not just an object, but she couldn't make herself believe it would help her now.

"Did you approach Don, or did he trace you? I know he was trying to find his family."

With the tip of his boot, Karl kicked back a log that had rolled onto the hearth. She wondered whether she could make it to the poker lying just out of reach. Then he spoke.

"I suppose it doesn't matter if you know now. I did, to persuade him to join us."

"Who is *us*? To do what?" Even if she died here, at least she'd know the truth.

"I had some paintings I needed to dispose of and I suspected I was being watched."

It was beginning to click into place—the stolen Nazi art. "No way would Don have helped you."

"Ah, but he was in a very difficult position." He gave an arrogant, cold smile.

"Why do you say that?"

"Because he had already spent most of his inheritance—and where did you think that money came from?"

Oh, poor Don. "Where?" she whispered, already sensing the answer.

"From my father. He was a Colonel in the *SS* during the war." Pride filled his voice, and his eyes gleamed. "He was put in charge of the Special Exhibit of *Intartete Kunst*, an important art exhibition. It opened in Munich and then traveled all over Germany. It included many German painters of the time."

So John Follet got it right. "I've heard of it. They surrounded the German Expressionist's work with graffiti and ridiculed them."

The gleam in Karl's eyes faded, and he frowned. "My father did a great service for the world. Just before the war ended, he saved a lot of the Expressionist's work. He took their paintings to Brazil."

"Quite the altruist." Casey started to understand. The paintings had traveled down the Nazi escape route to South America.

"You know five thousand pieces of art were destroyed at that time—burned. Otto Dix, Paul Klee, Max Beckmann, Kandinsky—many more. My father sent his paintings over to *Muti* one or two at a time for many years. She stayed in Germany to handle the sale of them. Then she became ill and could not continue. Before Father died, he sent the last to me."

Karl pounded his fist against the palm of his left hand, and Casey leapt in surprise. "I messed it up. It's become far more difficult now."

"I'm positive Donald would never have helped you. His hatred of Fascism is documented."

"He was thinking hard about it."

"He wouldn't consider it for a minute." She spoke resolutely. She would not let the cold seeds of doubt take root in her mind.

"He liked the money. Someone was trying to persuade him."

"Was it Reginald Jamieson? You sent the art to him, painted over somehow—to get them through customs. Am I right? He restored them and sold them into private collections."

Karl put a hand on her neck. His cold fingers bit into her flesh, and she shuddered. "How did you get this address? Who sent you here?"

"Did you steal Don's notes on his autobiography?" she asked in a strangled voice.

He let go, and she felt the bruise, warm and deep within the soft flesh, to her bones. It would hurt tomorrow, if she felt anything at all...

"I have no interest in such things. You will stand up now. Please come with me. I have a knife, and I don't want to have to use it."

Her heart thumped hard in her chest. He left the "yet" unsaid, but she heard it nonetheless. Despite this, she needed to know more. "Did you try to push me under the train? Did you throw that rock through my window in Richmond?"

He looked at her thoughtfully. "I sent a friend to follow you and discourage you. It didn't work, did it? Perhaps I should have let him do more. He was agreeable."

Casey took a deep, trembling breath. "A black man?"

Karl looked amused. "Hardly. We believe in white supremacy. The Nazi youth movement did not end with the war. *Muti* had very strong views. I was a small boy when she first took me to meetings—it has always existed and is growing in strength."

"You seem a disorganized lot to me," she said breathlessly as he hauled her along. "Does the right hand know what the left hand is doing?"

Ignoring her questions, he opened a door and gave her a shove. She fell awkwardly into a small storeroom, her hip stinging with the impact. She struggled to sit up and move, but the door slammed shut. A bolt slid into place. She rolled to all fours and then straightened, searching unsuccessfully for a light switch. A window provided the only light, but it was small and out of reach. She couldn't possibly fit through it, and even if she could, nothing in the room would reach it. If only her phone worked, but she'd left it in her bag beside her chair near the fire.

She tried to slow her breathing and forced herself to think calmly, resisting the panic curling through her and the sense of tightness across her shoulders. Where did the air come from? She fell to her knees, running her fingers along each crevice.

She tried to console herself by banging the walls, feeling how thin they were. It didn't help—she was caught. Walled in. She took a small measure of comfort from hearing Karl moving about, muttering to himself.

He obviously didn't believe in central heating. She pulled the sleeves of her anorak down over her gloved hands. What a fool she was to get herself in this position. No one would find her. Even if she escaped from this room, how far could she get with no money or passport and only a smattering of German, before he caught up with her again?

The light from the window began to fade. She could not face the thought of the deep black of a country night, of not being able to see her hand in front of her face. She leapt up, hearing the bolt slide back, and the door opened. Trembling, she prayed he'd change his mind, but Karl just shoved a plate into her hands. "Please let me go," she pleaded, but he silently closed the door.

For a moment, she brightened He wouldn't kill her. Not yet. The food was some unidentifiable, greasy, glutinous meat dish, which she ate greedily with the spoon he'd provided. She was hungry, and in the back of her mind, she hoped the food would also warm her and give her some strength. For what, she didn't know. She was too frightened to think about that. How long would he keep her here? Every moment, it seemed her lungs had to work harder to suck in oxygen.

She lost it finally, her temper almost visible as she closed her eyes, red hot, burning behind her lids. She threw the tin plate at the door. It crashed and bounced back, almost cutting into her leg. She yelled, "I need to go to the toilet!"

After what seemed hours, the bolt slid back again, and he pushed her through the house into a shabby bathroom. Her hopes for a bigger window faded when she found it was an internal room. She put her mouth under the tap and drank, then splashed water onto her face. A cracked mirror hung over the sink.

She looked around desperately for something to prise a piece of glass loose, but she saw nothing, and her short nails were useless. Her distorted face in the mirror made her feel lost, a tiny cog in the world that would vanish without a trace.

Soon Karl came to get her again, and she had a question ready to get his attention and hopefully forestall her return to the storeroom. At least here she could breathe. At least here she could be heard. She had a chance.

"Why did you fake your own death?"

Karl studied her for a moment. "I read about the knife used to kill Donald in the newspaper. It was identical to the one my father gave me. When I couldn't find it, I worried that the police would pin his murder on me."

It was all he would say. Remaining impervious to Casey's pleas, he locked her back in the storeroom. It was now so dark she could see little but a scattering of stars in the night sky through the small square of window. She sat and stared at it, hugging her knees.

In the early hours of the morning, she finally managed to sleep. She woke with a sob to the steely gray light of dawn. After another bathroom break and a rudimentary breakfast consisting of a slice of bread and ham, another long day passed. Her eyelids drooped with exhaustion, but she could only catnap, for the floor felt like a glacier. By the time it became clear she'd be in there for another night, she came close to a fully-fledged panic attack. But she quelled it with some fierce talk, her voice echoing around her like someone else in the conversation.

Karl came to escort her to the toilet again, and she pleaded with him to move her—to tie her up somewhere, but he remained impervious, shoving her back into the cold hole again.

With the coming of night, the temperature dropped, and she became perilously cold, shaking uncontrollably, her teeth chattering away in double quick time. Was it only a few months ago she'd been in Florida, her nights peaceful and her days filled with petty decisions?

She dropped off into a fitful sleep and dreamed she was dead. An angel had come to take her and hovered over her head. Gabriel—how beautiful he was. His face seemed familiar somehow. In some kind of metamorphosis, it turned into Rod's face. She reached up to touch him, but it changed again. Now it was Karl with his mad eyes glaring. She screamed herself awake.

She began to pray, but doubts kept flooding in, distracting her from her words. Did she believe in God? She'd attended Sunday school and occasional Sunday services when her father, not an avid churchgoer himself, decided she should. With a child's understanding of a father's shortcomings, she knew in a week or two, he'd forget and she'd be back on the beach again on Sunday mornings. She came to realize later that his faith had been severely tested by her mother dying so young.

In desperation, she prayed now to all the gods, not the false god who had killed Don, but the All Merciful, the Good the True and the Beautiful, Ruler of Heaven and Earth. She didn't neglect the pantheist gods, and for good measure, she threw in Buddha, Brahma, Mani, and Krishna, covering all the bases of salvation and deliverance.

She finished up with the Pagan gods lost at the birth of Jesus, and two other words swam into her mind: Alpha and Omega. She didn't want to die. After so many fallow years of abstinence, would anyone hear her voice?

Everything truly important now crystallized in her mind. Watching the sunset turn the sea to molten fire from the wharf in Key Largo. The call of seagulls—not the romantic, mournful cry of the gulls found on the Devon coast, the subject of poets—but something closer to familial squabbling.

She ached to be back there. The house still belonged to her.

Rod's face appeared again. Unsure if she was awake or asleep, she put out her hand to touch him. She opened her eyes, and his image faded. She knew now she should have trusted his good judgment, and that Tessa would rightly accuse her of deliberately sabotaging something good. It seemed her epiphanies had come too late.

She thought of Soc. What would happen to him without her to care? By the time the faint morning light came through the high window again, she was exhausted, and yet in some way, stronger—perhaps it was resignation. Karl was waiting for something or someone. Any moment, he could get instructions to kill her. It was only a matter of time.

The phone rang, and she jumped. She heard Karl answer it. She couldn't decipher his words until he raised his voice, his tone quite different, filled with a curious, boyish camaraderie. He spoke in English, and the words Casey could make out hit her like a jab of electricity.

"I can't kill this woman. You'll have to take care of it." She listened to one side of the argument, knowing it was about her. She wasn't sure who won it, but when she heard Karl say, "*Ja.* We all swore a covenant of blood that is worth dying for," she wanted to cover her ears.

Silence followed. And then Karl said, "I was being set up. I'll go away for a while, somewhere warmer, until everything settles down."

She strained to hear his final words, her ear pressed up against the door. "*Ja.* I know we need him." Then silence again. "The genius of Hitler was to act."

The room began to spin, and she sat down. Suddenly, everything became surreal. The man was mad, no question.

His extraordinary words burned in her brain. Now he would come for her.

She looked around wildly for something to use to save herself. She found nothing. Drained and helpless, she heard his footsteps stop outside the door.

"You are please to come out," he said.

She saw the knife tucked into his belt and wiped her dripping nose with a trembling hand. Her legs felt like rubber, and she had trouble walking. He gave her a push. She stumbled forward before she steadied herself.

"Outside." His voice and eyes were emotionless, empty. What would Hitler have thought of those eyes— flawed Eugenics? Would he have accused Karl of lacking Aryan perfection?

A car stood outside the front door with its boot open. Blinking in the light, she barely had time to register the horror before he lifted her into it and shut the lid. Doubled up, her knees under her chin, all the air squeezed out of her chest, she panted with panic. She yelled for help in the hope that someone would hear her, but she knew how unlikely that was. She wondered if the boot was airtight and if the exhaust fumes would soon kill her.

She tried to yell louder, but it was useless—the engine noise drowned out her cries, and fear made her voice weak. The car started to jolt its way down the potholed driveway. She bounced with it, hitting the lid of the trunk several times and cracking her head. Blood ran down her face, and she licked it away with her tongue.

The car slowed upon reaching the road, she supposed, and then accelerated at great speed. She remembered the state of the road through the woods. It seemed insane to drive this fast, but that was exactly what this man was. Insane.

She pushed her fingers down into the space beside the spare tire and held on, but the car swerved and sent her flying again. Her bruised hip banged against something in the corner. Crying out in pain, she grabbed at it.

The car finally slowed into a smoother ride, and she blindly explored the wrapped package, recognizing it as car tools rolled up in a cloth with a tie around them. Her fingers fumbled at the knot, plucking at it more and more feverishly the longer they sped on.

When it came undone, she opened it out carefully, feeling her way through the cold metal objects, until her hands curled over a screwdriver, small and sharp-pointed. She had just tucked this up the sleeve of her coat when the car swerved violently again and came to a skidding halt, rolling her painfully up against metal. She heard raised voices and took out the screwdriver again, banging on the lid and shouting. Minutes later, the boot lid flew up, and she slashed out wildly.

It wasn't Karl. A man jumped back, cursing in German. She'd hit him—a stream of blood curled from a gash across his cheek—but then she saw the police uniform and felt hysterical laughter bubble up in her throat.

The man dabbed at his face with a handkerchief and spoke to her again. She swallowed a giggle. He seemed to whisper, his voice nothing but a blur of foreign sounds.

He put his arms around her and eased her out onto the road. Her legs cramped, and her ears buzzed. She leaned against the car for support, still holding tight to the screwdriver, needing the feel of it in her hand.

The policeman gently prized her fingers away and extricated it from her grasp. She didn't understand his words, but the tone of his voice soothed her. He lay her down on the ground, placing a rolled-up coat under her head.

And then her eyes told her she really was dead. The angels she'd seen had been real. She couldn't believe what she saw: Karl cuffed and pushed into a van marked *Polizei*. Staring, she struggled to make sense of it all. This was a real policeman. She had fought him, cut him, and Karl was under arrest. She was safe.

Safe.

She looked up at the man still mopping his face with a weary expression. "I'm sorry."

He nodded, but she wasn't sure he understood.

"Does anyone speak English?"

"You are Casey Rowan?" another policeman asked her.

"Yes."

"We are acting on instructions from England," he said. "British police contacted our *hauptquartier*, someone from the Devon & Cornwall police—a Detective Chief Inspector Carlisle."

Rod. She hadn't shown up for lunch. How had he found her? Somehow, she found the strength to stand and, although she needed some help, make her way to a police car. They opened the car door for her, and she smiled wanly. She just wanted to be home, under her duvet. Now that she knew she was safe and Rod had done that for her, the relief mingled into something so dark and warm that she slept. She woke when the car pulled into the hospital grounds.

CHAPTER 30

Casey spoke to Rod on phone at the *wachstation*. "Are you okay?" he asked, sounding anxious.

She felt her head and grimaced. She hurt but felt better thanks to the third cup of strong, bitter coffer and hearing his voice. "It's just a slight concussion. I still can't believe you found me, Rod. How—"

"When you didn't show up for lunch and didn't answer your phone, I was bloody worried. We'd searched Jamieson's premises and found the boxes with the Farnberg address on them. That was the only place I knew to look. It was a close call, Casey. It makes me sick to think of it. How easily we could have missed you. The police only just arrived as Karl was leaving."

Casey shivered. "They're searching the Farnberg house now. Did you find those awful attempts at abstract art?"

"I'm no art critic, a lot of art looks bad to me," he said, his voice lingering, as though his thoughts were on something else entirely. She held the phone closer, wishing she could see him. It was far too hard to determine his thoughts when she couldn't see the expression in his eyes.

"Fly back as soon as you can," he said suddenly, and she felt released, softened by the understanding that seemed to travel between them. "Come and stay here for a bit, at least until we can sort this out."

"I'd love to," she said, warmth spreading through her. "But I'll have to bring Soc." He'd been at a cattery since she'd left London.

"Bring a whole menagerie if you like—just come."

∽∾∽

Casey put her suitcase down on Rod's sofa and released Soc from his cage. He stalked about, tail forming an indignant right angle. Rod folded her into a hug, and she rested her sore head on his shoulder. "You're late," he said.

She reluctantly pulled away. "Just a day or two."

"Would you like a cuppa?" he asked.

"Love it," she replied gratefully. "Tell me what you found at Jamieson's."

"The gallery had six paintings newly arrived from Farnberg. Scotland Yard has impounded them for examination. We'll hear soon."

Casey sucked in a breath. "I can't wait to see them." She frowned, and her fingers touched the bandage on her head. "I don't think Karl killed Don," she said quietly. She perched on a stool, enjoying the sight of Rod rinsing the teapot with boiling water before adding three teaspoons of her favorite tea, Russian Caravan. "Could it have been Reginald Jamieson?"

"His wife has given him an alibi. We have no evidence to the contrary."

"Have you been able to prove Lord Morris-Smythe burgled Fulham?"

"We've got SOCO back looking for anything we can connect with him, and we're checking for sightings of his boat. I'm confident something will turn up."

Rod added a dash of milk and handed her the cup. She took a sip. "Can't you arrest him?"

"Without proof, we couldn't hold him more than twenty-four hours."

"Do you think he killed Don?"

"I doubt it. Casey..." He hesitated. "Are you sure Donald wasn't involved in this conspiracy?"

"I'm positive. Karl would have told me. He had nothing to lose." She took another sip of her tea. It was heaven. "What do you think Karl had planned for me?"

"I don't think we should speculate on that." He gently lifted a lock of her hair away from the bandage on her forehead. "I'm glad you're here," he said and gently kissed the top of her head.

She smiled up at him. "I'm very glad to be here."

"I love the smell of your hair." He took the cup from her hands and placed it on the table. "It's so fresh—just like you."

"Who's fresh?" She laughed, grateful to be back in the land of the living, and silently thanked the gods for listening.

ཁ_ཁ_ཁ

Rod, gowned and wearing gloves and white protective covers over his shoes, stood in the middle of the lofty-ceilinged room. SOCO had protected the scene against contamination and the murder team wandered in and out, chatting. A mahogany desk with carved legs sat against one wall. A man's head rested on the desk's leather surface, as if he were taking a nap. Blood had seeped from his matted hair and dripped onto the delicate silk rug beneath. One hand hung down almost to the floor, still clutching a small antique gun.

A dark oil painting in a gilt frame hung on the wall behind him, it's subject so darkened with age, Rod found it difficult to interpret. He stepped closer and saw the image of a man lying dead in his bath, clutching a letter. It seemed Morris-Smythe had planned his death scene down to the finest detail. Rod glanced away through the set of tall windows looking out over the rolling green lawns and majestic trees of the park and wondered why someone who had all this would die by their own hand. He looked down at an envelope propped against the crystal paperweight on the desk. It was addressed to him.

CHAPTER 31

Casey was jotting down notes for a story when Rod rang. "I have some news."

She took a quick breath. "Tell me."

"Rupert Morris-Smythe has committed suicide, shot himself. He left a letter addressed to me."

"Like father, like son," she murmured. "What an odd thing to do, to write to you. What did it say?"

"He said he didn't kill Don. He confirms that the night of Don's death, after he'd parked in the street outside his apartment for several hours, he left about five a.m. and went to his office. He slept until nine, then went to the Hurlingham Yacht Club marina in Fulham.

"Apparently, when he lunched with Reginald Jamieson at Gorky's Restaurant, he heard Donald say he would be in Devon that weekend. Funnily enough, he always read Donald's column. When he found out Donald was writing his autobiography, he became afraid of what it might reveal about his father. As we suspected, he moored his boat at the Broughton's marina, broke in and stole Donald's records, thinking it could buy him more time."

"What did he do with them?" she asked urgently.

"There's no sign of them. So far, the assumption is he destroyed them."

"He wouldn't have deleted Don's encrypted file, would he?"

"We believe Donald did it himself, Casey. A program called *Evidence Eliminator* was used to wipe the hard disk."

"No. Why would he do that?"

"Perhaps he'd decided to join Karl? Perhaps he was afraid that if something went wrong, what was written there would incriminate him."

"You're *wrong*, Rod. Surely if Don had been involved, he'd still be alive."

She'd begun to feel cold and pulled Rod's jumper off the shelf, wrapping it round her. It smelled of him, as if his physical self were near. It comforted her.

"Okay, let's forget that for now. The full story about Morris-Smythe's father never came out. I went through the old post-mortem files. Lord Harold was a cocaine addict, had been for years. This was hushed up.

"In his letter, Morris-Smythe said he had a deal going to try to rescue his finances. He was broke, in danger of losing everything, and he needed money to get his wife back. He couldn't afford to divorce her.

"Claudette had something on him, too," he went on. "She threatened to reveal his Jewish ancestry. That would have shut tight many doors in the business world. Despite everything, though," he added thoughtfully, "I think he really loved her.

"Casey," she heard the tone in his voice change, "do you know where Donald got that painting, the Kandinsky hanging in the Fulham house?"

"Yes, from Jamieson."

"It's been missing since World War II."

"He wouldn't have known that."

"I'm sorry, love. I should have told you this when we were together, not over the phone," Rod said. "Are you okay?"

"I'm fine," she answered, but to her ears her voice sounded small and rather pathetic.

❦❦❦

Tessa asked Casey to come and check out an apartment in Chelsea with her, a conversion, half of a huge terrace. Casey thought its spacious rooms superb and the proximity to the King's Road to die for. After they left the agent, they browsed the shops and had coffee together at the coffee bar in Harrods food hall.

"What will you do now?" Casey asked, adding a teaspoon of sugar to her coffee for energy.

"Go on with my work, I guess. That's all I have right now. If only we'd had a child together, it would have changed everything, but Don believed the world was already too crowded. I think the fact that he didn't know his family history worried him, too."

Rightly so, Casey thought. She told Tessa about Lord Morris-Smythe's death. "Why do you think Don kept you in the dark about Karl and the art?"

Tessa looked at her for a moment and sighed. "I think Don was planning to leave. It was hard for us to face."

Casey leaned towards Tessa and took her hand. She found her trembling. "You both seemed fine when we got together that last evening."

"It was an act we'd just become good at. Since the episode with Arthur, he'd become...distant."

"He had other things on his mind though, didn't he?" Casey suggested gently.

Tessa nodded, closing her eyes. A spasm of pain crossed her face.

Casey had to ask it. "Tessa, Don wouldn't have become a party to Karl's activities, would he? He could never have changed that much, surely?"

Tessa hesitated and slipped her hand from Casey's, clasping it in her lap as if to stop the shaking. "Passion can take different forms," she said, her voice barely a whisper. She shook her head. "I don't know anymore, Casey."

On the crowded train home, Casey stood swaying, her hand gripping the hand rest on the seat in front of her, watching the landscape flash past. Through the dusty window, the slanting sun blurred and distorted the landscape, making the familiar appear strange.

She thought of Tessa's words, conscious of how little you really knew people. Even those you presume to be close to. The friendship the three of them shared had been very special. Perhaps Casey herself had filled a space, and her presence had given Tessa space, too, in which to find herself. The friendship had been important to Casey, and at that moment, she realized it had been important to the Don and Tessa as well. She just hoped she and Tessa could still find a place to be friends.

CHAPTER 32

Karl Baumann awaited trial for the murder of an alcoholic vagrant named Horace Small. The DNA testing had proved his to be the body in the car. Rod told Casey Karl wasn't talking.

Reginald Jamieson had been released on bail. The paintings from Farnberg had caused a huge media blitz. With the removal of the painted overlays, six of the paintings on Donald's list were uncovered. They caused enormous excitement in the art world, destined now to hang in the Tate while the fight over their true ownership began.

Rod had taken Casey to the art gallery on the Thames at Millbank for a private showing. How breathtaking they all were. If they'd found their way straight into private collections, as *Flower Girl* had done, they would have remained missing forever. She moved along the row, drinking in the beauty and uniqueness of each one. The soft purple shadows and golden lights of Monet; *Girl in a Blue Chair,* so true of Picasso's Blue Period; the haunting and poetic *Falling Angel* by Marc Chagall; the tender *Sleeping Child* by the Dutch artist, Van der Helst.

Karl's father had possibly saved two important German Expressionist works from destruction. And maybe many more that he'd sold years before, who knew? One was *Retribution,* with George Gross's wildly free brushstrokes depicting a furious image of a man-made hell, and the other, the unmistakable, caricature-like simplification of Max Beckmann, entitled *Spoils of War.*

Tears blurred Casey's eyes, and she grabbed Rod's hand. The whereabouts of the Mostaert painting remained unknown, but despite that, this cache of art, lost to the world for so long, had proved an extraordinary find.

e⁄sɔes

Casey decided to go back and see Jennifer Jamieson once more. She rang her, explained all, and said she hoped Jennifer would see her.

Walking through the doorway of that showcase of a house, Casey expected to find a beaten woman, but she was wrong—Jennifer looked years younger.

They had coffee on the terrace. Casey wondered how much Jennifer actually knew. She tried feeling her way to broaching the subject, but Jennifer began to talk.

"I always understood Reg was driven. He had what I suppose you'd call a fire in the belly. Early on in our relationship, I admired that about him, because he was so different from anyone I'd ever known. His involvement in the development of the Docklands never sat well with me, but I never dreamt he would sink so low."

She shook her head. "My only excuse is that he bowed me down over the years with abusive control. I was so emotionally exhausted, I let him overpower me." She smoothed her hair back off her forehead. "It's extraordinary how I can only see it now, and I know that for years I just buried it."

"You did leave him at one stage, didn't you?"

Jennifer looked at her but didn't ask her how she knew. "Yes, it was then that he seemed to realize how much he really loved and needed me. He persuaded me to go back, but his hold on me had begun to slip."

"You look like you're going to be fine without him."

She smiled. "I have my work. It's my life."

"Did you love him enough to cover for him?" Casey asked, wondering if the woman would answer. Jennifer looked directly at her with her Modigliani eyes.

"I didn't lie for him, Casey. He was with me that night. Jamieson didn't kill Donald Broughton. It's the one thing I'm sure of." As she spoke, her eyes widened slightly. Perhaps they'd both discovered how little they had known about the people they were close to.

രൗരൗ

Casey walked the length of her small garden, watching the morning sun squeeze rays of light through a band of tall conifers. Soc had found himself a perfect spot to lie in and lifted his head above a waving patch of grass. She bent down to stroke his sleek back. She hated feeling fearful and helpless. Karl behind bars didn't help—there were still others like him out there, perhaps lying low and waiting for orders. And where would those orders come from?

Her mind shifted away from Karl to Don. She tried to put herself in Don's shoes—what would he have done when Karl first revealed his plans? Leaving Soc in his grassy bower, she went inside to her filing cabinet and pulled out the photographs she'd taken at Heinrich Reinhardt's house, sorting through to make a small pile of the shots from Heinrich's study. Using a magnifying glass, she examined them closely, then checked the time and picked up the phone.

A man's voice answered. "*Herr Reinhardt?* It's Casey Rowan. Remember me?" She heard the doubtful tone in his voice and rushed on. "I know we didn't part under the best circumstances, but I *did* keep my promise. Nothing further has been published about your gallery's part in the sale of the Renoir."

"What is it you want, *Fräulein* Rowan?"

She looked again at the picture in her hand. "That SS Officer in the photograph with you and several of your friends, who was he?"

"Why do you need to know this?"

"I think it may have something to do with Donald Broughton's death."

"*Unmöglich!* Such a long time ago, how could it?"

"I promise I will explain it all to you, *Herr* Reinhardt, if you could just answer a few of my questions."

CHAPTER 33

By the time Casey hung up the phone, she knew she'd come close to the truth. Heinrich had been most accommodating. But she needed more proof. It took her the better part of a week to find what she sought. She had to delve into the archives of several newspapers, going way, way back. She found her efforts worth the hunt, however, and was convinced she knew who killed Don.

Now she needed to confront him. She rang and spoke to a member of his staff. "I have something important to tell him, which won't take long," she said. "He did an interview for my magazine, *Hers*. Yes, he was quite pleased with it. I think he'll see me."

Ordinarily it would take months to see the Chancellor of the Exchequer, if at all. But he let her come. She guessed he wanted to check her out, to see what she had learned from Karl. And she supposed he just wasn't afraid of her. She was so insignificant, he could swat her down any time he chose.

This meeting was to be at Number Eleven, Downing Street at six thirty in the evening. She hesitated, reminding herself he was a dangerous man. But surely it was the safest place in the world—he couldn't touch her there. However, he didn't need to. He could bump her off in a much more discreet fashion.

She quickly dismissed thoughts of that nature—before they made her turn back—and passed through the checkpoint with a carefree smile. The building seemed deserted but for a woman slipping on her coat, who showed Casey in. They entered Sir Henry's study to find him talking on the phone, surrounded by files and boxes.

"I'll be off now, Sir Henry."

He looked up. "Right, Jean. See you tomorrow. Come in, Casey." He motioned her to sit.

She suddenly acknowledged to herself the significance of where she was and whom she confronted. She was in Downing Street. The Prime Minister lived next door. She barely glanced at the wonderful porcelain caricatures of Disraeli and Gladstone she'd read about. Her facts now seemed extremely weak. With trembling knees, she sat down in a chair in front of his desk. He hung up the phone and offered a puissant smile, part of the softening-up process—a technique he was probably so used to wielding it had become unconscious. But Casey found, with relief, that she'd grown inured to it—and she needed to have her say.

"You must be worried about Jamieson and Baumann."

He leaned back in his chair and looked at her, eyebrows raised. "I don't know Jamieson. Karl will swear under oath, if he has to, that I was in no way involved in his activities. Why would I be worried?"

"Because you killed Don."

Sir Henry sat bolt upright. His face took on that pinched look again. "Where did you get a preposterous idea like that?"

Short of breath, Casey pushed on. "Not from Karl. He might suspect, but he doesn't know for sure, does he?"

Sir Henry's laugh sounded brittle. He checked his watch. "This is entertaining. Tell me what you've deduced, Detective Casey. Make it quick."

"You went to see Donald that night. You were well acquainted with his habits. After all, you were a *friend*. And you knew he was an insomniac, you told me so. You rang first from a public phone. And of course he let you in."

Sir Henry sat back again and crossed his arms. "Prove it."

She cleared her raspy dry throat. "I can't."

"Then get out, before I have you thrown out."

She stood her ground. "I don't think you will, Sir Henry, until you hear what I have to say."

He made no move to ring for security, so she went on. "I don't think Don knew about your involvement in this nasty business. When he went to Farrowham that weekend, Karl declared himself to be his half-brother. He must have told Don about his mother and the stolen Nazi art. How horrified Don would have been to learn that the family he had been so eager to find were frauds, thieves, and worse. I had to ask myself what Don would have done. My guess is he would have denounced Karl publicly."

She leaned forward. "But, before he could do that, Sir Henry, he would have contacted *you*. He had to warn you, to consult with you as to how best to deal with the situation. This he would have done, and at the same time set up that file entitled *Farrowham*—the place where he felt Karl hid the art. Then something made him hesitate. Perhaps you asked him to wait until you could see him. Perhaps he received a threat which included Tessa, and that's why he told her nothing about it."

She stopped and tried to swallow, the tension in her throat drying up her voice. She eyed the crystal water jug on his desk. "You must have been furious with Karl, and very worried because you knew that no matter what you said, Don would expose Baumann and Jamieson, even though it meant taking himself down, too. And although Don didn't know about your involvement, one of them would then expose you, to save their own skin. You couldn't have that. It would spoil your plans to cultivate a fascist government in Britain."

"Casey, you didn't strike me as a neurotic young woman when I first met you. Your ordeal in Farnberg seems to have filled your head with nonsense. I'll give you five minutes more of my time, which you are extremely lucky to get, to tell me where all this has come from, and then I don't ever want to see or hear from you again."

She forced herself to look into his eyes. She expected to find a hint of madness there, some confirming flash of fire, but she found gray fjords—cold and fathomless. "When I took shots of your uncle's home for that piece I did on you for *Hers,* I noticed he had a picture of himself in his uniform during the war, with a group of men, one of whom wore an *SS* uniform. I rang him and asked him who that person was. Your uncle, bless him, whom I suspect isn't that fond of you, told me it was a childhood friend of his, Fredrik Baumann, Karl Baumann's father. He, like many other Nazis, disappeared at the end of the war. Karl told me his father escaped to South America, taking with him a cache of very good art."

"So what if it was Baumann? You still don't have a shred of evidence to support your insane theories."

She plowed on, building an irrefutable portrait of a born and bred fascist. "Another person was in that photo. He stood out because he was the only one in civilian clothes. That man was Charles Richardson, your father, Sir Henry. At first, I thought your teenage years spent with your uncle in Germany shaped your thinking. But Heinrich was a war hero. He had no time for the *SS*. Your mother didn't send you to Germany to be educated—it was your father. He first met your mother in Munich, where he spent a lot of time mixing with the fascists just before the war."

Sir Henry gave a non-committal grunt.

"Some research I did on you threw up a small item about your mother and father's divorce," she continued. "Your mother had accused your father of being a Nazi sympathizer. At that time, I assumed it was just spite. But since then, I've dug further and turned up another piece, written by a tabloid in the nineteen seventies. Your father had died and couldn't sue them when they suggested he had an unhealthy association with the fascist Brownshirts before the war. It's not possible now to back this up with facts, but it set me thinking, as it will others. Your father would not have been the only Englishman to succumb to fascism, would he? Look at what's being leveled now at the Duke of Windsor, Edward VIII."

He shook his head. "You should write a novel, Casey. You writers live in a world of your own making."

She didn't expect a confession from him, but apparently she still had the floor. He must have had his own reasons for letting her talk. But she refused to dwell on what those might be. "That night, Don must have mentioned to you that Tessa was asleep. Maybe you told him not to disturb her—you wanted to speak to him privately. He obviously didn't tell you I was visiting. Perhaps you even hoped to the last he would change his mind and support you, that he could be bought."

She forced herself to meet his gaze. "You had to do it yourself. Karl wouldn't have killed a member of his own family—someone with the same blood in his veins. That was important to him. And anyone else might mess it up and incriminate you. You planned it carefully, giving yourself an alibi at Farrowham, but you left after everyone had gone to bed. You would have been back again before anyone noticed you weren't there. And I suspect you intended to frame Karl as well."

A spasm across Sir Henry's face told her what she wanted to know. "But he faked his own death and disappeared, spoiling your plan," she continued. "He saw a picture of that knife in *The Mirror* and couldn't find his. You know the one, Sir Henry, the unusual German knife you planted for the police to find. Karl suspected a set up. He was to be a scapegoat for the cause, and despite his fervent belief in this mad plan, he wasn't really prepared to go to gaol for it. So he baled. It was his car you drove that night, too—a perfect way to cover your tracks. Karl would never give you up to the police—you're much too important to the cause."

Her fragile voice began to desert her. She could hardly get the words out. "When Tessa came downstairs, you knew she would recognize you, so you had to kill her, too. And you would have succeeded if I hadn't been there. How you must have suffered, waiting for her to identify you. Luck was on your side, though—either Tessa didn't see you clearly, or the shock drove it permanently from her mind. You took Don's laptop, compact discs and notes from his briefcase, just in case the sordid truth was recorded there. And was it?"

She trembled as Sir Henry came around the desk and stood in front of her. She looked up and realized his actions blocked anyone's view from the door. He wrenched her handbag from her grasp and opened it. "Did you bring a tape recorder?" he murmured. His nearness made her head pound. He rummaged inside and, finding nothing to worry him in her bag, threw it back into her lap.

He gestured. "Are you wired?"

Casey stood and lifted her shirt.

He nodded, and she sank down onto the chair again, holding her breath.

Would he now say even one word that proved his guilt?

"Tell me about Donald, please, I have to know."

He perched on the edge of the desk close to her, speaking quietly. "Donald? He was an ideologue. It weakened him."

He dismissed Donald with a wave of his hand. Casey wanted to rage at him and strike him with her fists, but she curled her fingers into her palms and kept silent as he spoke. "The Americans have an appropriate name for it, Casey. Collateral damage. Donald's life, or Tessa's, Karl's, yours, or even mine when I'm done, doesn't matter—as history will prove."

She gripped the arms of her chair and watched him, waiting. His next question astonished her.

"How old are you, Casey?"

"I'm—thirty."

"Single—no children. And your friends—are they married? Do they have children?"

"Not yet."

"England is a predominately white Christian country. Sustaining this population requires each woman on average to bear two-point-one children. At present it's one-point-five per woman and falling. Are you familiar with the speech that destroyed the Tory politician Enoch Powell's political career?"

"The 'Rivers of Blood' speech? I read it once. He was against excessive immigration, wasn't he?"

Sir Henry crossed one elegant leg over the other, clasping an ankle with one hand. She barely listened. She was looking at his shoe.

"Allowing massive immigration into the United Kingdom was 'heaping up its own funeral pyre.' What Powell said back in nineteen sixty-eight was a true reflection of the future, Casey. Look what's happened since. I'm not about to make the same mistake he did by declaring this to the world. But I *must* head this government. Fascism is not the dirty word you think it—it's a way of bringing together left-wing egalitarianism and right-wing authoritarianism. There's no peaceful way of doing this. I am a man of the people, the right one to make the *very* hard decisions that prevent the loss of our traditions and our historic values. I've garnered an enormous amount of support from many quarters on this. I *must* be Prime Minister. For the future of England—for the generations to come. You must understand."

Now she saw the passionate glow of the zealot in his eyes. When he didn't see what he wanted in hers, some weakening of her resolve, he turned on her, his control finally deserting him. "Where are you going to take your unsubstantiated story? *The BBC?*" He stood above her, his hands curling into fists. It seemed for a moment that he might strike her down or put his hands around her throat, but he retreated to his chair, throwing himself into it.

"Get out." He said it quite calmly, but his face drained of color, and he suddenly looked old. "I strongly advise you to return to America."

She jumped to her feet, stunned by what he'd told her. Her mind reeled. This man was a criminal—a murderer.

She moved quickly to the door. "You're right about one thing, Sir Henry. I can't bring you down. As you say, if I wrote anything about this, no one would print it. I can only hope that Karl Baumann or Reginald Jamieson will do the talking. But just in case they don't, and you're of the mind that I should disappear, I have it covered. I've left a very enlightening letter with a solicitor, which I'm sure would bring some people in Scotland Yard down on your head."

Her teeth beginning to chatter, she walked from the room and made her way down the stairs and out through the doorway. She clamped her jaw and passed the friendly police. She was aware that Sir Henry might well become Prime Minister. But if he did make it, when it came to his fascist views, he would find a lot more opposition than he expected. Out on the road, ahead of her, a car waited, its engine running, exhaust belching fumes into the still air. She drew close, and the passenger door opened. She looked in at the driver's face and then jumped in.

"Are you satisfied now?" Rod's concerned face betrayed his anguish. She put her shaky hands up to her cheeks and found them burning. "You had to do it, didn't you, Casey," he admonished her, pulling her into his arms. "I told you to wait and let one of his own groups nail him. To let the law deal with him. It will happen in time. Have you *no* patience?"

Her breathing and her pulse slowed. Her part in it all was over. She took a bottle of water from her bag and drank thirstily. "He admitted it, Rod. You have your murderer. Can't you get him with that partial shoe print?"

"Even if he's the same size, do you think he'd still have that pair of shoes?"

"That's just it. I'm willing to bet he has all his shoes made from the same exclusive shoemakers."

"That wouldn't hold up in court, Casey."

"But it will rattle him."

"I'd need a pretty good reason to accuse the Chancellor of the Exchequer of murder, wouldn't I? Do you think my super's going to get the Home Secretary on his side with just a partial footprint as evidence?"

Rod pulled away and gunned the engine.

"I leaned one thing. Donald refused to be a party to their scheme. That's why Sir Henry killed him." She leaned back and shut her eyes, weighed down by fatigue, and he drove her home.

EPILOGUE

Smathers Beach Key Largo
September 2001:

Casey sat cross-legged on a towel on the white sandy beach, watching a pelican rise in stately fashion from the water. It was barely seven o'clock and the shoreline was deserted, except for a lone jogger emerging from the palm trees in the distance. Despite it being September, the hot sun burned the top of her head, and she reached for her hat.

She cut an article out of *The Times* and pasted it on the last page of the scrapbook she'd kept for years, a hard copy of clips of her journalistic endeavors. Some of Don's were also featured there, and she'd recently added some new items, not written by either of them, but still of great interest.

This one's for you, Don. The Times, dated June thirtieth:

Sir Henry Richardson, the Chancellor of the Exchequer, has had his trial date set. The extraordinary findings leveled at him and his associate Karl Baumann has blasted all other news off the front page for weeks. Both have been remanded on suspicion of murder and fraud in the Nazi Art Theft case. New forensic evidence taken from tissue and hair samples and a pair of shoes supports an alleged claim that the well-liked Chancellor murdered a friend in cold blood. The government is now in total disarray. Sir Henry was favored to be the Prime Minister, should the Tories have won the next election. The ailing Prime Minister, Lionel Sherringham, has already declined to stand for another term. Unless the party can pull a leader out of their hat to equal the charisma and talent of Richardson, it seems that Labour is now unquestionably the front runner in the election race.

She turned the page. The next was from *The Guardian*, dated July fifth.

Nazi Art Theft: Bombshell evidence is expected in the trial of the Nazi Art Fraud case involving Sir Henry Richardson and Karl Baumann. Reginald Jamieson, an art dealer, is set to give evidence under immunity from prosecution. Karl Baumann, employed as art historian by Sir Henry Richardson, has also been indicted. His murder trial date has been set. She smoothed out the new addition, and a fresh wave of pleasure coursed through her: *The Times*, September tenth.

Soon to take up his new appointment is Detective Superintendent Roderick Carlisle, responsible for solving the Nazi Art Theft case. His future looks extremely bright as part of the squad set up by Deputy Commissioner Gerald Channing to fight racist crime and terrorism. Channing has undertaken to target racists within society and within the force and has promised a new approach to deal with racist organizations such as Combat Eighteen.

The jogger grew closer, oddly surreal in the shimmering, hazy light. Casey grabbed her towel and walked down to the water's edge, the salt spray on her face and the crunch of wet sand under her feet. Rippling waves rushed up onto the beach and sank away again, pulling at her ankles, while her mind drifted into the past.

"Are you *ever* ready on time?" Rod said upon reaching her. His lightly tanned skin glowed from his run. He gave her a hard squeeze that took the breath out of her and the sting from his words.

"I'm all packed. I just have to hand the keys to the agent. He'll give them to the new owners at settlement time."

"But shouldn't you be dressed? Women take twice as long as men."

"Don't be a sexist pig," she said, flicking him with her towel.

He whipped it out of her grasp and looped it around her waist, drawing her to him for a kiss. She threw her arms around his neck, delighting in the feel of his warm skin against hers.

When she drew away, he looked at her carefully. "Are you sure you don't want to stay here?"

"What, and desert Soc?"

He laughed. Turning, he stared out to sea and said thoughtfully, "It's like staring into infinity."

She followed Rod's gaze out beyond the ultramarine depths to the silver rim of the horizon, her hand slipping into his. She acknowledged its grandeur, but her needs were simple. She knew she wouldn't miss it.

THE END

About the Author

Maggi Andersen and her lawyer husband are empty nesters, living in the country outside Sydney, Australia, with their cat and the demanding wildlife. Parrots demand seed, possums demand fruit, and ducks visit from the stream at the bottom of the garden.

Andersen always felt she was meant to be a writer, but raising three children and studying for a Bachelor of Arts degree and a Master of Arts in Creative Writing degree came first. Georgette Heyer has strongly influenced her historical romances. Her love of romantic suspense came from Mary Stewart and Victoria Holt.

Her current favorite writers are Elizabeth George and Sue Grafton. In her spare time, Maggi enjoys reading and watching movies. She swims and goes to the gym to keep fit.

www.ingramcontent.com/pod-product-compliance
Lightning Source LLC
Chambersburg PA
CBHW061540170626
46811CB00001B/33